SISTERS
AND
BROTHERS

Other Books by Janet Stevenson:

WEEP NO MORE

THE ARDENT YEARS

JOHN JAMES AUDUBON: PAINTING AMERICA'S WILDLIFE

MARIAN ANDERSON: SINGING FOR THE WORLD

SISTERS AND BROTHERS

A NOVEL BY

JANET STEVENSON

CROWN PUBLISHERS, INC. NEW YORK

To my sons and their friends
who will have to finish it. . . .

SISTERS
AND
BROTHERS

I

Talk around the Welds' supper table was always particularly animated on Fridays, when Theodore and Angelina came
home after their week in Lexington. They were both teaching in
Dr. Lewis's boarding school for young ladies, and happy in their
work—happier than they had been since the time they both thought
of as their "apostolic days." But they did feel cut off from the larger
world of public events, and they depended on the rest of the family
to keep them *au courant*.

Stuart, who was doing graduate work at Harvard this year, read
the Boston papers with scholarly thoroughness and gave his parents
a condensed version of all the news he considered significant. Old
Sarah read the religious and anti-slavery journals that came to the
house, clipped some items and marked others for reading aloud.
Angelina's daughter Sarah—young Sarah—usually had news of the
neighborhood and of their friends in Boston. Tonight she had a
letter from her fiancé to share.

But somewhere in the middle of her reading of it, her mother stopped listening.

No one noticed but old Sarah, who was still more sensitive to Angelina's moods than was anyone else in the household. She had, after all, a quarter of a century's start, even on Theo, for she had stood godmother to her baby sister, and acted as mother surrogate for most of the years of Nina's growing up. That stretched look around the temples now—that had been a sign of an oncoming headache even when she was a child. . . . Something must have happened at school this week . . . gone wrong. . . .

Angelina looked up and caught Sarah's eyes on her. She smiled affectionately, and made a slight movement with her head that Sarah read as a request not to call the attention of the others till they had had a chance to talk alone.

When supper was over, Theodore and the two children went into the kitchen to wash the dishes. Angelina had brought home a great stack of history examinations to mark, so she excused herself and went straight to the parlor, where the light was good and there was a warm fire in the grate. Sarah—who had prepared the meal and was therefore disbarred from the cleaning up—got her knitting and followed her sister.

"Have you read this week's *Standard*?" Angelina asked as Sarah came into the room.

"No. I looked for it, but I decided you and Theo must have taken it to school with you."

"Yes. I did take it. But I thought . . ."

Angelina's voice died away, and she sat so long abstracted that Sarah was afraid she was forgetting what she wanted to say.

"What was it in the newspaper that interested you, dear?" she asked.

Angelina roused herself and went to the table, sorted through her books and papers till she found a copy of the *Anti-Slavery Standard*. The article to which she pointed as she gave the paper to Sarah was signed by a Professor Bowers, of Lincoln University, in Oxford,

Pennsylvania. The type was so small and the lines were so crowded that Sarah had to go on a hunt for her spectacles before she could tackle the text.

"Have you ever heard of Lincoln University?" Angelina asked.

"Never."

"Nor have I. It seems odd that we shouldn't. The school was founded before the War, under some other name. It was changed to Lincoln only recently, after the President's assassination. Would you not think someone in Philadelphia—the Douglasses or Jane or Sister Anna—would have written us about an institution dedicated to educating Negro youth?"

Sarah had found her glasses and was running her finger along the lines of what seemed so far to be a rather effusive tribute to a student oration, pronounced at some ceremonial occasion by . . .

a young man but a few years removed from the chains of servitude, whose erudition and felicity of expression would be remarkable in any student in his sophomore year in any college with whose standards this writer is acquainted.

If he continues in his present course, what great things on behalf of the race he represents may not be expected of Mr. Grimké?

The name stopped Sarah. She blinked and stared and went back to the beginning. She had skipped too quickly over the opening paragraphs. . . . There it was: Archibald H. Grimké!

"Do you know who he is?" Nina's voice dropped almost to a whisper.

"I have never heard of him . . . never heard of the name Archibald in our family. . . ." Sarah's mind began to run down the list of their brothers and sisters, seeking one to whom this talented youth might once have belonged. There were, she was sure, no white Grimkés on this side of the ocean who were not members of their family. A number of slaves emancipated at the War's end—and even before it—had taken the name, but she and Nina knew them

5

all. They had made it their concern to keep track of them and give what aid they required, to reunite separated families. . . .

"Eliza and Mary never had any slaves." Nina was doing her eliminating aloud. "Sister Anna freed hers when she came north. We freed Mother's. We know all our brothers' people. None of them could be the father of this young man. If any of them had even heard of such a thing as a boy coming north to go to college, we would have been told."

"What about the hands Henry had on the plantation in St. Paul's Parish?" Sarah asked.

"I thought of them. But consider the time. Henry died, and the estate was auctioned off in 1852. This is 1868. If this young man was one of the Caneacres people, he was sold as a mere child. Why would he take the name of Grimké when he was freed? Why not the name of the master who raised him?"

Her tone sounded hostile, almost threatening, as if she were daring Sarah to avoid a trap toward which her questions were leading.

"Henry's sons were old enough to have slaves of their own by the time the War broke out," Sarah said. "This boy might have belonged to one of them."

"If he belonged to *anyone* in the family, why didn't Sister Eliza tell us about him when she came north? She left Charleston to come to us at almost the same time this young man must have left to go to Pennsylvania."

"He may not come from Charleston at all." Sarah grasped hopefully at the straw. "The article doesn't say anything about where he comes from."

"Are there Grimkés anywhere else?"

"Brother Frederick . . ."

"Who never owned a slave."

The shape of the trap was clear now. If Archibald Grimké was not the liberated slave of some white Grimké sibling, there was only one other way of accounting for his surname. Angelina was waiting for Sarah to put it into words, but Sarah's mind recoiled, went blank in a futile effort to preserve its peace.

There was a heavy silence in the parlor. Laughter and talk from the kitchen seemed to lose life as they filtered through it. At last, with a deep sigh, Angelina got to her feet. She took the newspaper back from Sarah.

"I am moved to write the young man," she said quietly, and went into her room.

II

Mr. Archibald Grimké,
Sir:

Angelina wrote the words of the salutation, and stopped. They looked alien, like words in a strange language, referring to strangers. It took an effort of will to force the connection between them and herself:

> *My maiden name was Grimké—Angelina Grimké—the youngest daughter of the late Judge John F. Grimké of Charleston. . . .*

Even that name looked alien. . . . Papa had been dead for half a century. It had been almost that long since she had spoken his name or tried to recall his face. . . . Her memory of Mother was fading too . . . of all of them, all the brothers and sisters . . . all dead now, except Eliza.

Tight-lipped, stiff-necked, and hollow-eyed with hunger, Eliza had come out of the conquered South at the War's end, to live in Massachusetts with the Welds. They did their best to make it easy for her, but Eliza could not reconcile herself to them or their world. After a few uncomfortable months she went back to Charleston, the new Charleston, governed by Yankees from Massachusetts and free Negroes ... went back without ever speaking the name of Archibald Grimké. ... Why?

Angelina went on with her letter:

> *Since the name is a very uncommon one, it has occurred to me that you have probably been the slave of one of my brothers. ...*

Or ought she to write what she meant? ... *the son of one of my brothers!*

That was the reason for Eliza's silence; and Eliza's silence was all the proof that was needed. For women like her—white women of the slaveowning class—there was only one defense against the shame of such a connection. That was to deny its existence.

> *I feel a great desire to know all about you, whether you have any sisters or brothers, who your parents are ...*

There! She had written it. She had put down the words of the question, and she could begin to let the answer form in her mind.

Who were his parents? Which of her brothers and what helpless black slave! Was it a woman Angelina had once known? A servant in Mother's house on East Bay or at the country seat in Bellemont? A mauma or a plantation hand? Or a woman bought for no other purpose than the violation of her womanhood?

As Angelina stared at the words of her question—suddenly and so strongly that it blotted them out—a face interposed itself. The Black Sister: the terrible invader who had spurred her to her hardest victories, and driven her to the brink of despair. ...

*   *   *

For Angelina the pious figure of speech "being one with the slave" had been literal truth.

In the very beginning, even before her recognition of the fact of slavery, was her oneness with a black child. Her first clear memory was of a playmate being punished—stripped naked and paddled till she screamed. Either Angelina was threatened with the same fate or she felt she deserved it. The pain—or the fear of it—and the shame blurred the line that separated her from the other child.

For years afterward, the scene recurred as a nightmare whenever her conscience was weighted with even the most trifling of sins. By the time she was old enough to understand that it was only slaves who were punished in that fashion, that she—a white child of the master class—was immune to such outrage, it was too late. She could feel only that the black girl was punished in her stead, for did she not know herself guilty of the same small crimes of omission and commission for which slaves were beaten? The double guilt drove her to her first secret act of defiance: stealing the bottle of soothing oil from her mother's medicine chest and slipping out to the servants' quarters to assuage the pain of a lacerated back, or—another time—of wrists and ankles chafed by chains. But neither that nor any of her other small penances brought relief from the guilt.

As she grew into womanhood, her hatred of slavery grew more personal and more intense. She sought out other troubled women—white women—the wives and sisters and mothers of slaveowners—and joined them in an infinite round of "good works." She conspired against the laws of the sovereign state of South Carolina by teaching one of her mother's house servants to read and write. But still she found no peace.

Then she heard the story of the Black Sister.

The man who told it was the minister of the Methodist Church on Calhoun Street, a good man, conscientious and kindly, troubled so deeply that he had to unburden himself and ask counsel of those to whom he customarily gave it.

"This woman is a slave," he said, "but a true converted Christian. There is no white member of my congregation in whose profession of faith I place more reliance.

"She came in great tribulation and asked me to tell her her duty. Her master had made illicit advances to her. A gentleman of the quality! And this, under the same roof that sheltered his white wife and children! The slave woman refused him. Next day, she was beaten severely by the overseer."

While the minister talked, Angelina saw the woman—her dark, sorrowing face, the curve of her shoulders and neck as she drew into herself to escape the blows, and the words that were worse than blows. The image was as real to her as the other women in the room —a handful of well-meaning, charitably inclined ladies of Charleston's élite, who were shaking their heads and murmuring soft distress.

"A few weeks later, when her back was healed enough so that she could return to her duties, her master again approached the woman and suggested a criminal intercourse. Again she refused him. This time the beating was more severe, and with it came a warning: that she would suffer the same punishment again and again until she submitted willingly.

"What was I to tell her?" the minister asked. "To rebel against the authority vested by God in her master? Or to sin against His holy commandment: 'Thou shalt not commit adultery'?"

"Ask yourself rather what commandment *you* sinned against when you left her to choose between the destruction of her body by the lash and the damnation of her soul!"

It burst out of Angelina with force that shocked the minister and the ladies, and marked her for the first time as "fanatical" in her opposition to what they all deplored.

The Black Sister stayed with her for weeks after that. Angelina had only to close her eyes, and the dark mask of anguish appeared before them. Sometimes with head averted, sometimes staring straight at her, pleading silently for mercy, for help.

It was harder and harder to be still, to deny, to draw away. Hardest of all at those times when she sat in the family pew at St. Paul's Episcopal and watched the Black Sister weep, while the minister enjoined his fashionable flock to love their neighbors as themselves. At last it was too hard.

She left the church in which she had been raised and joined the Society of Friends, as Sarah had done before her. It was the Quaker "witness" against slavery that decided her. The putting on of the plain gray dress and white cap was a declaration of personal war, not so much against the vanity of worldliness as against the far graver sin of asserting the "right" of ownership of a fellow man—or woman.

Next came the break with her family. The Black Sister goaded her to that, to each of the small clashes with her mother and brothers and sisters that sawed away at the cord of her affections . . . though the final break was over the mistreatment of a man- not a woman-servant . . . the quarrel with Henry, the last of her brothers who was still living at home. . . .

She could smell the sweet, storm-heavy air of the summer night and hear the sounds . . . the terrible sounds . . . Henry's grunt of effort and the different grunt of the man, Sam, as he resisted the reflex of pain. Sam was determined not to cry out. She could hear him take a long, shuddering breath now and then, but not a whimper, not a groan escaped. It was driving Henry to fury. He had not been really angry when he began, only doing his unpleasant duty as a master, training his boy by punishing him for a fault. Now he was caught up in a sickening contest of wills, his against Sam's. One or the other. Sam must give in or Henry was defeated. He was cursing like a wharf rat, as if he had to speak the language of the brute to play the part. . . .

Angelina stood on the piazza next morning, behind the screen of climbing Banksias, watching Sam drag himself painfully along the paths of the narrow garden, sweeping them clean of leaves and dead blossoms. The Draytons were coming to dinner, and the house was being tidied and garnished. Mother had sent to borrow Thomas's Cudjo to wait on the table, for it would be days before Sam was presentable before company.

"Does that shirt chafe your back?" Angelina asked softly, when Sam's sweeping brought him close to the porch.

"Yes'm, it do, some." He kept his eyes down, and his broom moving steadily as he added in an undertone, "But de oil duh heal 'um, an' I t'ank yunna fuh gib it, missis."

"What made him do it, Sam?"

Sam glanced up at her and then down again. " 'E say I duh let Prince go lame."

The horse was Henry's most prized possession, and Sam was a poor groom. Angelina suspected that he was afraid of Prince. She was. But whether it was fear or laziness or stupidity or resentment, or a combination of all, his fault was not to be cured by whipping. There would be another lapse on Sam's part, another occasion for brutality on Henry's. And it would be worse next time. These vicious circles always spiraled downward.

She must have let out her distress in an audible sigh, for there was a soft, placating voice behind her. "What's wrong, Nina dear? One of your headaches coming on?"

It was Henry's wife, Selina, a sweet, womanly woman who was bearing all the afflictions of a first pregnancy with the patience of Griselda. "Will you sit with me awhile?" she asked. "I declare it's getting so it's all I can do to drag myself around in the mornings."

"Sam has to drag himself around this morning with a back so raw he can't straighten up." Angelina was sorry before she had finished the remark. It was pure cowardice to punish Selina, who was not even an accessory to Henry's crime.

"I do wish he wouldn't be so hard on Sam," Selina murmured unhappily. "Still, I know Henry means it for Sam's good. If you don't show firmness, it's worse for them in the end."

The facile cliché annoyed Angelina. "Why is it?" she asked.

"Why, because . . ." Selina threw her a look of helpless panic. "Because nigras have to be taught to mind. Otherwise they'd . . ."

"They'd what?"

"Why, they'd . . . they'd just run riot, I expect. Hurt themselves and white people too! You know as well as I do, Nina—"

"I know no such thing!"

Tears started in Selina's eyes. She shook her head and looked away, trying to burrow back into the thoughtlessness that sheltered her. But Angelina was angry now, and determined to force the issue.

"Do you really love your husband?" she demanded. "Because if you do, I don't think you ought to sit by and let him risk his immortal soul without so much as a word of warning."

"I can't talk to him." Selina dabbed at her eyes and blew her nose. "I wouldn't even know how to begin. If it's really so bad— and I expect you're right, Nina—well, he's your brother, and you ought to help him. You're much better with words than I am. I'd only make a mess of it and end up crying."

And so it had fallen back on Angelina, the obligation to make herself even more disliked by the last of her brothers with whom she had any ties of affection at all.

The occasion came before she expected it.

Henry came into the parlor one evening, not a week afterward, in a towering rage. He had been sitting with some of his friends, drinking and playing cards, and his face was flushed.

"Where's Sam?" he demanded. "Where's that trifling, impudent black scoundrel? If I can lay my hands on him, I'll give him the sort of whipping I should have the last time! One he won't forget in a hurry."

Angelina suspected that he was venting his fury in words, and would do little of what he was threatening. But Selina turned pale, and Mother—who rarely reprimanded any of her sons—suggested that he moderate his tone and his language.

Henry calmed down and began to talk of something else. Perhaps he would have forgotten the whole thing, but in a few minutes one of the other house servants came to report that he had searched the quarters and stables.

"Stan' lukkuh Sam duh yere Maussa say 'e duh gwi' beat 'um an' 'cide 'e run off."

A snicker punctuated the last phrase. Henry jumped as if he had been stung.

"Probably just sneaked over to that brother of his, the free barber," Mrs. Grimké said. "Don't make a fuss over it, Henry. He'll stay there till he thinks you've forgotten about whipping him, and then he'll come home. Sam isn't fool enough to try to get to the islands in this weather. I wouldn't even offer a reward."

It was sensible advice, and Henry knew it. But he felt himself mocked, humiliated before his other servants. As the hours passed and Sam did not return, his threats grew more and more violent. Angelina could no longer hope they were empty. She began to think of running away herself, so as not to be a witness to the denouement. She hesitated only because of what she had promised Selina. But if she were to intervene with Henry in this high a temper, she was sure she would simply goad him to worse extremes.

She was still debating the issue in her mind on the evening of the second day, when she heard Henry come out of his room and pass her door on his way to the library. Everyone else had retired. It must be that he couldn't sleep and was going to try to read himself drowsy.

It was a sign.

Angelina believed much in signs in those days, assuming with the conceit of youth that whatever happened around her—natural law or its abrogation—must be intended as divine direction to her. If an opportunity to speak to Henry alone arose thus unexpectedly, it was because she was intended to speak. Now!

She made her way quietly to the library. The door stood open. Henry was seated at the desk, staring at some legal papers. He did not turn as she came in, but he heard her and knew who it was.

16

After a minute or so he reached up and touched her cheek, lightly and lovingly. The gesture started a flood of tenderness that threatened her purpose.

"I couldn't help overhearing some of the things you've said you'd do to Sam," she said quickly.

Henry twisted around in his chair and glared up at her. "And that's just what I will do! I've been too easy on him. What he needs is to be whipped till he can't stand. Cured once and for all."

"That would be treating a man as you wouldn't treat your horse."

"That's true. I wouldn't dream of whipping Prince. He's given me no cause."

Angelina backed away.

"You've no business meddling in this," Henry went on. "I don't meddle in your affairs. I say nothing about this outlandish way you've taken to dressing since you turned Quaker. Nothing about your manner to Mother or your rudeness to her friends—or for that matter to anyone else who doesn't suit your notion of what's right and holy.

"Charles has moved up to the country to get away from you. If it weren't for Selina's condition, I might do the same."

She tried to break in, to say she was sorry for having offended. "I have honestly tried to please you, Henry, even at the expense of my conscience."

"Oh, do stop that hypocritical cant! You enjoy making us all miserable. You must! Otherwise, why wouldn't you take your conscience north as Sarah has?"

"For only one reason!" she retorted, piqued to anger at last. "Because if I weren't here, you'd treat the servants even worse than you do. I stay to protect them. And to protect you, Henry. From the violence you do yourself!"

She expected him to be infuriated, but he closed his eyes, put his hands to them for a moment, then stood up. He walked slowly over to the window and looked out into the hot black night.

"If I do myself violence," he said without turning back to her, "it's because you have harrowed my feelings till I'm too wretched to know what I do."

It seemed the most unjust of all the accusations he had made, a perverting of her protest against his cruelty into an excuse for it. Angelina left the room in tears.

But Sam came home next morning, and Henry did not whip him.

She heard everything that passed between them. It was nothing. Henry told Sam to go about his business and not to provoke him again.

She felt one wild surge of elation. Here was proof positive of her sign. Proof of the power of the right word spoken at the right time. But almost at the same instant she heard the echo of Henry's charge: *. . . you have harrowed my feelings till I'm too wretched to know what I do.*

Not long after that, Angelina had a letter from Sarah in Philadelphia, begging her to come for a visit. She decided to go—only for a few months, at the most a year—but she never returned.

The Black Sister was responsible for that, too. It was her haunting, accusing face that distracted Angelina from the religious studies that were designed to lead her to a "ministry" within the Society of Friends. She had thought—as most people in Charleston did—that Quakers opposed slavery and the oppression of free Negroes as forthrightly as Garrison and the radical Abolitionists. It was a blow to discover the gap between profession and practice among the conservative Friends of Sarah's Meeting. Though she did her best to bear the yoke of the discipline to which she had submitted herself in joining the Society, Angelina could not obey the injunciton to "be at peace," with the Black Sister's accusing eyes always upon her.

That was why she was moved to write to Garrison at the worst moment of his personal ordeal, and was censured by the Elders of her Meeting for mixing in a public controversy. That was why she made the even more fateful decision to speak aloud in public on "slavery as it is . . . the truth of its evils and the desirability of its immediate abolition."

Until then no woman had ever spoken from a public platform in America. It was Quaker practice for women to rise in Meeting and speak as the spirit moved them, but not even in Quaker circles were they heard on a political subject. Not even in an audience composed entirely of other women. Sarah warned her that so audacious a step might lead to her being disowned by the Meeting, particularly if Angelina took it without asking leave.

"How can I ask leave to do what my mind is already made up to do?" Angelina asked, and Sarah said no more.

The announcement—which was made mostly from the pulpits of churches—said only that a meeting was to be held at such and such a time and place "to consider the formation of a Female Anti-Slavery Society." Not a word about Angelina's intention to speak! But the news must have been spread by word of mouth: that a white southern gentlewoman who had actually owned slaves herself was going to denounce the institution. The reaction was so intense and immediate that those who had the arrangements in charge began to look for a larger meeting place. It was obvious that no private parlor in the city was large enough to hold the crowd. At last, a Baptist minister who was himself an active Abolitionist offered the vestry room of his church to the ladies.

They accepted gratefully. But that made it public.

Within twenty-four hours—before Angelina and Sarah had been informed of the change of place—letters were dropped into their mailbox, denouncing them as immodest seekers after notoriety. Most of the letters were anonymous, but good friends and staunch Abolitionists came to plead with them to reconsider, not to hold the cause up to ridicule by such a departure from decorum.

Angelina was too troubled to decide the question herself. She went to consult the authority she most respected (of those within reach). Theodore Weld was the most famous Abolitionist orator of the day. She knew him only slightly, and admired him so much that it took great courage to approach him. Sarah went with her to give her strength.

"Slavery is on trial," Theodore told them gravely. "You are called as a witness to sustain the prosecution. What is needed is calm, deliberate, decided testimony from Southerners. If Sister Sarah is willing to add her witness, it will be even better. 'In the mouth of two or three witnesses every word shall be established.' "

To Angelina's surprise, Sarah agreed. They sent word to Maria Chapman and the other sponsors of the meeting that both the Misses Grimké would speak.

No further public announcement was made. But as the day drew near, excitement and opposition mounted till the question at issue seemed to be women's rights instead of the slaves' wrongs. On the morning of the day itself, there was a leaf-fall of angry handbills, referring to Sarah and Angelina by name, and calling on "all respectable members of the community to be on hand to give these bold southern women a lesson!"

Angelina was appalled. How was she to open her heart and give "calm, deliberate, decided testimony," in the face of such an uproar? But she could not back out now. There was no other business to come before the meeting, except the proposal to form a new Society, which was to be put to the assemblage after the sisters had spoken. If they did not speak, there was nothing. Victory for those who wanted to frighten all Abolition societies out of existence!

The moment came, and with it a terror that seemed to paralyze her limbs as well as her lungs.

The minister spoke a short greeting to the ladies (three hundred of them, packed into a room with space for half that number), intoned an even shorter prayer, and left.

Maria Chapman came forward to introduce Angelina. There was a commotion in the back of the hall, and the minister returned to eject a man who had attempted to conceal himself behind a large potted fern, hoping to spy on the mysteries to come.

Now Angelina was at the rostrum, standing erect but feeling that the slightest new disturbance would topple her into a faint.

"I feel a necessity upon me while I live and slavery lives, to testify against it . . ."

Her voice was so weak that it reached only to the first rows. Women farther back were craning their necks and stirring in their chairs.

"My flesh cries out, 'If it be possible, let this cup pass from me,'" she went on, still in a voice that was little better than a whisper. "Yet I know that if I hold my peace, the stone would cry out of the wall and the beam of the timber would answer it."

She faltered, shut her eyes, and breathed deeply. Suddenly, like the genie of the lamp, the image of the Black Sister appeared. Appeared to her and entered into her. Moved within her. Became her!

"Oh, the slain daughters of my people!" Her voice rang with a sudden new power that astonished her as much as it did her listeners. "They lie in all the ways: their tears fall as the rain and are their meat night and day; their blood runneth down like water; their plundered hearths are desolate; they weep for their husbands and children, because they are not; and the proud waves do continually go over them, while no eye pitieth and no man careth for their souls!"

She saw the women in the audience draw away, resist, and then—some more quickly than others—surrender, as she had already surrendered, to the woman for whom she pleaded. For she was no longer herself, but the Other, the Black Sister. She suffered, in her own person, all the humiliations and outrages, all the beatings, starvings, abuses without name. And the suffering was not of one, but of thousands, distilled into one.

The gift of tongues descended on Angelina to give them a voice.

It was a priceless gift but it was only provisional. Hers only so long as she was strong enough to bear the weight of anguish, and there came a time when she was not strong enough. Then it almost destroyed her. Then she had to expel the Black Sister, bar the door of her being, and retreat in fear to the farthest, darkest corner. . . .

* * *

For thirty years Angelina had kept that door closed, but the Black Sister was forcing it open now.

Not *the* Black Sister, the old anonymous abstraction, but *a* black sister . . . a real woman . . . victim of a real white man . . . a brother . . .

Angelina scrawled a hasty last paragraph to the letter to the young man at Lincoln University and went back to the parlor to consult with Sarah—and perhaps with Theodore—about the final draft.

Sarah was still sitting near the grate fire, knitting. Her steel-rimmed spectacles had slipped down her nose; she was not looking through them. Her fingers had eyes of their own after so many years. She was staring into the fire, and the rose glow of its reflected light fell like a blessing on her lined face and thin gray hair.

"Ah! There you are, Nina." She looked up and smiled with hard-won cheerfulness. "I was just thinking of coming in to you. The children have gone out visiting, and Theo is in the cellar looking up some old books. I wanted to ask you: have you shown him the article?"

"Not yet."

"Why not?"

Angelina was not sure, and it made her uneasy. In all the years of her married life she could not recall another time when she had kept a secret from her husband, even for an hour. "It seemed to me that this is a matter that concerns us—you and me—first and most directly. Thoda and the children only indirectly. I thought *we* ought to decide together what is best to do . . . what is possible. . . ." But the more she thought, the less defensible her silence seemed.

"How do you think Theodore will feel?" Sarah asked.

22

"Exactly as we do! And agree with a whole heart to whatever we decide."

"And Stuart and young Sarah?"

Angelina sighed. "If they are not prepared to accept *any* victim of oppression and injustice as their brother, then we have failed as parents—all three of us, for you have been as much a mother to them as I have." She put her letter into Sarah's hands and asked, "Will you look this over for me? I feel it is wrong—too brief and too cold. But I cannot do any better right now."

Sarah pushed her spectacles back into place and began to read. "You ask him to tell us whatever he is willing to about himself," she said, when she had finished. "Ought we not to tell him something about ourselves? Otherwise he may misunderstand our interest."

"You think he doesn't already know about us?"

"It has been a good many years since the close of our public life, and I doubt that the memory of it is kept green in Charleston." Sarah smiled with mild irony.

"You say 'we' and 'our,'" Angelina said. "I haven't asked you whether you are in agreement that a letter should go."

"Yes, I agree . . ." Sarah looked as if she were about to add something—a reservation or an explanation of her assent. But she changed her mind and said no more.

Angelina felt suddenly very weary. "Would you copy it over, Sarah, and make whatever corrections you think it needs?"

Sarah got pen and ink and a fresh sheet of paper and began to rewrite the letter, changing a phrase here, adding a line there, asking Angelina's permission in some cases, assuming the right in others, reading it all aloud as she put it down. Finally she paused to ask:

"What shall I say about Theodore?"

"Only that I was one of the early anti-slavery lecturers at the West."

Angelina turned and saw Theodore standing in the doorway.

23

She could not tell from his voice or the expression on his face whether he had heard enough to understand what was afoot or not. Perhaps he had known all along. Perhaps he had seen the article in the *Standard* and said nothing to her. It didn't matter now.

The benignity of his smile told her all she needed—if she needed anything—to reassure her. His devotion to her and to the cause they had both served fitted together into a ring of strength that would support her through any ordeal that was to come.

III

Archy and Frank slipped into their places at the table in the hush before the grace was pronounced.

It was an unusually long grace, lugubriously intoned by one of the theological students. The dining hall was cold, and the wheat porridge was solidifying in the thick crockery bowls before the students' spoons attacked it.

"Let's have Grimké to say grace the rest of the month," suggested one wag at Archy's end of the table.

"Me?" asked Frank.

"No, your brother."

"Archy? He'll make you an oration!"

"Not in the morning," said the author of the idea. "Look like he hasn't got a word to waste, even on the Lord."

There was general laughter, and Archy smiled to show that he took no offense. "Since we moved up to that corner room, I don't get thawed out till near about lunchtime."

Frank beamed his relief that Archy had taken the teasing with such good grace. "Let's get started," he said. "We got to go to old Bowers' study for Greek, and there might be a fire there."

"There is," said one of the first-year students. "I laid it myself."

On the strength of that promise, the entire second-year class wolfed down the last of the gelatinous porridge and pushed their chairs back. Professor Bowers lived a short distance off the campus, and the walk through the snow would take the minutes that remained before class time. As they were all slipping into their overcoats and boots in the entrance hall, someone called from the mail table:

"There's a letter here for you, Archy."

He came to take the small square envelope from his informant's hand.

"From Mauma?" Frank asked.

Archy shook his head. The handwriting was unfamiliar, and the postmark blurred. But in the upper left-hand corner were three initials, *A.G.W.*, and a street address in Fairmount, Massachusetts.

Fairmount . . .

He scowled at the name, and slowly it came into his mind that the young lady in the Freedom Office—long, long ago that seemed now—had said Miss Sarah and Miss Angelina lived in Fairmount. *A.G.W.* That would be her, all right. Angelina Grimké, now Mrs. . . . What was it? Wells?

"You coming, Archy?" Frank called from the door.

"Go 'long without me. I'll catch up."

He started to tear at the flap of the envelope, then changed his mind. Other students were coming out of the dining hall, and he felt a strong impulse to conceal. He slipped the letter between the pages of his *Introduction to Greek Grammar* and went upstairs, up to the room on the third floor that Frank and he shared. He would read Miss Angelina's letter where no one could read his face. Not even Frank. It was addressed, after all, only to him:

Mr. Grimké,
Sir:

In a recent number of the Anti-Slavery Standard, *I saw a notice of a meeting at Lincoln University at which a young gentleman of the name of Grimké delivered an address.*

My maiden name was Grimké. I am the youngest daughter of the late Judge John Faucheraud Grimké, of Charleston, sister to Miss Eliza Grimké, who resides in that city at present.

As the name is a very uncommon one, it has occurred to me that you have probably been a slave of one of my brothers or my nephews, and I feel a great desire to know all about you . . .

He had read down that far before the fuse of anger burned to the powder keg of his heart, setting off shellbursts of such brilliance that they blinded him to the words on the page. He saw only snatches of what followed:

. . . where you were born . . . who your parents are . . . everything you are willing to tell me about yourself . . .

Why, he was willing to tell her all there was to tell! Why not? Let her eat the answers to her incautious questions and see how they sat! He would put it all down . . . spare her nothing . . . from the very beginning!

*   *   *

The beginning was Caneacres.

He said the name over and over under his breath, rubbing it like a magic lamp till images began to form.

Sights. Sounds. Smells.

The feathery look of the rice fields between the dikes.

The gurgle of ditch water running through an open trunk.

Birdsong and frog croak.

Midges stinging at noontime.

27

The reserve—a great hall, pillared with cypress trees, roofed with high branches, festooned with moss, floored with a scum made up of millions of tiny floating leaves, cypress knees sticking up through it like hooded figures of men and women, wearing the gray garments of field hands, and kneeling to pray. . . .

He saw people, now, women with flails, beating at piles of rice grains, gold on a dark floor of dirt. He heard a rhythmic thumping from the mill at the water's edge. From the stables came an odor of hay and manure and horse urine. He was standing on the stoop of a little frame house, across the yard from the big house.

The big house . . .

Besides the name, all he could remember was its lower story—a sort of high basement—and the flight of steps that led up to the piazza. At the head of those steps stood a man, a very tall man with light hair and a stern face, brows that bushed out over eyes that were the color of evening fog.

There was a game they played together, he and the man. Archy stood at the foot of the steps and made a noise like a horse whinnying. Sometimes he had to make it many times before the man came out onto the piazza.

"Well, now," the man would say, "what does horse want?"

"Horse want 'e diddy."

"What's this?" the man feigned astonishment. "Horse can't talk, can he?"

Archy made the whinnying noise again. The man laughed and brought his hand from behind his back. When he opened it, something fell out and tumbled down the flight of steps. Sometimes it was a lump of sugar, sometimes a penny, sometimes a whittled toy. Once it was a marble that had whorls of brown and white like foam on swamp water. . . .

"Ellie, gib me some! Gib me some. . . . Me! . . . Me, too, Ellie!"

Black children crowded around him as Archy ran back across the yard, and he could hear the man on the piazza complaining.

"The boy's name is Archy. Why don't they call him by it?"

At some point (he could not recall when it was or who it was that told him) Archy learned that the tall man was called Maussa. He owned Caneacres and all the rice lands along the river. And that was not all! He owned a house in Charleston, which was a place far away—maybe as much as thirteen miles!—across and beyond the river. Maussa was connected in some way with people in that far place, people who sometimes came and passed a whole day at the big house but who never stayed the night. Mauma did not like these people. They made her fidgety and short-tempered. When there were visitors from Charleston, Archy and Frank were kept in for punishment on the slightest of excuses, or sometimes without any excuse at all.

The next thing Archy remembered clearly was the storm in which the big live oak tree was struck by lightning and fell, crushing three of the houses in the settlement and killing some of the people. He could still remember how the branches looked as they lay on the ground, with pretty ruchings of pale-green resurrection fern running the whole of their great twisted lengths. Archy had mistrusted live oaks ever since, and made sure to stay out from under them, even when the sun was hot and their shade would have been kind.

It was not long after the storm that Maussa took sick. Mauma was kept busy in the big house, even at suppertime, and the boys were sent to take their meals in the kitchen. Someone there told them Mauma had to nurse Maussa, who was very bad off.

Then suddenly everyone on the place was grief-stricken and frightened, as on the morning after the storm. "Maussa, 'e dead," someone said. "Now all t'ing duh gwi' be sol'. House and land and rice crop and people, all two!"

That was the first the boys knew that people could be sold. They knew it about pigs and chickens, because Mauma raised them. Now and again one would disappear, and when they inquired, they would be told it had been taken into Charleston to be sold. They had never been to Charleston, and they had no wish to go. It was a void into which pigs and chickens disappeared. Would Archy and Frank and Mauma now be sucked into that void, and lost?

"No," Mauma told them when they asked her. "We going Charleston, but not fuh be sold. We free. Maussa free us in 'e will."

"Then howcomeso we got to go Charleston?" they asked.

Mauma laughed and ran her hand over their heads and shoulders.

"Howcomeso you don' want to go?" she asked. "You go have it fine there. You go have cousins fuh play with, and the O'Hears and all the Wilkinson young uns."

These names meant nothing to the boys, and they were not appeased by the prospect of strange playfellows, however superior Mauma might consider them, in place of those they would be losing by the move.

"We go build our own house," Mauma promised next, " 'longside Uncle Frank and Big Aunty's house."

"Will it be as fine as this one here?"

Mauma said it would be finer.

"And you go have schooling. Learn you a trade. You never go have to serve, neither be sold. Remember that all times."

They did remember; and remembering made it hard later on, when the promises Mauma had made them began to be broken, one after the other, till there were none left to break. . . .

In the beginning they stayed—Mauma and Archy and Frank, and John, when he was born—in a large room over the kitchen of the Grimké house on Coming Street. That was because their own house was not built yet. (Mauma had bought the boards, she told them, but they must wait till Uncle Frank and his friends had time to nail them up.) There were lots of white people in this house on Coming Street: two old ladies, Miss Mary and Miss Eliza; a young lady named Miss Henrietta, who got married and disappeared; and two young white gentlemen, Montague and Tom. Montague was the elder, not as pleasant as Tom, but very kind and soft-spoken in those days, even to Mauma.

Archy's other memories of people were dim and uncertain compared to his memories of the city itself: a series of awesome revelations to a boy who had never been off a rice plantation in St. Paul's Parish. Archy could remember the first time they were taken to church on a Sunday, and he and Frank threw back their heads to look at the tops of the pillars, and got so dizzy they staggered. The first time they walked along the docks and were bewildered by the tangle of rigging and masts till someone taught them to see each ship as a separate entity. He remembered the marvel of crowds of finely dressed folk walking in the streets, not going anywhere in particular; of carriages drawn by two or even four horses; of clocks set high in church steeples; of iron fences and gates. He remembered the first time a door opened as he was passing a fine house, and he caught a glimpse of the long, shaded piazza that stretched back along the garden, which was as long and not much wider; the revelation that the houses of the quality turned a narrow shoulder to the street, and stretched out in luxurious privacy behind those wooden doors and brick walls. From that moment he imagined that the new house Uncle Frank was building would be something on this order, not as large, of course, but of the same fascinating design.

The reality was a crashing disappointment. The new house was nothing but the old house brought to town, the same size and shape, set up on the same short brick posts (though the river was so far away here it seemed unlikely it would ever rise high enough to flood underneath). True, the new house had partitions that divided it into three rooms: a bedroom, a kitchen, and a hall between, whereas the old house had been divided only by usage. But the old house had advantages that were missing in the new one. The yard, for instance, was infinitely superior as a playground. Here there was just space for Mauma's wash kettle and the lines where she hung out clothes. The boys had to play in the street or in the yard of one of their playmates.

One of Mauma's promises that seemed like it was going to come true was the one about school. It kept in a shack at the back of the Wilkinsons' lot, behind the pen where Mr. Wilkinson, who was a butcher, fattened the cattle he was going to slaughter. It was a white man who taught the boys there. Later, Frank and Archy and their cousin, Owen Weston, went to a different school, in the cabin of an old black woman who knew little more than her letters. They were warned that they must keep "shut-mouth" about these lessons, or the old woman would be punished.

Archy asked his Uncle Frank howcomeso, and was told it was against the law to teach colored children to read and write or to cipher.

"Then howcomeso we didn't keep shut-mouth when we went to the Wilkinsons'?"

"Law duh change back and forth," said his uncle with a brassy ring of bitterness. "Or they find a way round it. The Charleston quality makes the law for all Carolina, saving they own selves."

Soon after that, schooling stopped altogether.

Neither Archy nor Frank minded. Life was school enough in those days, full of interest and promise. If there were hard times— days when there was not enough food to fill them, nights in winter when the little house could not be kept warm—such times would pass. They might come again, but they would pass again. Poverty was the only enemy the family had to fight, and they fought together, deeply united, and confident of eventual victory. For the boys believed that all they needed was to grow. Once they were big enough to play a man's part, they would provide for themselves and for Mauma as well.

They had almost reached that point, when the most important of Mauma's promises was broken, in a way for which she could neither be blamed nor entirely forgiven.

It happened on a day that began like any other. They came, Archy and Frank, to deliver Montague Grimké's laundry to the side door of the Coming Street house. Miss Eliza met them as usual, but instead of taking the clean linen from their little wagon, and giving them a bundle of dirty laundry and some money, she told them to come on into the house.

"Wash your faces and hands at the bowl there, and wipe them on the towel I've put out," she said. "I want you to come meet your new mistress."

They had no idea what she was talking about. "Mistress" was a word they had heard, but its meaning had been of no concern to them.

"You're to make her a bow," Miss Eliza said. "Do you know how to do that?"

They did not.

"Scrape your foot and drop your head. . . . No, not like that! You don't have to bend double, for goodness' sake! Just make a little bob! . . . There, that's more like it. And say, 'How de do, mistress, how glad we are to see you.'"

They followed her up to the parlor on the second floor, and there was Montague, staring in a sicky-sweet way at a lady who sat with her hands in her lap, smiling back at him, and smelling like violets.

"Now then!"

Miss Eliza gave them a little shove forward. The boys made their bows, as she had taught them, but they could not bring themselves to repeat the nonsense she had lined out for them.

As soon as they could, they escaped and ran home to tell Mauma the story and ask her what it meant.

Mauma glared at them as if she suspected them of making it up, though they kept interrupting themselves to assure her that it was all true. "What Montague say?" she asked once.

They couldn't remember that he or the young lady had said anything.

"Must be that 'e new wife," Mauma said, when they were done telling. "Folk say 'e go all the way to Alabama to fetch 'um."

That was all. The boys were still full of questions, but Mauma looked queer around the mouth and eyes, as if she were suffering from toothache and might snap the head off anyone who pestered her. They let the questions sleep, and before very long had forgotten them.

At breakfast one morning, some time later, Mauma told them that Montague Grimké wanted them to come and serve in his house. She looked even more queer now, her mouth drawn tight as if she'd been eating persimmon skin, and her eyes shuttered down on the inside. Again the boys had questions they dared not ask. They did what Mauma said: washed themselves, put on fresh clothes, and walked up Coming Street, feeling self-conscious, like people dressed for church on the wrong day of the week.

They knocked at the kitchen door and were met by Miss Eliza, who was full of even more crazy notions than before. She and Miss Mary spent the whole morning instructing them in the duties of houseboys, some of which were interesting, others downright silly. But the significance of all this did not dawn on either of them till late in the afternoon when they were sent to be measured by a tailor for suits of livery.

They understood then, all right. They had seen other boys dressed in such suits, made of fine flannel, with brass buttons in double rows down the front of the tight-fitting jackets. Boys who served in the fine houses along the South and East Battery. Boys who were despised and pitied, made the butt of taunts by the free urchins with whom Archy and Frank played. Boys who might be better fed and clothed than most of their tormentors but who were slaves.

"You told us we free!" They faced Mauma with it when they got home for supper. "You said we never go have to serve."

Mauma did not look up from her ironing.

"It ain't right," she said. " 'E daddy tell me on 'e dyin' bed: se, Montague my eldes'-born son, and I put the charge on 'um to carry out my wish; se, treat you like 'e own kin, see you never duh want!

"That what 'e daddy say on the day 'e die. Montague know. All the Grimkés duh know.

"They ain't never bother theyself what we want fuh. Ain't never give me a cent but what I earn washing they clothes. I ain't never ask more: only be let alone and raise my children up free."

Mauma set her iron down on the stove lid with a heavy deliberate hand, and sank into a chair, her face turned so the boys couldn't see the look on it. She took a big breath, held it, and then blew it out. Her anger seemed to blow out with it. Her voice was softer when she spoke again.

"It ain't right. But they's nothing to do. You too small yet to try and make it away."

So it began, the long war, the private war that lived within the womb of the public one, separate, yet ultimately dependent on the larger outward event. A war carried on by two boys, ten and eleven years old, against four adults and a whole system of laws, prisons, policemen, and professional torturers. A war that would have been doomed to early defeat if the enemy had not been engaged in a desperate, losing struggle on the outer front.

They fought in different ways, Archy and Frank. Archy's tactics were hardly subtle enough to merit the name: a simple, silent, stubborn refusal to learn the lessons of servitude that he had been raised to believe he would never have to learn. Day after day Miss Eliza would take him into the dining room and show him how the table was to be laid: where the plates and napkins went, the water tumblers, the saltcellars and pepper shakers, the vinegar cruet, and so on, till finally, with exaggerated ceremony, she unlocked the silver chest with a key from the bunch she carried at her waist and revealed the serried ranks of knives and stacks of forks and spoons.

Archy did as he was directed just as long as his mentor stood over him. As soon as he was left alone, he made mistakes. Not the same mistakes every time. Sometimes by accident—none at all. When that happened, Miss Eliza would congratulate him and reward him by saying he could do it on his own from now on. But the very next time, he would make a mistake and there would be a hullabaloo. Sometimes he was punished, struck on the hands or the top of his head with the sole of a house slipper, not hard enough to hurt him much, but enough to humiliate and embitter him.

Frank's strategy was, in the beginning, more devious and more successful.

In the matter of the hateful brass-buttoned suit, he won an easy victory. Miss Julia (the new Mrs. Montague) had cautioned the boys about taking care of the suits, which were expensive. They were to wear them only on duty, not going and coming from home (an economy that spared them the shame of being seen by their old playmates in this telltale garb), and they were never to kneel in them except at prayers, lest they stretch or tear the trouser legs.

Frank was careful to obey all these commands, but he managed to fall down the cellar stairs and rip both trousers and jacket so badly that they had to be sent back to the tailor. He was not punished for this mishap, but sent home to have his scrapes and bruises poulticed by Mauma. (Archy was consumed by envy. He did not arrange to have a similar accident only because he foresaw that the ruse would be exposed by repetition.)

When the suit came back, Frank wore it only a week before he stumbled while carrying a bucket of lye water. Next day great holes appeared in the fabric. This time he was whipped, but whipping had remarkably little effect on Frank. He had a natural stoicism, an ability to draw into himself so that he presented an almost impervious surface of body and spirit to the lash. Montague exhausted his arm and his anger without the satisfaction of a whimper from his victim. And Miss Julia decided to punish him by "letting him go round in that raggedy old suit, instead of looking nice and smart, like Archy!"

Frank did his best to conceal his satisfaction, but Montague caught a glint of it. The gage was down. From then on, they confronted each other like duelists between whom no honorable compromise is possible.

The entire Grimké family seemed to consider that it had a duty to break Frank's resistance, but the ladies did not approve of corporal punishment. Montague was forced to experiment with alternatives, and eventually he hit on one that was explosively effective: locking Frank in.

The first time it was because Frank had forgotten (or simply decided not) to blacken and polish Montague's riding boots. He was scolded and taken up to the third floor, locked in a room with the boots and some rags, and told he had better be sure the chore was done, and well done, by suppertime, when he would be let out.

To be confined in a small space was unendurable to Frank, so he went to work to free himself. The door was latched on the outside, of course, but he found a long hooked rod, made for closing window shutters, reached it over the transom and lifted the latch. He walked downstairs, and what's more—he bragged at supper that evening—as he passed Miss Julia's chamber door he made a face at her back.

Next time he was locked in a shed in the yard behind the kitchen. There was no transom, and there was a padlock instead of a latch. But the shed was set on brick posts like a plantation cabin, so Frank turned his attention to the flooring. He found a board that could be pried up, wriggled his thin body through the opening, and wormed his way out between the floor and the ground. He got a bad scratch that festered and gave him a fever. But it was not too high a price for such a triumph.

For some reason (perhaps because the Grimkés were a little afraid of a showdown with Frank), it was Archy who drew the first real fire. Miss Eliza lost patience with his "stupidity" and complained to Montague, who dragged him the whole length of Coming Street to shake him under Mauma's nose like a rat.

"You're behind this, Nancy," Montague shouted. "You put the brats up to it!" And he began to spew out oaths more shocking even than his anger.

No one in Mauma's house used profane language. The boys had been raised to believe it was a sin that condemned the transgressor to eternal damnation. There was solace in the thought of Montague plunging toward the fiery pit, closer and closer with each word he uttered, but there was terror, too. For by the same token he was no longer "quality," but a creature like an overseer or a constable, beyond the reach of morality, capable of any atrociousness.

Threats of punishment rolled like thunder in the little kitchen. Worst of all was the unspoken threat that Mauma would lose her temper. Montague had twice raised his hand as if to strike her. If he did—if he made even the smallest move to bring it down—Mauma's hands would be at his throat! Archy knew that the penalty for striking a white man was death. Mauma knew it too. She was wrestling with the demon of her anger. Archy closed his eyes, bowed his head, made himself small, and prayed. But he could still hear the quarrel, even through his prayer. Words that beat like bludgeons or cut like knives! Words that made a sourness rise in his throat, so that he was afraid he would vomit right there in the small, stifling space where the two confronted each other.

". . . you' own blood brother you taken fuh slave!"

"That's a lie!"

"No lie! You daddy tol' you, and you know."

*　　*　　*

Archy's revery was broken by the group of dark figures that suddenly moved across the white expanse of snow at which he was staring from his dormitory window. It was Frank and the rest of the Greek class, coming home. They were laughing and clowning, like children, making snowballs and threatening in pantomime to hurl them at the president's house or at the newly erected statue of the martyred President for whom the college had been renamed.

Frank was very much part of the group. Yet he was noticeably lighter than any of the others. As light as Archy. Almost light enough to pass for white.

He looked up just then and saw Archy in the window, and waved. He was coming up, instead of going on to the algebra class that was next on this morning's schedule. Probably because he was curious about the letter.

If Frank had not already seen it, Archy would have been tempted to conceal it . . . just as he was tempted to ignore it . . . to let it go unanswered forever now that his first impulse of anger had burned itself out.

Oddly enough, that was Frank's first suggestion when he had read it through.

"You going to answer her?" he asked. "I wouldn't, if it was me."

Archy shrugged noncommitally. "You know what I been thinking about?" he said. "Changing our name to something else besides Grimké."

If Frank was taken by surprise, he hid it well. The step was not unusual among students at Lincoln. Many came directly from slavery, bearing the name of the last master to whom they had belonged. As their horizons expanded and other possibilities opened up, they frequently made a different choice. Lincoln was a common one. Washington was another, or Sherman or Sheridan or even Jefferson.

"What for?" Frank asked.

Archy frowned. Frank knew what for as well as he did. For any number of reasons, beginning with the one Miss Angelina's letter raised with such brutal directness—the question of their paternity.

"For one thing," Archy said aloud, *"she* wouldn't ever have written us if I hadn't gone by that name and got written about in the papers."

"You don't have to answer her," Frank said again. And then, in a tone of studied casualness, "What would you want to change to?"

"I don't know. I'd have to think some. Weston, maybe," Archy said.

Frank looked as if he wanted to say something, but couldn't make up his mind to it. After a moment or two he picked up his books. "You going to miss another class?" he asked. "Just on account of that old letter?"

Archy shook his head. He jammed Miss Angelina's letter into the drawer of his writing table, picked up his books, and followed his brother down the hall.

IV

Old Sarah was determined to keep herself so busy that anxiety would have no chance to sink a roothold into her heart. She would have gone to Boston with young Sarah—who had a new letter from her fiancé to share with his mother—and spent the time paying visits to some of the old friends she seldom saw of late. But this was the day Stephen had promised to come for the heavy house-cleaning, and he needed supervision, so she stayed to give it.

Stephen was the one almost complete failure the sisters had suffered in their long campaign to rehabilitate the slaves they had freed and brought north. After a quarter of a century, Stephen was still shiftless and slovenly and unreliable. No one else would employ him, and it was a sacrifice on their part to do so.

As the morning wore on and he did not put in an appearance, Sarah tried to pass the time doing those of his tasks that were within her strength, but her old legs kept giving out so that she had to sit and rest. Each time she did, she found herself slipping into a silent dialogue with her absent sister. Actually, it seemed to be going on all the time and to be covered by the "cheerful noise" of her movements only so long as she worked.

"You ought not to have acted in such haste, Nina," she was saying sternly now. "You could have made inquiries. There is an office of the Freedman's Bureau in Boston. They could have put us in touch with the Bureau in Charleston. Or you could have consulted with Parker Pillsbury. His brother and sister-in-law are in Charleston. They could have helped us find out a little more before writing directly to . . . to . . ."

Even in her mind Sarah could not bring herself to choose words that would define the relationship. She got to her feet again with a sigh.

What she must do was keep moving at chores that would not tax her so that she had to rest again. She decided that if she took the stairs very slowly, she could make any number of trips from cellar to second story with small loads of coal to fill all the bedroom grates.

But soon the rhythm of the steps, ascending or descending, insinuated itself into her train of thought, and she found herself telling them off like beads on a rosary, naming each step with the name of one of her brothers.

John . . . Thomas . . . Charles . . . Frederick . . . Benjamin . . . Henry . . . Over and over, till one after another they dropped from the list of "possibles," like losers in a game of musical chairs.

Charles could hardly have been the master of the young man, for he had never owned anything but the right to live off his parents and brothers. . . .

Frederick never owned a slave while he lived in the South. He moved to Ohio after he graduated from college, and rose to prominence as a judge. It was possible then to own slaves in some parts of the North, but Frederick—who wrote learned defenses of the rights of southern states to legalize slavery—had taken a firm personal stand against it.

Thomas owned many slaves—though Sarah and Angelina believed he was on the point of emancipating them when he died. His two sons inherited all his chattels, and the young man who called himself Archibald Grimké might have belonged to one of them, except that they had both changed their surnames to Drayton, in order to inherit from their maternal grandfather. Their freed slaves would go by the name of Drayton, or some other . . . not Grimké.

That left Benjamin, Henry, and John.

Benjamin died young. Sarah and Angelina had long ago bought and freed all of his servants.

They had done the same for John's and for their mother's. Henry's people from the Caneacres place had been too many for them, but—as Nina pointed out—they would have taken the names of later masters.

That left only Henry's two sons. They might have purchased young slaves to serve in their houses before the War. But Eliza had lived at one time or another in the households of both these nephews, and if two of their liberated servants had achieved such distinction, she would surely have spoken of it at some time during her stay. . . .

Sarah groaned. Must she now go over the list again, testing the name of each of her brothers against the other premise? Must she ask herself which beloved brother had hidden the sin Nina's rashness was about to expose?

What if it should prove to be Thomas? the hero of Sarah's girlhood, who had defied the secessionists of his state and stood up to the mob that came to punish him for it. What if Thomas were now to be revealed a hypocrite and a profligate?

Or Benjamin?—the gallant one whose life was thrown away in an attempt to save others from a shipwreck. His son and daughters worshipped his memory. Were they now to be shamed?

But it would be just as bad if it were Henry or John, both of whom had left children and grandchildren. Even if it were Charles —of whom it was easiest to believe evil—all of them, all the Grimkés would be shamed. . . .

"If you persist in the course you have set out upon, Nina," she said aloud, "you will bring shame on all of us. And what is to be gained? Nothing. Not even by this . . . by Archibald! It would be far better for him to pass as an ex-slave—to call himself by another name."

"But he chose to call himself Grimké," Nina answered in the silence. "Does that not give him the right to our consideration? Think how many others we have given to, without stint. Would you deny *him?*"

"He hasn't asked for our help! He could have written us when he came north."

"Perhaps he never heard of us. You said yourself, there is no reason to believe our memory is kept green in Charleston."

It was true. Sarah had said something like that, but the more she thought of it, the less likely it seemed. And certainly after the young man came north, to a school that must have on its faculty many of the old anti-slavery comrades or their sons, it was impossible that someone should not have called his attention to the fact that the name he bore had once been famous. For Angelina Grimké had once been the most talked-about woman in America, and Sarah a close second.

Sarah's legs were giving out again and she had to rest. She went into her own chamber and lay down on the bed. The dialogue took up again.

"You ought not to have done it, Nina," she said. "It can do no good, and it may do harm."

"What harm?"

Sarah could not answer. She was getting lost. She had not felt like this for many years. It waked her old envy of her sister, and the anger that accompanied it. For Nina was never lost. She had always known better than Sarah, who was thirteen years older. Even as a child, Nina seemed to know with the certainty of revelation which was the path of righteousness, no matter how covered by contradictions or hidden by brambles. . . .

Only once had Sarah dared to differ with her precious child, to range herself with Nina's critics and detractors, and the memory of it appalled her even now.

*   *   *

It was in 1835, after Nina came north and was received into the Philadelphia Meeting. A black year, when the whole country rocked with fury against Abolitionism. Newspapers carried accounts of mob attacks on the homes of its partisans, of assaults on free colored families, of a theology student stripped and flogged for carrying anti-slavery tracts in his valise, a schoolmistress jailed for accepting a dark-skinned pupil, a gibbet large enough to hang two, raised in the street opposite Garrison's Boston home.

Sarah heard the commotion only dimly, engaged as she was in a desperate inner struggle of her own. It was a tenet of the Quaker faith that when the spirit of the Lord moved in one of His children —man or woman—it was a command to minister. Sarah felt such a command, but she could not speak. She tried again and again, but the words that came to her lips when she rose in Meeting were unacceptable as inspired truth. Those Friends who loved her urged her to be patient, to read and meditate and pray that she be made a worthy vessel; then, in the Lord's good time, the message would frame itself without effort on her part; the words would come of themselves. Those who did not love her spoke reprovingly of her pushing herself forward, and hinted that she committed the unpardonable sin of writing out and committing to memory what she said. The Elders of her Meeting came as close to bidding her be silent as the usages of the Society allowed.

Insulated in her own ordeal, Sarah was nevertheless conscious that her sister was undergoing a different one. There was not the slightest doubt in Angelina's mind that she was called to the ministry, but the Friends imposed a probationary period during which she was to "be still and invite the peace that passeth understanding." To be still and at peace was a contradiction in terms for one of Angelina's temperament. Into the vacuum imposed by this discipline, a new concern was intruding itself: the political spirit of Abolitionism.

Sarah was not out of sympathy with the cause itself. By the time Angelina was born, Sarah was old enough to have come to the conclusion that slavery was evil. Like Nina, she had been attracted to the Friends in the first instance by their witness against slavery, and like Nina she had been shocked to discover that, in Philadelphia at least, the majority of the sect was content with denouncing the evil in the abstract; that when it came to the practical matter of acting on their concern, members differed so radically that discussion of the issue was forbidden, lest it bring disunity into the Meeting.

Sarah suffered this disappointment with humble patience. Angelina did not. She turned—and this was what alarmed Sarah—more and more in the direction of the extremist group around William Lloyd Garrison.

Garrison was the archfiend or the archangel of the movement, depending on one's view. Sarah had no view of her own, but those whose guidance she accepted in other matters condemned him. It distressed her that Nina should subscribe to his polemical *Liberator*, wait each week for its arrival with unconcealed eagerness, devour it as if it were manna for her starving spirit. It distressed her even more because this disrupted the program of study and meditation that was supposed to be preparing Nina for her ministry. Was it not Sarah's duty to remonstrate, to "be faithful" to this beloved child? As godmother, she had taken responsibility for her sister's spiritual life. Was she not bound to exercise that office now and help Nina achieve the goal she herself had set?

It was not hard to convince herself that this was indeed her duty, but Sarah was timid of trying her powers of persuasion against Nina's obstinacy. Less and less sure of her own vocation, more and more dependent on human affection, she dreaded any clash with the being she most loved in all the world. So she found reason after reason for postponing the painful discussion, until—with almost no warning—Nina decided to leave the city for the summer, and go to live with a family of Friends in Shrewsbury. She made no arrangement to have the *Liberator* forwarded.

Sarah was deeply relieved. Either Nina had lost interest in the sort of news and opinion Garrison printed, or she had decided to reject his gospel. Either was good enough. Sarah drew her ration of reassurance from each copy that arrived and was laid away by her, unread. She was, therefore, unprepared for the thunderbolt when it struck.

"Friend Evans has come to see thee," said Catharine Morris, in whose home Sarah was living that year. "He is waiting in the front parlor."

Elder Evans was chief among Sarah's detractors in the Meeting, and there was no possibility that this was a friendly call. Her mind darted over all her deeds and words, even her thoughts of the past few days, as she made her way downstairs to greet the aged Friend and receive his granitic nod in return.

"Thee has seen thy sister's letter?" he asked, in the manner of one inquiring whether the next of kin has viewed a corpse.

"What letter?"

"Thee knows very well that she has written a letter which Garrison has printed," he said irritably.

"Angelina? Wrote Garrison? And he printed—"

"Yes, yes! If thee does not know, say so, instead of repeating my words like a parrot!" It was obvious that he did not believe her innocent or ignorant, but to cut matters short he ran briefly over the dreadful facts.

The current issue of the *Liberator* contained a communication signed by Angelina, who was identified as "a member of the Philadelphia Society of Friends, and the daughter of a prominent South Carolina family." As for the contents of the letter, it was so offensive that the outraged Friend could not bring himself even to summarize it.

"Thee must read it for thyself," he said, and thrust his copy at Sarah. But before she could compose herself enough to obey, he was reading it to her in snatches, directing her attention to first one and then another shocking expression, making it impossible for her to follow either Angelina's argument or his objection to it.

"*Respected Friend*—thus she addresses Garrison! *It seems as if I was compelled at this time to address thee* . . . and so forth and so on . . . about her fear that he might be driven back by the force of the public opinions he has roused against himself. Now where is the place where she says . . . ? Ah! Here! *Judge then what were my feelings on finding that thou stoodest firm in the midst of the storm. I thank God, desiring that thousands may adopt thy language!* Mark that! Adopt his language! which is as offensive as it is wicked! Hate and contentiousness cloaked in Scripture quoted against itself!

"And mark this too! *The ground you stand upon is holy ground.* Might this perchance be idolatry, does thee think? . . . *holy ground! Never surrender it. If you do, the hope of the slave is extinguished and the chains of his servitude will be strengthened a hundredfold!* Did thee ever hear such wicked untruth?"

He glowered expectantly at Sarah, who could think of nothing to say in Angelina's defense or her own.

"It is extravagant . . ." she began timorously.

"I am gratified that thee finds it so," he said with weighty irony. "I trust that thee will also find extravagant her hope that the blood of Abolitionists may be spilled to secure them the crown of martyrdom!

"But this is not the matter I came to discuss with thee. It is, rather, thy failure to be faithful to thy sister in the—" He broke off and stared at Sarah accusingly. "Thee would truly have me believe thee knew nothing of this letter?"

Sarah nodded her head.

"Neither thy sister's purpose to write nor her opinions and sentiments?"

"We have spoken of our concern for the slave," Sarah confessed. "And for the suffering of our free colored brethren here in the North."

"Yes, yes, we all share that concern." Elder Evans cut her off impatiently. "But Friends are under discipline not to enter public controversy. Not to publish on any subject without submitting the article to responsible Elders. Not to attack the practice of our Society, and certainly not in such a periodical as this!"

"But surely Nina has not attacked—"

"Indeed!" Again the printed evidence was thrust at her. "Read where she speaks of the persecution of Abolitionists serving to *purify the church* . . ."

"I assume she speaks of other churches or the church in general."

"She is identified as a member of the Society of Friends! Those who read what she writes will assume she speaks of what she knows! Read this about *false brethren such as the Apostles had* . . . Can you assume that she speaks of any but the brothers in her Meeting, who are not infatuated into unity with her and Garrison?"

Sarah's knees were trembling and she felt close to fainting, though she had never fainted in her life. She begged to be excused to read the letter carefully and pray over her duty. But Elder Evans had more to say.

"If thee truly had no foreknowledge . . . ?" He paused for her third denial (which she gave with a shake of her head, and found herself listening for the cock's crow). "Then perhaps thee had best go and counsel with her. It may yet be possible to mend matters."

The amends he wanted was a public admission by Angelina that she had erred, and an alteration of the passages in her letter that might be construed as criticism of Friends. Also, if it was true (as

Sarah believed and he doubted) that the letter had not been intended for publication, that Angelina's permission had not been asked or granted, Garrison ought to be urged to admit as much in print. "It will save thy sister's character among Friends in other Meetings who will have no opportunity to hear her explanations."

Sarah agreed to go immediately to Shrewsbury and try to persuade Angelina to follow this advice—though some of it seemed questionable. What wrong Garrison might or might not have done was his affair, and so was the question of what measures he should take to expiate it. Angelina had sins enough of her own to expiate. For she had disobeyed the discipline to which she submitted herself when she joined the Society. She had used her own judgment in defiance of the consensus of her Meeting. She was guilty of the sin of pride.

Angelina was surprised and delighted at the visit.

"Thee had best read this before we talk," Sarah said, and put the *Liberator* into her sister's hand.

Nina scanned the page, saw her letter, and said only, "I did not expect it would be printed. But I should have had to send it in any case." Then, with no show of embarrassment or regret, she settled herself to read her letter through from start to finish.

Sarah watched her closely for signs of repentance—or at least of uncertainty—but Nina had never seemed more profoundly at peace with herself. She was poised, alert, beautiful. Sarah felt herself awkward, stupid, plain. . . .

It was not the first time she had surprised herself in envious comparisons of this kind. Usually she thrust the thought from her as one more evidence of her own lack of grace. But today she tried a different stratagem: exposing the ugly thing to realistic appraisal, paring away the layers of illusion and self-pity to get at its evil core. For the envy was not rooted in a great difference in their physical endowments. Sarah was already past the bloom of her youth, while Angelina was at the peak of hers. But in her day, Sarah had had the same delicate fair skin, blue eyes, red-brown hair that curled into ringlets if not forcibly restrained, the same strong, slender body and graceful carriage. Why then was Nina always the more admired and loved?

Not more loved! (Sarah caught herself in a falsehood.) More admired. Nina kept even those who were most drawn to her at a distance. Sarah was more accessible, quicker to win and hold the affection of others. It was not love she envied Nina. It was . . .

Light!

Angelina gave off light. Sarah only reflected it. Nina burned like a star, generating her own radiance, indifferent whether it was or was not reflected back to her in the form of approval by others. Sarah had to warm herself—if she was to be warmed—at her sister's and others' fires. This was at the heart of her struggle to achieve her ministry. She wanted to depend solely on her Saviour, and this was denied her. What she had most envied her sister was that the path between her spirit and the Divine One seemed to stand open. But was this really so?

Friend Evans did not think it was, and the weight of proof seemed to be on his side. For Angelina had undoubtedly written her letter in the conviction that she was moved by her inner light. If she could be wrong once, she could be wrong any number of times. Her inner light might be a stubborn *ignis fatuus*.

Angelina looked up from the *Liberator,* and Sarah loosed the volley of condemnation she had stored up for this occasion. She spoke quickly lest she lose her courage, but not quickly enough. As soon as she saw pain in Nina's eyes, the words no longer came of themselves. They had to be forced out, tumbling over each other in such disorder that nothing came clear. It was she, not Nina, who was blushing guiltily; she who was suffering shame!

When Sarah had finally blundered to some sort of close, Angelina began to speak, keeping her eyes down so that the lids veiled them. "I am willing to stand condemned without a hearing by all except thee," she said quietly. "To thee I owe the duty of vindication—

though I doubt I can fulfill it, seeing I already stand condemned by the judgment of Friends thee regards as infallible." She stopped to blunt the edge that was creeping into her voice. "If I had written as I did in a church capacity, they would have the right to censure me. But I spoke for myself alone, and I shall tell thee under what compulsion."

In a tone as impersonal as a lawyer's brief, Angelina set out the successive stages of her decision to write to Garrison. It had first come into her mind when she read—not in the *Liberator,* but in a leaflet that came into her hands purely by chance—his "Appeal to the Citizens of Boston." Before that, at the beginning of the summer, she had determined to cut herself off from the whole Abolitionist agitation and concentrate on her neglected religious studies. Four weeks had gone by without her scanning a line of any periodical except the conservative Friends' journal that came into the house where she was a guest. It was in one of its issues that she read of white mobs breaking into the Charleston post office to look for Abolitionist tracts, which they confiscated and burned in the market square; of handbills distributed at the scene, setting a price on Garrison's head; of a reward of $5,000 offered by the Georgia Legislature to anyone who would bring the monster into the state where he could be arrested, tried, and convicted.

Next day she saw his "Appeal."

It was the voice of a man who stood on the brink of martyrdom. The howl of the Charleston mob was echoed by its counterparts from New England to Illinois. Yet Garrison appealed, not for mercy, but for liberty. For freedom to go on speaking in the same inflammatory vein! His lines moved Angelina to tears, and she felt an impulse to write to him at once. But remembering her vow not to be diverted from her studies, she suppressed the impulse and turned back to her books.

Only after several days of struggle had convinced her she would never be able to resume her meditations till she had relieved her mind did she permit herself the luxury of setting down her thoughts. She did so without any intention of sending the result.

"I laid the letter away in my desk and tried to study. But for two days I passed through such agonies of indecision that at last, on Second Day night, I knelt and asked divine direction.

"Next morning I felt easy to send the letter. And after committing it to the post office, I felt all anxiety removed, as if I had nothing more to do with it."

The calm assurance of Angelina's expression piqued Sarah into asking, "Does thee not question whether it was divine direction or thy own willfulness?"

"How can I question the light I have?"

Sarah saw the trap her own question had laid for her. She shifted her ground. "I believe that thee had no expectation of seeing thy letter in print. But others cannot know that. Friend Evans feels it is but right that Mr. Garrison acquit you of the charge."

"How?"

Sarah repeated the elder's words like a charm that rang hollower and hollower against the sounding board of Nina's silence. ". . . print an admission . . . retract the allegation . . . refute the slander . . ."

"Do you know what you are asking?" Angelina broke in at last. "I wrote Mr. Garrison imploring him to stand his ground though it cost him his life. Shall I ask him now to retreat to save *my* good name among hypocrites?"

Forced onto the defensive, Sarah permitted herself the liberty of anger, and it betrayed her. "Thee has no right to use thy name to please thyself!" she declared. "A disgrace to it is a disgrace to all who bear it."

Angelina raised her eyes, and blue lightning struck Sarah even before the thunder rolled.

"Thee stood accused of disgracing the family when thee first put on the dress and speech of the Friends," Angelina said. "Thee did not consult Mother's comfort, nor any of our brothers or sisters or others, when thee saw the light. And thee counseled me not to listen to them when I was making the same choice."

"But that was a matter of thy spiritual life or death."

"Does thee think this is not?"

Angelina went on to denounce (in language as intemperate as Garrison's) the spiritual cowardice of the Philadelphia Society and the practice of leading Friends. "Why does thee suppose they will have nothing said or written that might disturb the tomblike quiet of their minds? Is it not that they fear to offend the southern slave-holders with whom they trade? What else would lead them to subvert the foundation of their own faith and deny freedom of conscience to their own saints?

"Has this not brought us to the verge of spiritual death?

"Ask thyself, my sister, why it is that in our own Meeting brothers and sisters of color are herded into a separate pew under the stairs! Why a Friend stands guard to prevent their passing beyond it to take a better seat, or any white person from entering to share their humiliation! And no voice is raised in protest! No, sister, not thine nor mine!"

Like specters summoned by Angelina's wrathful magic, the faces of two Negro women Friends rose in Sarah's mind. There they sat, alone and despised. How was it she had never till this instant seen that her own place was next to them?

"There may be some shadow of excuse for those who have kept themselves in comfortable ignorance," Angelina continued relentlessly, "but thee and I are exiles on this very account. Yet we speak no word, perform no act of witness."

Sarah bowed her head before the storm.

"We both despaired. We believed that nothing would ever convert the slaveholder to sacrifice what he calls his property. We believed that only the horrors of servile war would wash away the wrong. We sickened at the thought of how many of those we love would perish.

"But now I have a better hope! It may be that the lives of a few score Abolitionists will redeem the rest. That our blood will be spilled instead of the blood of thousands, innocent and guilty!

"I pray for the strength to suffer such a fate. For if this is not a cause worth dying for, I know of none."

*   *   *

Sarah came slowly to herself, lying on her bed in the chilly upstairs chamber of the Fairmount house. Her body was stiff and aching, but there was a warmth in her heart that had not been there before.

It was good to relive the old times for the lessons in them, especially that one lesson which she had learned so late in her life and at such a cost of wasted years.

. . . a little child shall lead them.

That little child, for Sarah, was the sister over whom she had watched and prayed. Angelina had led her—once she gave herself to be led—to peace in the last place Sarah would ever have looked for it: in the very heart of the storm. All Sarah had to do was trust her, or trust the light that still lit Angelina's way.

Stuart came home on Friday morning, when Sarah was again alone in the house.

"I forgot some books I needed," he explained. "I could have got them in the library at college, but the undergraduates make such a racket one can hardly read there any more."

He went to his room and got the volumes and brought them to the table where Sarah was working. Stuart was not demonstrative but he showed his affection in ways that touched his aunt the more for their indirectness. It was one of the compensations for the disappointments of her life, early and late. The love of Nina's children —no longer children now—gemmed her sky with stars that shone brighter as it darkened. It was a blessing enjoyed by few spinsters at her time of life. That she had earned it made it even more precious to her.

"May I ask you a question, Aunt Sai?"

She looked up and saw that Stuart had laid down his book. He had been staring at her for some time, it seemed.

"Of course, my dear."

"What was it that made Mother give up making public speeches?"

"I don't know that she gave up . . ." (There was something in Stuart's voice that disturbed Sarah, a note of something like hostility, almost like disrespect.)

"Isn't it true that she'd been lecturing all over New England before she and Father were married, and then she stopped and never appeared on a platform again?"

"That's *almost* true," she conceded. "It was not a decision she made. It just turned out that way. Speaking was a great strain on her, and there were other ways in which she could serve the cause. We both helped your father—"

"I know about all that," Stuart interrupted. "It was only about the speechmaking that I was curious."

His choice of words shocked Sarah. It was as if someone speaking of Joan of Arc had reduced the magnificence of her passion to a cant phrase about playing soldier! But she fought down her impulse to scold Stuart. How could he, or anyone who had not lived through the glory and terror of those years, be expected to know? What she ought to be doing, instead of rebuking him, was thinking of a way to bring the past alive for him, relate it to something in his own life.

The trouble was, there was so little in Stuart's life to compare it to. He had faced only one choice that might conceivably have tried his soul: to fight or not to fight in the War just past. He chose to resist the draft. It was not for Sarah, who had preached the Quaker doctrine of peace to him in his childhood, to question his stand. But she was uncomfortably aware that Stuart had chosen, not action, but inaction, not suffering for a principle, but safety, comparative comfort, and ease. . . . How different were the choices that had shaped his mother's life!

*   *   *

For months after her letter to Garrison and the storm it provoked, Nina had seemed so quiet and submissive that many of the Philadelphia Friends (including Catharine Morris in whose home both sisters now lived) concluded that she was working out her penance. Sarah was sure this was not so.

She was sure Nina did not regret her support of Garrison. The mob that ripped his clothes, dragged him at a rope's end, and came close to hanging him would strengthen, not shake, partisanship like hers. If Nina was quiet, it was because she was waiting, seeking a path that would lead her to greater usefulness, listening for the inner voice that would direct her—perhaps to martyrdom.

News of mob violence in the South and the West was growing more frequent and more ominous. Lovejoy was murdered in Illinois, and his friends feared to mark the spot where they buried him. The conscience of New England was shocked into audibility at last. Men like Channing addressed public meetings. Even the Elders of the Philadelphia Meeting began to shift their stand.

When Catharine Morris said as much to Angelina, she answered abstractedly, "It is too late. A few martyrs will not redeem the soul of the nation now. If it is not to go down in blood, some tremendous effort must be made. . . ."

But of what the effort must consist, or who must make it, she said nothing. Silence spread around her like a heavy odor. Both Catharine and Sarah were growing alarmed, but when they asked, ever so gently, if she were not feeling well, she responded by assuming a false cheerfulness that was even more disturbing.

Then one evening, when the whole Morris family was sitting in the kitchen, each occupied with his or her own reading or quiet chore, Nina suddenly groaned aloud.

"Is there nothing I can do?"

Everyone looked up, but she seemed unconscious of having spoken. She sat a while longer, and then rose to bid them all good night, making her usual round of the family with a kiss for each. When she leaned down to kiss Sarah, tears fell from her cheeks.

No one spoke. It was as if she had woven a spell that held them all enchanted and enchained.

About an hour later, Sarah said her own good nights and went up to her room, which was next to Nina's. She prepared herself for bed, moving quietly, as if she were afraid of waking a sleeping child. Yet, although there was no sound from the other side of the connecting door, Sarah was sure Nina was not asleep.

She lay down on her bed, and waited.

The story of the disciples who slept while Christ wrestled with his despair in Gethsemane came into her mind. If they had been women instead of men, would they not have watched through that hour? If they had loved their Master as Sarah loved the sister for whom she watched, would sleep have tempted them?

At last she could no longer breathe without the feeling that she lifted a stone. She got up and went to the door. By leaning her ear against it, she could catch a faint sound of sobbing. Her hand went to the knob, but she did not turn it. If Nina was muffling her sobs, it was because she did not want a witness to her travail. Sarah withdrew without making a sound.

She tried to sleep, but could not. Again she waited till she could not breathe without effort. Again she went to the door and listened. Nina was still weeping on the other side. Sarah turned the knob and looked into the dark room.

There on the floor, in a wide shaft of moonlight, lay Nina, still fully dressed, her face buried in a pillow, her whole body shaken by the violence of her weeping.

Sarah knelt beside her, afraid that the slightest sound or lightest touch might be too cruel a shock. But when at last she did call softly, Nina responded with astonishing *sang-froid*.

"Oh, my dear," she said. "I've kept thee awake! Forgive me. Go back to bed. So will I. I promise."

They kissed again, and Sarah returned to her room. There was no further sound of weeping, and at last she dozed off.

In the morning Nina came down to breakfast with a face as clear as a summer sky. Her body was vibrant with energy, but no longer tense.

"It has all come to me," she said. "I see what it is I must do."

That was said to the whole Morris family. Later, when she and Sarah were alone, Angelina drew from the pocket of her dress a much-creased letter, which she handed to Sarah without comment.

It was an invitation from the Executive Committee of the National Anti-Slavery Society to come to New York, "to meet with Christian ladies in their parlors and converse with them on the subject of slavery as it is, the truth of its evils, and the desirability of its immediate abolition."

Sarah looked up from the last line and saw the expression of almost seraphic beatitude on Nina's face.

"All these weeks I have been asking what I can do," Nina said. "And lo, a door is opened that I did not even know existed. To speak to women! To rouse them to their sacred duty! What a glorious work!"

"But thee has had this letter for some time."

Angelina admitted it. "I couldn't share it, even with thee, till I had wrestled with my own weakness.

"I would gladly face persecution for the sake of the slave—at least I hope I would. But I find it almost more than I can bear to suffer public ridicule or the censure of those I love. What is asked of me now is to go among strangers who will laugh at my gown and cap and my 'thee' and 'thine,' as well as at what I have to say. And it may also earn me the censure of my Society, and force me to leave it."

"To break thy vows?" Sarah was aghast.

"I will not break them," Angelina said. "The yoke I put on I will carry. But in matters of conscience I have made no vow except to myself. It may be that following my own light, I shall cause myself to be disowned."

"It is quite decided, then?"

A shadow crossed Nina's face. "It is decided, except that I did hope to visit Mother this winter. It costs me something to give that up, for it comes into my mind that I shall not see her again in this life."

Sarah had recovered herself enough to put up a token struggle against what she regarded as an act of unbelievable rashness. She put her objection as mildly, but as gravely, as she could, and in the form of a question:

"Is thee sure thee can do what is asked of thee? Remember, most of those to whom thee will be speaking are as prejudiced against the notion of women's preaching as against the doctrine of Abolition."

Angelina smiled. "Surely *women* can be persuaded that they are as much creatures of God as the sons they bear. As for being able to do what is asked, I am not sure. But I shall put my trust in Him. If He sends the words, I shall not fear to speak them."

It was not a tactful answer. Nina could not help but know that Sarah had struggled for nine long years under the conviction that she was commanded to speak, but He had never yet sent the words. Sarah tried to stifle her resentment, to separate her own disappointment from her sister's hope.

"Before thee can throw thyself on His mercy, thee must be sure thee has prepared thyself as well—"

"I thought of the same thing just now," Nina interrupted eagerly. "I must marshal my thoughts! Clarify my arguments! Give instances! That is the great thing! Instances!

"I want to write an appeal to the women of the South before I address myself to the women of the North. I see just how to go about it. I must point out that it is in their *interest*. That their own lives and their children's and husbands' and fathers' and brothers' depend on their being roused to do justice before it is too late!"

As Nina went on, glowing with excitement, Sarah found herself growing cold with dread: not of the consequences of Nina's rashness—that would come later—but simply at the thought of this being who was her anchor to life slipping away. She wanted to throw her arms around Nina's neck and beg her not to go. To cry out in pure selfishness, "What is to become of me?"

"What does thee think?" Angelina finally stopped for breath. "It is a bold step, but might it not succeed?"

"Thee has already decided to take it, as thee has already decided to take the much bolder step of speaking in New York." Sarah answered with a frigid evasion.

"I have not *decided*. I have seen a vision. I can't unsee it. I can't resist. I must go."

"Then I must go with thee."

Sarah had not an instant's warning of her own decision. If she had pondered it, she might have wavered. But Nina was embracing her, and weeping, and Sarah staved off terror by drying those tears.

"There will be much I can do to help thee," she said. "Pick up the chips so that thee has more strength to give to thy meetings."

It sounded so small and so easy, but she felt that she was promising to risk not only her mortal but her immortal life. The decision was bringing her no surge of joyful strength. She was not choosing, as Nina did, between right and wrong. She was choosing one love over another: her sister over her Saviour. She was throwing away whatever gains she had made in nearly ten years of the most painful spiritual travail, turning her back on the goal for which she had sacrificed every other prospect of happiness and usefulness—even that of marriage and motherhood—and facing in her middle age into a stormy dark.

* * *

"I've said something to upset you, Aunt Sai. I'm sorry. Forgive me."

Sarah came to herself, blind with tears. Stuart's arm was about her shoulders. She patted his hand and dabbed at her eyes.

"It's you must forgive me. You see what a foolish, weak old woman I've come to be. You were asking me something . . ."

"It doesn't matter," Stuart said, going back to his place and picking up his book.

"Please, my dear," she insisted. "I shall blame myself for not having answered you."

"It distresses you to talk about those days," Stuart said. "And it was really of no particular importance."

"It does not distress me. It is a tonic to me!"

He hesitated a moment longer and then gave in. "I'm not sure it's worth the fuss we're making about it. It's just that I get a feeling sometimes that other people know something I don't. As if there were some sort of mystery—some terrible ordeal or accident or tragedy in Mother's life . . ."

"Who talks to you of her in that way?"

"There are lots of people in Cambridge who remember her. They talk about what a blow it was to the movement when she was lost to it."

"There's no mystery about that," Sarah said.

"But why was she lost? Why did she stop speaking? Was it . . . ?" He faltered, blushed, and finally managed to ask, "Was it having *us* —her children—that broke her health? Is that what no one wants to come right out and say?"

"Bless you, no! You mustn't think such a thing!" Sarah's denial was more fervent than her conviction on this point. But it would not do to have the boy take such a burden on himself. "I won't deny that the births were hard on her," she said. "Your mother was old to begin bearing children, and as you know, she had a bad fall not long before you were born. She had to wear a brace for some time afterward.

"But if any one thing was to blame for her troubles, it was exhaustion. She had worn herself out the year before she married. When I think back on that time now, it's a wonder to me that either of us survived it. We spoke sometimes nine or even ten nights without a rest, and traveled all day between meetings, in all sorts of weather, in open wagons as often as in carriages! There were months when we slept in a different bed each night, and never ate two meals in succession at the same table!

"And besides speaking, we were writing. Your mother was answering Catharine Beecher's attack on us, and I was answering the Congregational clergy."

"But you were doing all that Mother was doing," Stuart said. "You're older than she and certainly no stronger. And you didn't break down."

"Indeed I did! Long before Nina! I came down with typhoid fever the middle of the second winter, and she had to nurse me and carry out her tasks and mine. If she had spared herself then, she might not have suffered later."

Stuart was thoughtful for a moment. "It's curious," he said. "I keep forgetting that you lectured, too. And you stopped and never went back."

"You forget because you hear no one bemoan the loss," Sarah said wryly. "I'm afraid I was not much account as a speaker."

"Always the modest one, Aunt Sai," said Stuart loyally.

Sarah shook her head. "I was a corroborating witness, and that was of value. And sometimes, when Nina was not there to dazzle, my light was strong enough to illumine the dark of northern ignorance. But that was all."

"It's interesting that you use a word like 'dazzle,'" Stuart said. "That's the sort of hyperbole everyone seems to resort to when they talk about Mother. You'd think she was one of the Seven Wonders!"

Again there was that note of hostility and disparagement. But memory had uncovered just such a sharp edge in Sarah's own secret thoughts. Why was it, she wondered, so hard to admit the marvelous in those closest to us? To tolerate idolatry of those we love?

"She was a wonder," she said softly. "You had to stand off a little from her to see it, and it was not often I could do that. When I did, it was a revelation. . . ." (If she closed her eyes now, she would hear Nina's voice ring like the trumpet of Judgment, see that beloved and familiar face transfigured past recognition, and lean forward with the rest, straining not to lose a word or an instant's play of expression.)

"I have to believe you, Aunt Sai," Stuart said in a tone of resignation. "I can't imagine it, but I have to believe what all of you say is true."

"Don't you suppose most young people feel the same thing when they hear their parents described by those who knew them in their prime?"

Stuart shook his head. "It's not the same. For instance, I've never heard Father speak with the great voice everyone says he used to have. But I can imagine him as an orator. I can see him holding a crowd spellbound, swaying it this way or that, persuading people and converting them."

Sarah got up and went to the hall closet where she and Nina kept the box full of mementos and clippings from the New England campaign, (and the scrapbook in which they had been intending to paste them in some sort of order all these years). She brought the box to the table, wiped the dust from the lid, and opened it. Stuart watched her as she took out packet after packet of clippings, leaflets, and letters—all carefully tied with bits of ribbon or string. At the very bottom was a file of old *Liberator*s and some odd copies of other Abolitionist periodicals.

"Maybe it will help you to see your mother through the eyes of strangers," Sarah said. "There are all sorts of reports of our meetings here. Some friendly, some quite the contrary. And in the *Liberator*s you will find the whole text of some of her addresses, as well as eyewitness accounts of all that went on."

Stuart looked a bit dismayed by the quantity of evidence being offered, but he picked up one packet at random, untied the string, and spread out the clippings.

Sarah began on another packet. Hers seemed to consist entirely of comments on the great meeting at Lynn. There was the usual mixture of praise and blame, adulation and vituperation:

Over a thousand people packed in at some danger to the joists of the flooring. . . .

That was true enough! She remembered the boys hanging like bats to the window frames that night. And there were as many men as women in the audience, with no explanations made and no apologies offered.

And yet the heavens did not open to rain thunderbolts on their impious heads, nor the earth to swallow their iniquity! !

Sarah chuckled to herself. But it had been nothing to chuckle at at the time. All that had sustained them against the hurricane of criticism was the conviction that their mission must be divinely sanctioned or it would not have mushroomed so quickly from its modest start.

*　　*　　*

The start was the gathering of ladies in the vestry room of the New York church. Out of that came a second meeting, which overflowed into the body of the church itself. There was a new chorus of outrage. St. Paul's admonition to women to be unheard and as nearly unseen as possible was quoted—it seemed—from every pulpit in the city. But the impact of the Grimké sisters' testimony had shocked the sluggish liberal conscience awake at last. A movement was under way, and the sisters were carried before it like twin figureheads on a ship.

The Female Anti-Slavery Society commissioned them as its agents, unpaid but accredited, and calls for their services began to come from all over New York, and—as the news spread—from even farther afield. At first they spoke to women only. To groups which were formed to hear them, but which often stayed together afterward to become the nucleus of a local anti-slavery society.

More and more often men appeared in their audiences. They were asked to leave, but as time went on, with less and less insistence.

Finally there came an evening—at a meeting in a Negro church in Poughkeepsie—when they both felt easy to speak to their colored brethren as well as to their womenfolk. From then on, men began to flock in greater numbers until the meeting in Lynn. . . .

*　　*　　*

"What do they mean by a promiscuous audience, Aunt Sai?" Stuart's question broke into her revery.

"One in which there are both men and women."

"Is that all?" Stuart smiled with the tolerant amusement of the young for the foibles of their elders. "This person writes of *the dangers which at present seem to threaten the female character* as if you and Mother had been some sort of debauchées."

"It sounds like the Reverend Mr. Nehemiah Adams," Sarah said.

"It is. Who was he?"

"A Congregational minister in a small Massachusetts town, a person of no prominence or influence. But the letter you are reading was passed as a resolution by the General Association, and that gave it great power. We spoke mainly in churches, and after the 'Pastoral Letter'—as it was called—many that had been open to us were closed. One minister said he'd as soon be caught robbing a henroost as letting any unnatural females into his pulpit."

Stuart laughed. "And who is the man he was berating for *encouraging females to so far forget themselves as to bear an obtrusive part in measures of reform?* Was that Father?"

"No. That was Brother Garrison."

Stuart had started on another batch of clippings. "Here's one that calls Mother *a pretty Quakeress who converted me to 19/20ths of an Abolitionist!*"

"And 'pretty' is not a word you think appropriate to anyone as old as your mother?" Sarah teased gently, and Stuart had to smile at himself.

He went on through the clippings till he came to one from a Boston newspaper that he recognized. "Listen to this: *She uses facts and arguments lucid and weighty, accurately adjusted and powerfully driven home* . . . , and then he goes on about how expressive her face was. I've never heard any speaker praised like this. Not even Mr. Phillips!"

"That was written after Nina addressed the Legislature," Sarah said. "Before her great public meetings at the Odeon."

"Tell me, Aunt Sai. How did it happen Mother was asked to do a thing like that? Did the Legislature actually invite her to come and speak to them?"

"You would have to understand what else was going on at the time," Sarah said. "There were many different measures being advanced by the different sections of the anti-slavery movement. And a good deal of controversy over what was the best path to follow— but that is a different question, and moot these many years." She resisted the temptation to expatiate on what had been an engrossing concern in the days she was reliving. "One of the measures being pushed—in Massachusetts especially—was a petition to Congress, asking that slavery be abolished in the District of Columbia. That was not a question of the right of an individual state to make its own laws, you see, but the right of Congress, which represented the whole country."

Stuart nodded as if this were all familiar to him, but Sarah was not to be hurried. She explained how the petitions were circulated, how signatures were collected—many hundreds of them at meetings where the two sisters spoke, how when they were ready for presentation to the Legislature in Boston (for transmission to Washington), it was decided to ask for a formal public hearing so that the petition's sponsors could present their case not only to the legislators but also to the interested public of the city.

"This was at the time when I was recuperating from typhoid fever," Sarah said. "We were staying with our friends, the Philbricks, and Henry Stanton came to pay us a call. He said, so casually that I assumed it was in jest, that there were the signatures of

67

so many women on the petitions that he wondered if Sister would like to speak at the hearing on their behalf.

"I thought no more of it, but a day or so later Nina told me that it had come into her mind at that very instant that she ought to say Yes, and she had decided to go to the office of the Anti-Slavery Society and tell Brother Stanton so."

There was consternation in the inner councils of the Society. No one had the courage—or the effrontery—to tell the most effective Abolitionist speaker in the country that she was not wanted, but there was a new round of the old debate on whether presenting a woman in an arena where no woman had ever appeared before would help or harm the cause for which she spoke. When Angelina learned of this, she cut through the arguments with a sword of scorn.

"She told them she would bear the responsibility wholly herself. She made independent application for permission to speak *after* the brothers who were representing the Anti-Slavery Society had finished—as a woman, a Southerner, and a moral being!"

"And they gave her permission on those grounds?" Stuart asked with an admiring smile.

"They did. But by that time the fainthearted in the Society had been shamed. Henry Stanton made a request that Miss Grimké be included on their list, and that was also granted. I was so caught up in the excitement that I offered to bear my witness, too!"

"You spoke to the Legislature?" Stuart asked in surprise.

"No. When the morning came, I was not well enough. I ought really not to have gone at all, but Nina needed me, for she woke up that morning weak with fear."

"Mother was afraid?"

"Perhaps that is not the word for it." But Sarah could think of none better. "You see, she depended entirely on the inspiration of the moment. She prayed before she spoke each time, asked our Heavenly Father for guidance and strength, and she was always answered. But sometimes it was not till the moment of addressing her audience that the spirit moved in her."

"You mean to say she had nothing written out? Not even notes?"

"I believe she did put down a list of the points she wanted to cover, but she rarely looked at papers once she had begun to speak."

"I don't wonder she was frightened," Stuart said. "It frightens me to think about it. To get up after men like Mr. Stanton had finished, to speak *ex tempore* to the highest governing body of the state!"

"Those are almost the words she used that morning," Sarah said. "She blamed herself for having suffered a madness of vanity when she offered to speak, and there was nothing I could say to comfort her, except that He, who had supported her through so many other trials, would not desert her in this one.

"For there was more at stake than the accepting of the petitions, you understand. Or even the winning of important converts to the cause. What Nina had undertaken to do was important to women, to our country, to the whole world. To succeed in it meant the end of old shibboleths. To fail . . . Well, it did not bear thinking of."

"Yes. I see that." Stuart's aloofness had entirely dissolved, and his face was bright with curiosity. "You went to the State House with her? Tell me how it was."

"We set out together," Sarah said slowly, "a mighty sorry-looking pair, with me holding Sister's arm to help her walk. The halt leading the blind it must have seemed."

* * *

And to make things worse, as they neared the State House they began to meet crowds coming away, who told them that there were no places left. By the time they arrived, the press around the doors was so dense that a sergeant-at-arms had to clear a path for them, and even so they had to walk over seats to reach the places assigned to them.

Nina sat with her head bowed, and Sarah knew she was praying.

69

There was an interminable wait, while the chairman of the committee in charge of the petitions puttered with papers and wrote notes to his secretary. But finally he looked over at the sisters and nodded. Sarah touched Nina's arm and whispered to her that it was time.

Angelina stood up, looking very pale, as if she might faint, and at that moment a great hissing was heard from one of the rear doorways. It seemed to be directed at her, but it was impossible to be sure, for there was a great deal of confusion in the part of the hall where the public was seated. The chairman pounded angrily with his gavel, but the hissing only grew louder, and soon the spectators who were shocked by the breach of decorum were making as much noise as the provocateurs.

The chairman invited Angelina to come forward and stand directly below his desk, facing him. Sarah went with her, in case her sister should need physical support. But by now there was a little color in Nina's cheeks and she was no longer trembling. But when she began to speak, her voice was not strong enough to carry above the hubbub, at least not to the members of the committee, on whom she was forced to turn her back.

* * *

"The chairman asked her to come forward and take the desk of his secretary, which was directly below his," Sarah said. "That way she faced out toward the committee and the public, too. But now the chairman could not hear her, for her back was to him. So he interrupted her again and invited her to come up and take his place! I was invited to come with her and sit in the chair of the Speaker of the House while Nina stood at his desk to make her address. There was a sight to set the world by its ears! Not one, but two women in the place of highest honor in the Commonwealth!"

"And this time Mother was allowed to speak without interruption?" Stuart asked.

"She spoke for two solid hours! Her voice was as strong as any man's. But toward the end the quiet was such that she could have been heard if she had only murmured."

"How I would like to have heard her!"

"Brother Garrison printed the whole of that first day's address." Sarah pulled out the old *Liberators* and looked till she found the right one. "Here it is. And here is the passage that had the greatest effect. I marked it, I see. *Do you ask what I mean by emancipation?*" Sarah's voice cracked as she strained to get the effect of Nina's. "There! I could never sound the trumpet, no matter how it echoed in my heart. You read it, Stuart. Aloud, if you please."

Stuart took the paper from her and began to read, woodenly at first, but with more and more fire as the swing of the phrases caught him:

> "Do you ask what I mean by emancipation?
>
> "It is to reject with indignation the wild and guilty phantasy that man can hold property in man.
>
> "It is to pay the laborer his hire, for he is worthy of it.
>
> "No longer to deny him the right of marriage, but to let every man have his own wife, and every woman have her own husband.
>
> "To let parents have their own children, for no one else has any right to them.
>
> "No longer to withhold the advantages of education and the privilege of reading the Bible.
>
> "To put the slave under the protection of equitable laws.
>
> "Now, why should all this not be done immediately? Which of these things is to be done next year, and which the year after?
>
> "I have seen too much of slavery to be a gradualist. I dare not, in view of such a system tell the slave-holder—as some do—that he is PHYSICALLY UNABLE to emancipate his slaves.
>
> "I say he IS ABLE to let the oppressed go free, and that such

heaven-daring atrocities ought to cease now, henceforth and forever."

Stuart finished, took a breath, and sighed it out. "Did she speak more than once?" he asked.

"Yes. It was six o'clock when she finished the part you have just read. She had other points to make, so she asked for a second hearing, and a day was set for that. But it was not enough. She spoke three times in all."

Stuart was no longer listening. He had gone back to the *Liberator,* and was reading the text of the address from the beginning, not skipping a line.

Sarah watched him for a while. What would have happened, she wondered, if this excursion into the past had taken place five years ago? Before Stuart faced the choice between risking his life in the "cause worth dying for"—and whatever it was he had chosen instead. Would it have made any difference? If he had felt the strong pull of his mother's evangel then, would he have volunteered —as the Garrison boys did—to carry out the logic of his parents' life rather than their "peace principle?"

No use to ask "what if?" The past was settled. The future held enough questions, pregnant with pain. Sarah wondered, not for the first time, how Stuart and his sister would take the blow that was almost surely going to fall when the letter came from Oxford . . . if a letter ever came.

Perhaps what Stuart was drinking now from the well of his mother's passion would strengthen his soul against that ordeal.

V

Archy had never tried to write anything that caused him as much trouble as the answer to Mrs. Weld.

A dozen times he had decided to follow Frank's suggestion and ignore her letter. But there was a mounting pressure of anger in him for which he had no other outlet. What he wanted was to loose a volley of facts that would explode in the quiet of her life, shattering its peace, avenging the insult of her questions. The trouble was that to marshal his facts he had to make himself relive scenes and sequences of events that he had done his best to forget.
... *who your parents are* ...

Each time he looked at that line in her letter, each time he took his pen and wrote the name *Henry Grimké,* his mind jumped ahead to the moment when Frank would look at his letter. They had never spoken of their father. Archy was sure Frank must know, but who had told him? And when?

One thing was sure: neither Frank nor John found out the way Archy did, from Mauma's quarrel with Montague Grimké.

*   *   *

Neither of his brothers was in the little house then. They came in later, when everything was quiet. Mauma was going about her ironing, pressing the shirt on the table before her without really seeing it or her flatiron.

The younger boys caught the smell of trouble, and looked to Archy for an explanation, but all he could do was shake his head. Something terrible was about to befall, but he had no idea what it was, not even whether it was any use to run.

Mauma went on ironing. The suspense and the silence stretched tauter and tauter, like a fiddle string getting ready to snap, till it was almost a relief when at last there was a knock at the door.

It was a constable, come to fetch Mauma, and right behind him the Grimkés' coachman come for Archy and Frank.

"You best go 'long to you' uncle," the coachman said to John. "You can' stay on here alone, little as you be."

The days that followed were filled with a terror that had no name.

Archy and Frank were not badly treated. They were too stunned to give cause for rebukes, and the Grimkés themselves seemed a little subdued. But now and then, coming into a room, Archy would catch the tag end of an urgent, low-pitched conversation. He was sure it was about Mauma they were talking, but he could never learn anything: not where she was or what was to become of her, whether they would ever see her again. It went on and on, a nightmare, till Dr. Faunt came and mercifully cut it short.

Dr. Faunt was the Grimkés' family physician. When Archy let him in that evening, he supposed the doctor must have come to see Miss Mary, who had been keeping to her bed most of the week. But he was not carrying his little bag, and he told Archy to show him up to the parlor, where the family was sitting as if they expected him.

Miss Eliza made a point of telling Archy to run along, and the parlor doors were shut before he was well out of the room. That was enough! He ran to get Frank, and they crept as close as they dared, and held their breath to listen.

They could not catch all that was being said, but they pieced together enough to answer their awful, unvoiced question.

Mauma had not been sold away! She was in the workhouse. She was sick. Very sick. Like to die!

"There are some people so constituted that they cannot live in confinement," Dr. Faunt said. "Nancy is apparently one of them."

Montague said something about its being her own fault.

"I can't understand you, Montague," Dr. Faunt said sharply. "The woman raised you after your mother died. Yes, she did. You were older than Tom, but not too old to need mothering, and you got it from her."

Montague answered back, but Miss Eliza started talking too, and everything was a jumble till the doctor's voice reasserted its authority.

"You may believe what you choose, but I know better. I was Mrs. Grimké's physician all during her illness, and I know how Nancy nursed her and how grateful she was."

"Nancy was impudent," Miss Eliza shrilled. "So impudent that my brother once had to whip her!"

"That's got nothing to do with it," said the doctor. "I don't care how many quarrels there were or what punishments. Human beings don't dwell together all their lives in perfect concord, neither white nor colored, slave or free. What matters at this moment is that the woman is sick. If she's not taken out of that hellhole, she may die. Do you want that on your consciences?"

He won his point.

Mauma was released, and Archy and Frank were permitted again to go home at the end of each day's work. But it was not long before the war was on again, not long before another catastrophe could be felt gathering like an electric storm.

"I've locked Frank in the attic," Montague announced to Miss Eliza one afternoon in Archy's hearing. "This time I'll be sworn he'll stay there till he's had a change of heart, if it takes the rest of this day, tonight, and tomorrow."

Less than an hour later, something dropped past the window near which Archy was working, and landed with a thud on the roof below. There were people in the room whose attention he didn't want to draw by looking out, but he was almost sure it was Frank. How could Frank have got out of a windowless attic room? And from what height had he jumped? The roof of the house was at least twenty feet from that of the kitchen ell.

Frank was at home when Archy got there, happy to answer these and any other questions.

He had discovered an opening in the attic chimney left by the builders, who anticipated that it might some day be finished as a bedchamber. He tore away the boards that closed the opening and climbed up and out on to the high, hipped roof. The jump to the kitchen was awesome, but he would have made it all right, if he hadn't landed crooked with one foot taking all the shock. He sprained his ankle, and had two more jumps to take: one, from the kitchen roof to the yard; the next, over the fence into the neighbors' yard. These neighbors were slaveholders, and if they had seen him, they would probably have given the alarm. But Frank had luck. He made it safely out their back gate, down the alley, and all the way home, on his throbbing, swelling ankle.

It took weeks to heal so he could put his weight on it, and by that time the Grimkés had decided they did not want Frank back. They had come to the conclusion that he was incorrigible, or—as they put it to Mauma—"not to be trained by any means *we* care to indulge in." So they hired him out to a man with fewer scruples, a man known for his success in subduing unruly servants by a combination of beating and starving. There was no coming home at night or on holidays any more. Frank disappeared from Archy's ken as if he had died or been sold away.

Archy had made a vow never again to do anything that would bring trouble on Mauma, but with Frank gone there was no hope of keeping it. Nothing he did—or omitted doing—pleased the Grimkés. The next storm gathered quickly and broke over nothing, over a fire that wouldn't burn in the dining-room grate, so that the family came down one morning to a cold breakfast table.

Before Archy knew what was coming, blows from a leather strap —Montague's belt—were raining on his head and shoulders. He shrieked a protest that brought another round of blows. He was told to hush, but he wouldn't. If his screaming angered his tormentor, it was a weapon. He had no other. He screamed and screamed.

Miss Eliza began to beg Montague to stop. "The whole neighborhood can hear him! It's a disgrace!"

Miss Julia said the same thing.

At last the women prevailed, or Montague tired himself out. The belt was thrown against the wall in one last venting of rage, and Archy was ordered to go down to the kitchen, wash his face, and get on with his chores.

Some time later in the morning, the bell rang and Archy went to the street door.

"Does Mr. Montague Grimké live here?" a man asked.

"Yes. But he's not home."

The man grabbed Archy by the arm. "It's you I've come for, then."

It was the constable who had arrested Mauma.

Archy was led along the same route to Calvary that she had walked, down streets he always tried to avoid. For the workhouse filled him with dread even before he knew what it was. There was something menacing in its very shape: squat and bulky, with crenellated towers at its four corners and buttresses against its walls. On one occasion when an errand had forced him to pass close, Archy had imagined he heard groans and cries from its barred windows. Today, however, all was as silent as if everyone inside were dead.

The constable opened a small door cut into one half of the large wooden gates that closed the main portal, and pushed Archy through ahead of him. To the left was an iron door that opened into the jailer's apartment. Montague was waiting there with the jailer, a small, pale man who seemed to suffer a helpless distaste for his office and all with whom it brought him into contact: not only constable and captive, but complainant as well.

"This the boy?" he asked wearily.

Montague nodded, avoiding Archy's eyes. "I want him given a lesson that'll remind him not to scandalize half Charleston next time he's punished."

The jailer's face twitched in a grimace of disgust; he signed to the constable to be gone, and to Archy to follow him. The way led through another iron door, down a corridor that was as cold and evil-smelling as a tomb. On either side of it were cells so dark it was impossible to make out whether they were occupied. Archy thought of Mauma locked up in such a stone coffin, and his legs gave way under him. A shove from Montague sent him stumbling ahead, around a blind corner and into a large chamber, harsh with light.

It was crammed with implements and structures whose purposes were so plain that, although Archy had never seen any of them before, they took his breath like a fist in his belly. He could not cry out. It would have done no good anyway, for there was no one to hear. The windows looked out on a bare, sun-seared courtyard, empty of everything but the shimmer of noon heat.

And now, from the jungle of lashes and paddles and chains, a black man emerged. His face was disfigured and expressionless, as if he had been maimed and muted by some act of calculated cruelty. He kicked a pair of rough wooden ankle stocks across the floor till they lay directly under a tall wooden frame that had a reel for a crossbar. The jailer directed Archy to stand inside the frame, and—docile as in a dream where one is powerless to avert the omen of doom—he obeyed.

The black man knelt to close the wooden circles around his ankles, and stood to lock a pair of iron wristlets on his hands. There was an eye in the chain that linked the two wristlets. Through this the man now threaded a rope that he passed up over the reel. He gave a few quick turns to the crank at the reel's end, and Archy's arms were drawn up over his head till his feet barely touched the floor. A filthy woolen cap was pulled over his head and face, blinding him, suffocating him. For one awful moment he thought he was dying. Then the beating began.

His skin, stretched tight as a drumhead, seemed to part at the first blow of the paddle. The pain was excruciating, but it unleashed anger. In a moment that was all he felt.

Anger kept him conscious through the whole agony, repeating over and over the word that would inflict the greatest damage on his adversary:

"Brother!"

When at last it was over, and the woolen gag was removed, anger hissed loud enough to carry the shaft to its target.

"Brother!"

He saw Montague flinch, and it gave him joy—though he hated himself for it later when the anger had burned out.

When Archy got home that night, he told Mauma he could not go back to the Grimkés.

"I got to run off."

He was prepared to counter Mauma's objections, but she made none.

"Can' hardly do much running till you' back heal up," she said, and set about dressing the raw flesh so it wouldn't fester, and making him comfortable enough to sleep.

Before dawn, she waked him and took him next door to Big Aunty and Uncle Frank's. She would start right in looking for a better place for him to hide. Meanwhile, if worst came to worst, Uncle Frank's was easier to run from than Mauma's little house. Uncle Frank's had an upstairs room with windows overlooking the path by which any slave hunter must approach, windows that could also be used in an emergency as an escape route.

It was during his stay at Uncle Frank's that Archy came to know Liby and to hear her tales about Mauma in the days before he was born.

Liby was a Gullah-speaking Johns Islander who had been sold in the Charleston slave market to some member of the Grimké clan, and sent to work on the family's up-country holdings at Bellemont. It was there she first knew Mauma, who used to come up with Maus Henry's family when they stayed the winter holidays. They met again, she and Mauma, several years later, at Caneacres. Liby and a number of other hands from Bellemont were brought down to work the rice fields, and they were sold with the other goods and chattels after Maus Henry's death.

Liby's life since then had been a succession of different masters and overseers, each meaner than the last, till she was driven to the desperate expedient of running off. Uncle Frank took pity on her and was harboring her till a "shipment" was ready to cross battle lines to the Union Army camp out near Fort Moultrie. Harboring fugitives was perilous charity for free people of color.

Archy did not know how perilous till he read the advertisement that listed him and Frank as runaways. It was printed in the *Charleston Mercury,* which had a regular column devoted to such notices, and it contained, besides a description of the two boys and the offer of a reward *for each or both, delivered to me at my home,* an unusual and ominous finale:

> *I have traced one of the boys out in several places in this town and I am certain that he is harbored. This notice is given that when he is taken I am determined to punish him till he*

*informs me who has given him food and protection, and I
shall apply the law to my own satisfaction on those concerned.*
E. MONTAGUE GRIMKÉ, ESQ.

Archy read this aloud to the group around Big Aunty's table. (It
had become his weekly office to read the column, since he was the
only one in the house who could read with any ease.) The silence,
as he finished, was as intense as if everyone had stopped breathing.

"What 'e mean 'bout the law?" asked Cousin Owen.

"Law say you ain't to harbor," said Uncle Frank curtly. "Free
colored can lose they freedom for such."

Owen looked at Archy as if he had just been exposed as a carrier
of the plague. "You mean they might could take us all just for
keepin' him?"

"Shut you' mouth," said Big Aunty. " 'Sides, Montague Grimké
ain't know a thing 'bout where Archy is, nor Frank needer. If 'e do,
'e don' spend money fuh put advertisement in paper. 'E sen' constable fuh catch 'um."

Young Owen was about to dispute this when his father turned
the talk to something else. Later, Uncle Frank took Archy aside
to assure him that the danger he represented to the family was
trifling. But Archy read the advertisements in the *Mercury* after
that with a depressing sense of guilt.

The next one he found that held any special interest described
Liby, without naming her:

RUNAWAY *Negro wench about 35 years old, very dark color,
wears a handkerchief tied about her head to cover scars on
neck and ears. Said girl was sold by Messrs. Wm. Payne &
Sons as the property of an estate in St. Paul's Parish, to a
Thomas Priestley of Edgefield, of whom I bought her on the
17th of April. She may be lurking in that district as she is said
to have young children on plantations there.*
A. WATSON, ESQ.

81

Liby reacted to the reading of this notice with a snort of amusement. It seemed to Archy that she took too much comfort from the fact that her master had made a poor guess as to her whereabouts. But Big Aunty and Uncle Frank also seemed much reassured. Little by little, as they talked and joked about it, Archy began to understand what it was that underlay their optimism.

Free and slave alike, these dark people had taught themselves to read the mind of the white enemy the way a swamp dweller reads the trail of an invader or a prey. What delighted them was not that Liby's master believed her to be in St. Paul's Parish but that he was able to give no real description of her.

"Mus' be t'ousan' 'oman on de streets ob Charleston got kerchief fuh cover dey mark," Liby sneered. "Constable duh gwi' stop ebery one, fuh carry 'um so Maussa can see?"

Next week, however, the *Mercury* carried an amended version of the same notice, which shook her confidence. Mr. A. Watson had gone to the trouble of consulting with one of Liby's former owners or overseers, someone who had held her longer or paid closer attention to her person. Mr. Watson had no reticence about publishing the results of his research:

> *. . . and much scarred about the ears and neck and on the rump by whippings. One ear notched, think it is the left. Has a number of black lumps on her breasts. Marked with the letter C or G on the inside of both legs . . .*

Liby spat, as Archy finished reading, and said something in her fast, clicking speech, something that had to do with the brand marks.

Shy as he was in such matters, Archy was compelled by his curiosity to ask, "The letters . . . do they stand for Caneacres or for Grimké?"

"Needer one. Maus Henry yent mark 'e people wid bran'. No time. 'E duh beat 'um, eeder lock 'um in de stock. But 'e don' use iron fuh burn 'um. Needer 'low 'e obshay do so."

"He did have them whipped?"

Liby gave him a curious oblique glance. *"Dede,"* she said (meaning, yes, indeed!). "All 'cept you' mauma. 'E yent 'low 'eself be whip by no buckra. 'E too proud."

Liby glanced at Big Aunty and then back at Archy. There was something mocking in her voice as she asked him, "Yunna yent neber yere 'bout de time Maussa go fuh beat you' mauma?"

Archy said No. Then he remembered having heard Miss Eliza say Mauma was whipped for impudence, but it was too late to correct himself, for Liby was already launched on her tale-telling, and he had to use all his energy to follow the unfamiliar cadences of her Gullah speech.

"Dis yere back in de ol' time, 'fore Maus Henry duh buy de rice lan's. 'Fore Miss Selina duh die. Dey all come to Bellemont fuh spen' Chris'mas. I he'p in de kitchen. Dat howcomeso I mek 'quainted wid you' mauma, howcomeso I yere all what duh fall out."

She leaned back and rocked a moment or two, letting the tale work itself loose from the tangle of other memories, her eyes half shut to block out interference from the present.

"One day Miss Selina tell Nancy: se, yunna grown now, good healt'y 'oman, time yunna start mek *dindi* for Maussa. I gib yunna good husban', mek *sampa* in church.

"But Nancy mek answer: se, Don' want fuh tek husban' in church, needer lie wid no man fuh mek *dindi*."

Big Aunty clicked her tongue at that and shook her head. A look passed between her and Liby whose meaning eluded Archy and made him uneasy.

"Well, den," Liby continued, "Miss Selina tell Maus Henry: se, Call Nancy, gib 'um good whippin'.

"Maus Henry say, Whaffuh?

"Miss Selina mek answer: se, 'E duh sass me, don' mind what I tell 'um.

"So Maus Henry call Nancy and tell 'um: se, I duh gwi' gib yunna whippin' fuh sass you' missis.

83

"Now den!" Liby poked a stiff forefinger at Archy's heart. "What yunna t'ink you' mauma mek answer?"

Archy had no idea. He could imagine the look on Mauma's face at such a threat, but no words from her mouth.

"Mebbe yunna t'ink 'e beg: se, Please, Maussa, don' give me whippin'. I bery sorry. Yent go fuh sass missis! Please, Maussa, do have mercy on po' Nancy!" The burlesque whine in Liby's voice made it perfectly clear that she shared Mauma's contempt for such groveling.

"Dede!" (The word was used here in pure irony.) "Nancy stan' shut-mout'. Yent speak a word. Yiz look in 'e eye. Maussa raise 'e han' wid switch fuh strike 'um. *Bim!*"

Liby's palm slapped the table like a pistol shot.

"Quick as snake, 'e duh grab 'e han', twis' 'um twill de switch fly, an' t'row Maussa on de groun'!"

Everyone gasped. Then burst into laughter.

"Don' tell me Nancy duh throw Maussa down," said Big Aunty, wiping her eyes and rocking back and forth. "Howcomeso she strong enough to do so?"

"Nancy strong!" said Uncle Frank. "No mistakin' she strong. And she fly off the handle so quick, nobody got time to get 'self set."

Liby nodded and grabbed her own forearm, pinning it to the table, her fingers wriggling helplessly.

"What 'e do, 'e yiz hol' 'um wid all 'e stren't'," she said. "Maussa kick an' t'rash twill 'e bus' 'e braces and pop all de button off 'e trouser!"

Laughter rose in shrill peaks. Big Aunty slapped her thigh again and again, as if she were punishing herself. Uncle Frank threw his head back so hard he almost tipped over in his chair.

"Atter while 'e stop kickin', Maussa do, an' Nancy let 'um up. Now den!" Liby paused dramatically. "What yunna reckon 'e duh say now?"

"Reckon 'e didn't have nothing to say," was Uncle Frank's guess. " 'E be too condemned!"

Liby shook her head scornfully. "'E straight' 'e clo's, look at Nancy bery stern, and speak out loud fuh all de people duh yere: se, Yunna better go see 'bout you' task now. An' don't sass you' missis no mo', eederso I gib yunna anoder whippin'."

Laughter lacerated the air again.

"What Miss Selina believe?" Big Aunty asked, when she could get breath enough. "That Maus Henry gib Nancy whippin', or not?"

Liby shrugged. The point of the tale, so far as she was concerned, lay in a different direction. She looked at Archy. "You' mauma yent 'low 'eself be rule' by no buckra. Needer obshay nor maussa. 'E too proud."

Archy had stopped laughing long ago. He could not understand the others, Mauma's own kinfolk! laughing on. Did they not see what must also be true, if this was: that Mauma was able to defend herself against this man—to whom she had borne not one but three sons. That she was tempery enough to take the risk, however dreadful, if her pride was infringed upon. Or was it that they did not know what Archy knew: that he was the son of the man who cut such a ludicrous figure in Liby's tale?

*　*　*

Archy began the letter to Mrs. Weld again, and this time he did not stop till it was finished.

He read it over once, crossed out a word or two and wrote his correction on the line above. He decided not to copy it over or show it to Frank. He put it in an envelope and walked in to Oxford, bought postage, and dropped the letter into the office. All without letting himself stop to think!

On his way back up the hill of the campus, he passed President Randall's house, and on a strong, sudden impulse he turned in at the path, knocked at the door, and was admitted to the parlor that served as a waiting room.

It was one of the self-conscious traditions of the new school that the door to the president's study always stood open. Any student with a problem to discuss was welcome, but the open door inhibited many, for whatever was said in the study could be heard by whoever was waiting his turn outside, as Archy was waiting now.

Perhaps President Randall counted on this to limit the traffic. Few students were willing to go into as much embarrassing personal detail as the one who was in there now. Archy tried not to listen. Not out of regard for the other's privacy, but to protect the urgency of his own concern. He did not want it diluted or dissipated before it was time to put it into words.

He tried to concentrate on the pictures that hung on the parlor walls. There was one of Jesus standing very straight and tall, bending his head to the verdict of Pilate. It reminded Archy of Mauma. He could see her avert her face in silence from the verdict of those who ought to have known better . . . like Big Aunty and Liby, who marveled that one as sternly upright as they knew her to be should have accepted the sinful and degrading role of a concubine. They clucked their tongues and shook their heads and even laughed a little . . . Archy heard them the very next morning after Liby told her tale . . . and because he was listening to them, the terrible thing occurred.

*   *   *

Liby was taken.

Archy was upstairs at the time, and he ought to have kept an eye on the yard and the gate that led to the street. He didn't see the constables coming. When he heard Liby's scream, they were already at the door.

It was too late to warn her, too late to save himself by jumping from the window. One of the men was standing a few feet from where he would land, if he did. Archy was cornered. Guilt and terror struck from opposite sides, paralyzing him.

Then Liby ran out the front door.

Straight at the constable she ran, and past him, in a crazy dash for freedom so unexpected that she was out the gate before the

86

constables thought to reach for the pistols they carried at their belts. They cursed and started after her. Out the gate! Out of sight!

There was a tremendous commotion in the neighborhood now. Sounds of shutters banging. Doors opening and slamming shut. Voices calling. Mauma came out of her house and went into the street.

Big Aunty came out her front door. She stopped and looked up at the window where Archy was standing, straight into his eyes. Her astonishment struck the chains from his limbs. An instant later he was out the window, over the fence into Mauma's yard, standing at the door to her kitchen.

There he hesitated.

The plan in which he had been carefully instructed was to get under the house, not by crawling in from the yard, but by dropping through a trap, cut in the floor of the hall. There, under the exact center of the house, was a clutter of discarded building materials, artfully arranged to trick the eye of anyone peering in from the side. There was space enough in it for a boy of Archy's size to conceal himself completely.

Archy hesitated because for the moment he was lost. The door looked alien—as if it belonged not to Mauma, but to someone else whom he had never seen but of whom he had heard ill.

He ran around to the back of the little house where there was an old privy, long abandoned. There were planks leaning against its sagging, hingeless door. He worked his body under them and slid inside, leaving most of the cobwebs undisturbed.

From here he could see nothing, but he could hear everything: Liby's screams as she was brought back and her loud, repeated lies. She was declaring that she had only this morning come to Big Aunty's house by mistake, seeking someone whose name she spoke but who—Archy was certain—had been invented to serve the purpose of the moment. Big Aunty and Mauma picked up the lie and carried it forward. Both of them swore they had never seen the woman before.

"How about that boy of yours, Nancy?" one of the constables asked Mauma.

She denied having seen Archy since his disappearance. So did all the neighbors, some of whom were telling the truth, and some not. Mauma invited the constables to enter and search the little house, if they did not believe her. But they had their hands full with Liby, who was struggling violently. They would come back, they told Mauma, but Archy knew it was unlikely. He was—for the present, at least—almost safe.

The hubbub subsided into a quiet that seemed exaggerated, and the day slowed down to a crawl.

Mauma came and went, hanging up wet clothes, taking in the dry ones. Big Aunty was in her yard, beating rugs. Neither spoke. For a while Mauma sang.

"Take one brick out of Satan' wall . . ."

But mostly she worked in silence. Vegetable vendors cried their wares in the street, and fish peddlers theirs. The white woman at the corner (who was Mauma's enemy) called to her children to come home for their dinner. Otherwise it was so still Archy could hear leaves fall and chickens scratch.

The only way he could tell time was passing was by the knives of light that cut between the warped boards of the outhouse. They moved slowly, painlessly, across his cramped body, leaving no scars. At last they were withdrawn. It was growing dark.

Archy had made up his mind to leave as soon as night came, but now he could not make himself start. He could picture in his mind every step of the escape he ought to be making: getting out of Mauma's yard, slipping down to the wharves, stealing a skiff and drifting with the tide till he was far out in the harbor, rowing the rest of the way to the swamps from which he could make it on foot to the Union encampment. What he could not picture was the scene that must come before: the moment in which he told Mauma goodbye or left without doing so.

He slumped down and dozed off. . . .

Mauma was calling his name.

It was late. The world was silent. The moon was rising. Mauma called again in a whisper, and he realized that she was standing just a few feet from the outhouse door.

"Archy? You in there?"

He stirred, and the dry boards creaked.

Mauma's voice sharpened. "Come on now! Quick! 'Fore the moon light up the whole place."

He slept that night in his old place at the foot of Mauma's bed, slept soundly, knowing that she kept watch. She was the all-wise, all-loving Providence to which he had only to deliver himself to be secure. She would hide him till it was safe to make it away. She had already found him a new place of refuge. She would find a way to get him there. All he had to do was to trust her, and sleep.

Sometimes it seemed to him that it was more than a year before he wakened from that sleep . . . that he dreamed all that happened in the interim: the escape from Mauma's house late at night, the walk—disguised in girl's clothes—right through the whole of the city, all the way out to Line Street, the family named Cole who now became his keepers in the little coop of a house where he lived, cut off from everything and everyone he had known . . . week after week . . . month after month. . . . Allowed to go outside only in the dark of the darkest night, and then only into the small fenced yard. Penned like a calf, wondering from which side the butcher's bludgeon would strike him down. Reading the war news in the Charleston newspapers, forced to believe that the South was winning, that slavery would be fixed forever, not only on himself and Mauma and his brothers but even on free colored, like Uncle Frank and Big Aunty and the Coles who had three generations of hard-bought liberty behind them.

What kept Archy sane in those days was the life he lived in books. There logic imposed itself on the chaos of experience. There right triumphed, albeit sometimes tardily. Good was rewarded, evil punished. The balance might be lost for a time, but it was always redressed in the end. Real life was a poor thing by comparison. It had no meaning. Or what meaning it had was madness.

Even at the end, when the news was good, it was still crazy. Even when the guns from the blockading fleet began to speak in tones no Charleston newspaper editor could gainsay. Even—or most of all—on that very last morning, when the Yankees were said to have taken the city. Not by storm from the land, but peacefully, by invitation, from the sea.

It was said that the City Fathers themselves had sailed out across the harbor, under a flag of truce, and asked the Yankee commander to come and save the town. The Confederate garrison was making ready to blow up all the public buildings, beginning with the arsenal. The conquest that Charleston had resisted for so many months it now begged as a boon. The Yankees obliged. It was crazier than a crazy man's dream.

Archy found himself that morning alone in an empty house. The Coles and all their neighbors had gone down to the wharves to welcome their deliverers. They would have taken Archy with them, but he was not ready to go out. The change was too sudden. It was nearly two years since he had been abroad in daylight. Two years since the door had stood ajar. It made him fearful just to see it like that.

But slowly, slowly, the quiet grew weightier than his fear. Slowly, with his heart pounding and his legs tingling, he walked out and stood in the street, letting light settle on him, thick as the silence. Slowly, he started to walk toward the center of the town.

Everything looked altered or distorted. There was grass growing thick and bright green between the paving stones, so that at a short distance the street looked like a lawn. He passed what had once been a solid block of fine buildings, all gone now, with a thick bramble of Banksia roses covering the ruin. And the silence persisted even here, as if the heart of the city had stopped.

An owl hooted. On Meeting Street, just before noon!

Archy shuddered, turned, and walked down toward the docks. Here were sound and bustle, but the sense of unreality was no less oppressive. For the men who were moving about their tasks looked familiar enough—the faded uniforms they wore could have been Confederate as easily as Federal—but their speech was so strange that it was a shock to catch, now and then, a phrase he could understand. Brisk, cheerful aliens, who were more at home here than he. Clearing the blocked streets, mending the shattered sewers, putting out fires, carrying in supplies, bringing the city to life again. Freeing the bondsman, jailing the vandal, burying the dead. . . .

Then he saw Frank.

Frank, in a brand-new blue jacket with braid on the shoulders, mounted on a fine horse and holding another by the reins. Archy gaped, wordless and motionless, till at last his brother turned. Saw him. Recognized him. Called him by name.

Then at last he came awake, knew himself and where he was, knew that the nightmare was over: the war, the hiding, what he had hid from, all over and done with! A new life was beginning, different, and better than the old.

That was when he should have taken the name of Weston or some other, then at the very beginning of the new life, or on the first morning when he and his two brothers ascended the steps of the school and were asked how they were called. If only he had stopped then to think!

But the moment was too overpoweringly exciting.

The new Yankee mayor—Mr. Gilbert Pillsbury—had proclaimed that all Charleston children of whatever color or previous condition were henceforth to attend the school closest to their homes. For Archy and Frank and John that meant the Morris Street School, an impressive two-story stone building that overlooked and dwarfed the old shack school in the Wilkinsons' slaughter yard. They complied in a mood of religious awe, walking softly like neophytes admitted to a forbidden temple.

For Archy that mood was never really broken. He had fallen in love with learning in his days at the Coles, and now he was permitted to indulge his passion with the blessing of the occupying authority. He prepared his daily lessons as a burnt offering to the deity, through the medium of its priestess, a young Yankee schoolteacher. Nothing in his out-of-school life impinged on his consciousness with anything like the force of Miss Harriman's approval or disapproval of what he did or said or wrote. It was this long-sustained effort to impress her that brought him—and Frank, too—the offer to go north and to college.

Miss Harriman asked each of her pupils to prepare and give in class an oral report on a book he had read. Archy spent days trying to decide which book, and fixed at last on one called *The Impending Crisis,* by a man named Hinton Helper.

It was one of the many books Uncle Cole had borrowed (or stolen) for Archy from the houses of the white families for whom he did cabinetwork. Helper identified himself in the very first pages as a North Carolinian whose people had been slaveholders for more than a hundred years, and set himself down as opposed to the "peculiar institution," whose early doom he predicted. The polemics of a white native son were strong drink in the midst of a war that he had also predicted, and whose end he foretold. Archy's thirst drove him through some of the most difficult reading he had ever attempted.

He went back to it now, reread it from start to finish, summarized its arguments, and committed one of its more dramatic passages to memory. He recited this as the finale to his oral report:

"And now, Sirs, we have thus laid down our ultimatum! Our motto—and we would have you understand it—is the abolition of slavery and the perpetuation of the American Union!

*"If by any means you do succeed in your treasonable attempt
to take the South out of the Union today, we will bring her
back tomorrow! If she goes away with you, she will return
without you!"*

"This prophecy and many others made by the author have since
been fulfilled," Archy wound up with a flourish. "It remains now
for the South to catch up to the rest of the nation, as Hinton Helper
promised she would, once the chains of bondage were stricken from
her limbs!"

There was applause, tempered by envy, as he returned to his desk.
Miss Harriman beamed at him proudly, and the next day he was
sent for by the principal.

All the way up the stairs to Mrs. Pillsbury's office on the second
floor, Archy swung between extremes of hope and fear: imagining
himself about to be punished for some inadvertently committed sin,
or—just as possibly—to be rewarded for some inadvertent achievement. But all the lady seemed to want to talk to him about was the
Grimké name.

"I don't suppose there was a more famous name in the whole
country, when I was a girl," she told him.

Archy thought she was going to ask him how he came to bear
it, and the muscles of his stomach cramped. But Mrs. Pillsbury
sailed on into a highly emotional account of the "martyr days, when
the wrath of the mob was unleashed against Abolitionists and
people of color, while the law stood back and laughed!"

She was the largest white woman Archy had ever seen close up,
and one of the ugliest, with a red, unpowdered face and thin gray
hair, a huge, shirted bosom, festooned with chains and ribbons,
some leading to eyeglasses of different sizes and strengths, some to
keys, one to a watch pocket in the belt of her skirt, and some leading so far as he could determine—nowhere at all. She smelled
strongly of witch hazel and faintly of perspiration, and each time
she drew breath to power one of her long sentences, the little room
seemed to be sucked dry of air.

She was advising him now to pattern his life on the example of those "two frail, saintly women whose name you have the honor to bear." Her bosom heaved like surf, and her eye fixed reproachfully on him. He was doing his best to look absorbed, admiring, awed, or whatever it was she wanted. There was no price short of downright deception he was not ready to pay in order to propitiate so august and benign an authority. If only she would let him know what would please her. Ought he to say that he knew about Miss Sarah and Miss Angelina, or that he did not? Ought he to claim a connection, or deny it? How much of the truth did she want?

He never did find out. When Mrs. Pillsbury finally ran out of reminiscences about Abolitionist celebrities she had known, and events in which she had been associated with them, she switched abruptly to the subject of Archy's book report. Did he know the history of *The Impending Crisis*? Did he know that it had caused a riot in the halls of Congress, before secession had cleansed that body of the partisans of slavery? That it had been used—or misused —in Mr. Lincoln's election campaign? That it had been illegal to possess a copy in any part of the Confederacy, at the time Uncle Cole had brought it home? Archy answered No on all counts.

"Now, about Mr. Helper's prophecy for the free South." Mrs. Pillsbury fixed him with another of her stern glances. "Have you thought about the part you want to play in that?"

Archy was not sure what she meant.

"There will be need of real statesmen and leaders of all types— lawyers, doctors, ministers, teachers—from among your people," she explained. "That's why it is important that young men like you should prepare themselves. You do want to go on and complete your education, I suppose."

Archy had only a vague notion of what "complete" implied in this context, but as Mrs. Pillsbury talked on, he saw into a world of wonders. The white world of the North. A world from which no impassable barrier separated him. A world to which he could raise himself by his own efforts: by improving his appearance, correcting his speech, filling in the gaps in his knowledge. Freedom, which he had thought of till now as the breaking of irksome bonds, assumed new and alluring shapes in his imagination. Ambition mushroomed in his soul.

He tried to share his new hopes with Frank, but Frank seemed impervious to them. He acted as if he thought Archy a fool to expect anything from any white people, even Miss Harriman and Mrs. Pillsbury. There was something stubborn and unreasonable about his indifference . . . at least, it had seemed so then. Later, Archy came to understand why Frank felt as he did, and eventually to feel the same or more so himself. . . .

When Mrs. Pillsbury came to see Mauma about sending Archy north to go to college, he was surprised to hear Mauma put in a plea for Frank, and surprised that Frank made no objection. " 'E not so likely a student as Archy, but 'e got a need fuh learn," Mauma said. " 'E studying 'bout being a doctor, eeder a preacher."

For John, Mauma made no plea. When he asked her, "How-comeso I don't get to go north?" she answered, "You got to grow some first, and I don't mean taller nor wider, needer." John laughed easily and let it go at that.

Soon the news was spreading like smoke—momentous or menacing, depending on one's point of view—that two young freedmen were going all the way to Massachusetts to be educated. Folks began dropping by with advice. Among them was Lieutenant Miller, the officer to whom Frank had hired himself and whom he had deserted at the end of the war.

(Archy heard while he was at the Coles' that Frank had run away from his brutal taskmaster, passed himself off as free, and hired his time to an officer stationed out at Castle Pinckney, in Charleston harbor.

The good luck went to Frank's head and he began to press his luck. On one of his trips into town to see Mauma, he was betrayed by an informer who wanted the reward money, arrested and locked up in one of those terrible black cells on the ground floor of the workhouse. He came near dying there, would have for certain if Mauma had not humbled herself to go and beg on her knees till the Grimkés relented and let her take him home.

What happened while he was getting back his strength, Archy heard much later from John. John had been taken to serve in his brother's place and to wear the hateful brass-buttoned suit, and he was in the upstairs parlor when Montague came home one day and tossed a bundle of paper money into his wife's lap.

"Where did all this come from?" Miss Julia asked.

"I sold Frank to that lieutenant he's been working for," he said. "We're rid of the trouble, and you have a fine present into the bargain."

John ran home to tell Mauma and Frank, expecting to create a sensation with his news. Instead there was silence, heavy and cold.

"Ain't you glad of it?" he asked Frank. "You don't never have to go to the Grimkés again. And you like Lieutenant Miller. You always saying how fine you get on. And he must think a lot of you, for it was a heap of money he gave."

Frank did not even ask how much.

"Just acted like he was mad at me for something," John complained to Archy.

He couldn't understand Frank, but Archy could. To be sold! Like a pig or a chicken. Sold by one white man to another! It was something you could never forget, never forgive either of them. It explained many of the changes Archy had sensed in his brother since their lives converged, and why the explanations could not be made directly, by Frank, in words.)

Lieutenant Miller had forgiven Frank for disappearing in the confusion of the retreat. If he knew that Frank joined the enemy army and served in it for several weeks, he chose to ignore it. He came now to offer him employment at wages that were fair enough, as things went in the bankrupt South.

"The boy won't find anything better up north," he told Mauma with unmistakable conviction in his voice. "I know the rumors that are running around Charleston: what the pay is up there and what it will buy. But I can tell you this much: no Yankee has the slightest interest in the Negro except as a laborer who can be hired for less than a white man. Factory owners don't think twice about turning out their hands to starve, black or white."

Mauma bowed in courteous deference to this opinion. "Most likely you in the right. They been all kinds of masters in slavery time. Must be all kinds in freedom. We got to have hope our boys find as good as you been to Frank." And no more was said of the lieutenant's offer.

Mauma used the same deft diplomacy on other advice-givers, and the preparations went on. Conferences with Mrs. Pillsbury (and sometimes with her husband, the mayor) became more frequent. Anticipation of the future grew so bright that the present was dimmed, and the past completely shadowed. Until the night Archy heard Grandmauma taunt Mauma, the night the boys were taken to say good-bye.

They did not know till then that they had a living grandparent. Mauma explained that it was because Grandmauma was never allowed to leave the up-country plantation where she lived, though most of her children had been sold away or bought themselves free. On this, her first visit to Charleston, Grandmauma was staying with the most prosperous of her sons, Uncle Jacob Weston, a tailor who owned a combined house and shop on Queen Street in the fashionable center of town.

Neither Mauma nor Uncle Frank were on good terms with this brother, so the boys had never been inside his establishment. They were awed in spite of themselves. And Grandmauma was as awesome as the house.

Tall, very thin, dressed all in black except for her scarlet head rag, she was so dark that her face was featureless against the stark white walls of the kitchen. Only when she turned toward the fire did it spring to life, a portrait drawn in flame-colored lines on ebony.

Archy looked from the old woman to Mauma and back again, comparing. They were alike and not alike. Both held themselves very straight, as if they were balancing something on their heads. Both had a face shaped like an Indian's, with high bones under, and sharp ridges over their eyes. Their noses were beaked. Mauma was lighter in color, and her hair was brown and wavy. She wore it uncovered, parted and pulled back in a knot. Grandmauma's hair was hidden by her kerchief, but Archy guessed that it was white and kinky-curly. Both had brown eyes, but Mauma's had lights in them: points of light when she was angry, a glow like sun on swamp water when she was sorrowful or loving, as now.

She presented each of her sons in turn. Grandmauma sat in a high-backed rocker and examined each boy with interest but no show of affection, her breath whistling in and out between her teeth and tongue in time with her rocking. The only comment she made was about John. " 'E a Weston by looks," she said.

Then she and Mauma started to converse in a curious way that was like quarreling behind a curtain. Archy's interest was provoked by the deliberate obscurity of their words, and he listened long after Frank and John had moved to the other side of the fireplace and begun to roast goobers on the coals.

At first the women talked about the boys going north. Grandmauma was against it. She saw no sense in such a move when the Charleston schools were open to them as well as to the white children.

"Fewer of the whites coming every day," Mauma told her. "Soon they be none. Pretty soon they be teaching nothing but how to work better fuh the white man."

"Maybe dey teach nigger children *be* white men in de North?" Grandmauma inquired with elaborate irony.

"Just so they teach 'um be men, I ain't mind 'bout what color," Mauma said.

At that, Grandmauma blazed into rage. She seemed to consider that Mauma had insulted someone: Uncle Jacob or Uncle Frank—perhaps both—and some other kinfolk of whom Archy had never heard before. "Ain't take dey freedom from no buckra, needer Yankee nor Secesh! Dey buy deyself free!"

"What good it do 'um?" Mauma asked. "Spend they whole life working like slave to buy freedom. I want better for my sons."

There was no sound for a moment but the whistling of Grandmauma's breath.

"Maybe you studyin' to get married," she said suddenly. "Maybe dat howcomeso you hab so much hurry fuh lose you' sons."

Mauma denied it, but the old woman persisted.

"You young 'oman yet, and handsome, too. Must be plenty nigger mens in Charleston take you fuh wife. Hard-working mens! Don' leave you weary youself washin' and ironin' all day and night fuh buy vittle."

"I ain't studying to get married," Mauma said again.

"Why so? Nigger men still ain't good enough?"

Mauma pressed her lips tight together and her eyes fairly glittered. Her head jerked toward the boys to remind Grandmauma of their presence, but the old woman only shrugged.

"Still hankerin' after de buckra and what gif' 'e give for 'e pleasure?" she sneered. "Stan' lukkuh you learn somethin' more 'bout the wages of sin—"

Mauma's wrath boiled over suddenly, and she talked back to Grandmauma in words even harsher than those she had used on Montague Grimké. Archy could not understand some of what she said, but one thing stood out as clear as a pillar of fire: Mauma had done no sin. She was—as Liby had said in a different context—too proud. The core of her being was love: not a gentle, yielding sort of love, but an awesome force that burned away all dross. It could be cruel. It had driven her to punish the sons she loved for small transgressions, to hold them to a standard of conduct that had seemed utterly unreasonable at times but had brought them through trials in which other boys—whose greater liberty Archy had once envied—were destroyed. It was driving her to punish herself most terribly by sending them away from her now. And even to defend the man who betrayed her and her love! For that was what she was doing. In the face of Grandmauma's malicious disbelief, she was standing up for the father of her sons, blaming Montague.

"Stan' lukkuh 'e daddy know how Montague duh gwi' do," said Grandmauma dryly.

"'E trust in 'e own son, firstborn! What more 'e can do?" Mauma demanded.

"Set yunna free," said Grandmauma.

Mauma grabbed Archy by the shoulder. "Come on!" she said. And to Grandmauma: "I bring you' grans fuh see you, but you got no good word. Best we get on home."

A smile showed Grandmauma's jagged teeth, and then went out, leaving her face as black as the night sky.

* * *

"Ah, Archibald! Come in!"

The boom of Dr. Randall's voice brought Archy to his feet in a daze. He could not get his bearings in the present fast enough. The white man seemed to be talking to three people at the same time: to him—inviting him to make himself comfortable in the wing chair beside the grate; to the departing student, inviting him to come back when he had "considered the proposition"; and to Mrs. Randall, who was asking something about tea. Archy felt that the confusion was deliberate. An attempt to deflect him from the purpose for which he had come. To waste the precious moments before someone else took his place in the anteroom. What was it he wanted to say? He must lose no time.

"I come about changing my name!"

Dr. Randall smiled as if that was understood beforehand, suggested again that Archy take the chair near the fire, and told his wife they could both do with a cup of good hot tea and perhaps a piece of her freshly baked bread. He drew his own chair slightly closer to the fire and settled comfortably into it.

"Now then," he said, "let's think about this a little together."

"There's no reason I can't change my name if I've a mind to, is there?" Archy demanded.

"No reason at all."

Archy was conscious that he sounded much too belligerent. But Dr. Randall's manner was like a wall of slippery marble or a hill of sand. It gave him nothing to grasp or to push against, no chance to get his balance back.

"The only reason we took it was we were told to put down a name. When we first came to the school in Charleston, I mean. So we did. All three of us. We didn't need to put down Grimké, and I wish now I hadn't of."

Dr. Randall nodded again, still with an air of imperturbability in which there was something faintly insulting. As if Archy's agony and indecision were too contemptible to take notice of, as if it were beneath the dignity of a white gentleman to show either sympathy or curiosity about such a step on the part of a man who was only half white.

"Does Francis feel as you do?" Dr. Randall asked casually.

"I—reckon so."

"Have you discussed it with him?"

"Some."

It should not have been difficult to say that the discussion had been left unfinished, that Frank had no idea Archy was coming to the president about it, that Archy himself had had no idea of doing so when he left his dormitory. But the tea tray arrived just then. Grateful for the interruption, Archy gulped the hot liquid too quickly and burned his mouth. Tears came to his eyes, and he was ashamed to wipe them away.

VI

The letter from Pennsylvania came on Wednesday. It was addressed to Angelina, so Sarah propped it up on the mantelpiece without opening it, but she found that she could not sit comfortably in the same room with it. Even when she passed on her way to or from some errand, it drew her eye and her mind to the threat it embodied. Not till she had laid it flat, face down, was it possible to forget its presence.

Young Sarah's midweek domestic-science lesson helped.

Ever since she engaged herself to be married, the girl had been studying the arts of homemaking with the one member of the household who could presume to teach them: Betsy Dawson, who no longer lived under the same roof but who would always consider herself, and be considered by the family, to be part of it.

Betsy was the first of their mother's slaves that Angelina and Sarah had freed and brought north. She had lived in and helped them to keep the little cottage on the banks of the Hudson at Fort Lee where they lived after Theo and Nina's wedding. Eventually Betsy married and left them to found a family of her own, but for all but a few of the intervening years the separation had been only a matter of a mile or so. She had played an important part in the bringing up of the Weld children, and the initiation of young Sarah into the mysteries of baking was an office she took with seriousness. She set aside one day every two weeks, and the two Sarahs did the same.

Old Sarah loved these days for the warmth of the kitchen, the smell of bread that blessed the whole house, and the flow of memories that was evoked. It seemed stronger than usual today. Everything she touched: the handle of the coal scuttle, which she filled to save Betsy's time for more skilled pursuits; the table on which she spread a clean cloth for the kneading, the chair in which she sat to watch the two white-aproned priestesses, one white-haired and dark-skinned, the other dark-haired and fair-skinned, bending over the mounds of dough—all these took Sarah back to the days when she had written out and sent to Theo the lists of goods to be purchased and furniture to be made for the new household:

> *Let the furniture be of cherry and the simplest possible design, Nina says. A table with six legs is sturdier than one with four. On no account let the cabinetmaker turn fancy wobblings into the legs . . .*

> *Getting the sort of table and chairs we want may prove difficult* [Theo had replied]. *For everything nowadays is so gewgawed and becurlicued and tipped with all sorts of colors that even the older cabinetmakers seem to have forgotten how to work in the chaste style which all three of us admire. . . .*

"Now! Grease the top of the loaves so they won't dry out while they're rising," Betsy instructed her pupil. "It takes a good while with this coarse kind of flour. White flour rises quicker. 'Course, in this house you' not supposed to know things like that."

She looked over her shoulder to see whether the shot had scored. Young Sarah laughed. The diet regime of the household was a battered fortress in which the general outline of the old Graham plan was still discernible, but compromises and concessions to many sets of invalid guests (as well as years of dwelling in communal colonies) had worn away most of the battlements. The children made great fun of what remained, and Betsy egged them on.

"I ever tell you how your brother Stuart come near starving to death?" she asked young Sarah. "They was feeding him out of that book of theirs, and the child was pitiful! I don't believe we ever would have raised him if it hadn't been that your daddy was called down to Washington to see something about the Congress. He was away most of that winter, and it give me a chance to talk some sense into those two poor ignorant women.

"They'd been feeding the poor little thing two spoonful of milk porridge at a time, and letting him whimper for two hours in between. First thing I did was make up a pot of gruel, and I give him a cup of it! Mind you, a whole cup! Well, he drank it all down and fell off to sleep with the last drop and a smile on his little mouth. I did the same thing next day and the next and the next.

"Time his daddy come home for the spring plowing, there was roses in his cheeks, and they stood out, so!

"Now let me tell you something I don't want you to forget." Betsy frowned sternly at young Sarah as she reached the moral of her tale. "Time you come to have babies of your own, Lord only knows what sort of fad and foolishness may be going on. You pay it no mind. Hear? Grown folk can defend themselves, but a baby's got nothing to do but take what's given him.

" 'Course, you going to want to nurse your babies, and most likely you can. But your mother had to stop with Stuart. Things happen when you don't look for them to. Nobody's fault. All I say is, no matter how you feed your babies, feed them full!" She turned to Sarah with a challenging, "Ain't that right, Sister?"

Sarah said Amen.

"I don't know what we would have done without you, Betsy. Poor ignorant women we certainly were in those days."

"Not much better now, when it comes to cooking," said Betsy tartly. "You supposed to be beating some air into those yolks."

"Here, let me do it, Aunt Sai. I'm finished with the bread for a while." Young Sarah took the bowl and wire spoon and began to whip vigorously. "Why is it that you and Mother didn't learn from Betsy when you were young?" she asked.

"Young ladies weren't taught to cook in Charleston," Sarah said. "At least not in the sort of home we had. Our mother thought a lady's only duty was the giving of orders to servants."

"But after you left her home, you had no servants to give orders to. Weren't you very poor?"

"Not poor as it is generally understood, child. We never wanted for the necessaries of life. We had small incomes from our father's estate, and few needs. As Friends, we were always invited to make our home with other Friends."

"Didn't you help with the housework in the houses where you stayed?"

"We did our best, but that is not the same as keeping a house. For instance, we both sewed tolerably well. It was easy to make our contribution in that way and do little of other domestic work.

"Still, we did learn some things. I remember I learned to wash plates the first winter I stayed with Catherine Morris, and to iron shirts the second. What a victory I thought it when I had learned to do that well!" She caught Betsy's eye and amended, smiling, "Tolerably well."

Betsy shook her head. "Never in my born days saw such a pair as they were when I first come," she said. "Couldn't boil a pot of beans without burning it. It was a blessing that book of theirs said to eat everything raw, or they'd have lived on pure charcoal."

And so the morning flowed on.

The two old women renewing and being renewed by the bond of memory that joined them, the young one filtering their talk through the rosy crystal of her own expectations. Tribulations and triumphs, the wisdom of hindsight, the afterglow of strong emotions and tender ones . . . "Do you remember how it was?" . . . "Do you know how I want it to be?" . . . "When the children were little, . . ." "When I first came to freedom, . . ." "When I have my own home . . . my husband . . . my babies . . ."

After the loaves were slid into the oven to bake, Betsy went home, leaving detailed instructions about when they were to be taken out and how they were to be cooled.

"And don't go off somewhere and forget about them," she warned young Sarah. "Like your auntie and your mama used to do. They'd go for a walk along the river and stop in to see a neighbor who was ailing, or set themselves down in the front yard to read or write something. Come in the house I don't know how long after and surprise themselves to find an oven full of hard burnt bricks!"

The Sarahs promised to stay within smelling distance of the kitchen, and bade Betsy goodbye at the front door. As they crossed the parlor on their way back to the kitchen, young Sarah noticed the envelope on the mantel and stopped to examine it.

"Who is this from?" she asked. "A. Grimké, Oxford, Pennsylvania . . . Who is he? Or is it a she?"

"You'll have to ask your mother," Sarah said. She had decided this was something for Nina to explain to her daughter and her son at whatever time and in whatever way she thought best. But it made Sarah uncomfortable to evade a question from either Stuart or his sister, or to answer with less than the candor they expected from her. She was relieved when young Sarah's next question pointed in a different direction.

"What's wrong with Mother lately?" she asked, as she followed her aunt toward the kitchen. "She doesn't seem herself."

"She is wearing herself out with this teaching, I've told her and told her. The trip back and forth is too hard, especially in winter. And she doesn't rest well away from home."

"Oh, I think she does! I think Mother's happier when she has things to do that take her away from home."

Sarah turned in surprise. Her namesake was staring dreamily out the kitchen window, her head tipped slightly to one side and a little frown on her forehead. She was not a pretty girl, but there was an intensity of goodness about her that made her lovely at moments. This was one of them.

"I don't know how you can say that," Sarah reprimanded her tenderly. "When in your whole life has your mother ever been away from her home? She has devoted herself to you children and your father to the limit of her strength."

"I'm not *blaming* her, Aunt Sai. And you're right, of course; she hadn't ever been away till we moved here and she began to teach in Lexington. But there were times—like when we lived at Eagleswood —when Mother had nothing to do with making a home, and I think those were the times she was happiest."

"You speak as if she had failed in her duty!"

"I don't mean to," young Sarah insisted. "I only mean she doesn't enjoy keeping a house and taking care of little children. We would have had a hard time of it when we were small if we hadn't had you to mother us."

To hear herself spoken of as mother made old Sarah's heart melt and run like water. But it also woke an old guilt, a vague feeling that she had robbed Nina of something that was rightly hers.

"You know," young Sarah went on after a moment, "I think it was hard on Mother, feeling she had a duty to love us—more than she loved Father and the things she did before she had us—trying to devote herself to us instead of them."

"What a way to speak!" Old Sarah was truly shocked now. "How it would wound your mother if she heard you!"

"I wouldn't speak this way to anyone but you, Aunt Sai. And truly, I don't *feel* anything that ought to wound Mother. I love her, and I know she loves us. Not as much as she loves Father but—"

"That is wrong of you! Quite wrong!" Old Sarah's alarm broke out in voluble indignation. "This 'more' and 'less'—this meaning and comparing! It is not at all the way to talk of love! Or even to think of it!"

"Maybe I shouldn't have said 'more' or 'less.' What I mean is—there are *different* ways of loving. And they seem to change. For instance, loving William has made me feel different about everyone else. Even you."

"Well, that's perfectly natural," Sarah said, mollified.

"Is it? I sometimes wonder if there is such a thing as 'natural' and 'unnatural' above love. Is it right to have rules laid down about who you're supposed to love, and how, and when?"

"What rules are you talking about, child?"

"You know them, Aunt Sai. When you're little, you're supposed to love your mother and father first and most—or best, or whatever you want to call it. Then you're supposed to love your brothers and sisters, and then your uncles and aunts—and grandparents, I suppose, if you have any.

"But when you grow up and get married, it's all supposed to change. Your husband is supposed to come first if you're a woman. Your work is supposed to come first if you're a man, and if it's anything important and worthwhile that you do. Then, if you have children, it's supposed to change again. They're supposed to come first because they need you most.

"But what if you don't change? Is it right to force yourself against your nature?"

"I don't understand you at all," Sarah said severely. "Are you saying that it is not your mother's nature to love her blessed children? That she had to force herself?"

"Let me see if I can say it in a different way," young Sarah said patiently. "For instance—you remember the time you and mother got up that petition—a Declaration of War Against Slavery, or something like that?"

Sarah inclined her head.

"There was supposed to be a campaign to get thousands and

thousands of people to sign, so President Lincoln would have to do something about emancipation. I remember I and some of my friends were already carrying it around the neighborhood, when the President announced his Proclamation, and there was no point in going on."

"I remember," Sarah said.

"Well, do you remember what Mother was like then? There was something so—'exciting' is the word that comes into my head, but it was really more than that. She was almost inspiring! Then, after it was over, she was taken sick and . . . Well, she's never been like that again."

"We do grow old, child," Sarah said softly.

"Of course. But Mother *seems* older than either you or Father, and she's not. I've wondered lately if maybe it's because she's been starving her spirit all these years. Or feeding it the wrong food. You taught us when we were young that it's a sin to mortify your body, to deny it food and air and rest and exercise. You still scold Father and Mother about abusing their strength. Why isn't it just as much a sin to abuse and mortify your spirit?"

Sarah felt a sharp jolt at the foundations of her peace. If young Sarah was right—and she was certainly right when she guessed that her mother had been struggling against her nature all the years of her married life! If that was a sin, then Sarah was the sinner! For it was she who had commanded Nina to mortify her spirit. She had seen it as faithfulness, as helping her beloved sister to find peace by accepting the yoke it was her duty joyfully to bear . . . the motherly offices that she, Sarah, performed with such pleasure and success. Had it been selfishness instead? Had she revenged herself in secret against the being she loved more than herself?

"I think I'm one of those ordinary women who are made to love in the ordinary way," young Sarah's voice came sweetly through the tumult in her aunt's heart, quieting it. "I've always loved you most, Aunt Sai. Now it's William. And one day it will be my babies, I suppose.

"But if it turns out to be different . . . if I always love my husband more, for instance . . . I'm not going to punish myself. Because I think if God made us, and if loving is the most important thing He gave us to do, it must be right to do it in whatever way He made natural to us.

"If you don't . . . if you try to make yourself love the way *people* say you should—the dutiful way—then you sin against His way, and you suffer for it. You end up not being able to love at all. Or— if you're a very strong person—you break your own heart."

Sarah got to her feet and went to look at the bread. It was time to take out the pans of rolls and move the large loaves back into the hottest part of the oven. Her hands trembled more than usual, and she felt near tears.

But she was not unhappy. She was remembering the time when the walls of her life were shaken by Nina. Only good came from that. Good would come of this, if she was not too old to rebuild . . . in love.

VII

Theodore's first morning class was one described in Dr. Lewis's catalogue as "familiar lectures in Mental and Moral Philosophy." In practice this meant that Theodore was free to discuss any aspect of human character or life, any problem or solution that interested him or any of the dozen young ladies of the senior class who had elected to spend this hour with him.

It was a particularly attractive group this term, all keen-witted and curious. The girls' questions to him and debates with each other had the sharpness and sparkle of the coeducational classes he so much preferred. (In Theodore's own school, which he closed to go back into harness as an agitator for emancipation during the War, he had insisted on a natural proportion of boys and girls in all classes, and the results confirmed his belief that the reciprocal action of male and female minds was an essential part of the educational process.) But if Dr. Lewis discriminated on grounds of gender, he did not on grounds of color. There were always a few Negro girls in the student body, and the one presently in Theodore's philosophy class was most interesting to him.

Her name was Harriet Morgan, and it was rumored that she was related to James Forten, the Philadelphia shipbuilder who was the first Negro to make a fortune in the American commercial world. Harriet was physically delicate—in all probability she had been sent to the Lewis school because of its unusual program of physical education and corrective gymnastics. She was also very shy. She volunteered little in class discussions, but when Theodore put a question to her, her answer was quick and accurate if it was a matter of fact, original and courageous if opinion was involved. He felt drawn to her not only for these reasons but also by a quality difficult to define: something at once pitiful and admirable, as if the girl was putting up a heroic struggle against heavy odds. He did not think it had only to do with her color and the world in which she was placed. He had often wanted to question her, to probe a little into her personal circumstances, but so far he had not found the right opportunity.

He was, therefore, surprised and pleased when she took the initiative by coming to his desk before class on a Monday morning.

"I should like to ask your advice," she said in a prim, reedy soprano. "You've been talking to us about opportunities to be of service . . . things *women* can do . . . besides just the ordinary things that are expected of them, like being wives and mothers."

" 'Besides' or 'instead of'?" Theodore asked with a smile. "That is a sore point with some of the ladies of my acquaintance, married and spinster."

Harriet smiled back and continued, a little more at ease: "I've been thinking I should like to offer myself as a teacher in one of the schools in the South where they teach ex-slaves."

"Admirable!"

"I want you to tell me whether you think I am qualified. You've said so much about the vocation of teaching, how not all who profess it have the gift . . ."

"You would make a splendid teacher," he said with real enthusiasm. "In addition to your other qualities, the fact of your being a Negro is an incalculable advantage. The example you set—simply by being what you are—will be worth a thousand exhortations!"

"Would you write me a recommendation?" Harriet asked.

"With the greatest of pleasure." But he was caught by an afterthought. "Except for one thing. Your health. Is it equal to the strain of such a situation? I assume you are thinking of one of the schools on the islands?"

Harriet nodded. "It's on that account I've held back," she admitted. "The schools that interest me most are on the Carolina and Georgia coast, and the climate is said to be hard for persons with a tendency to weakness of the lungs. For a while I thought I ought not to attempt it, lest I break down and become a burden. But yesterday in church . . ." She hesitated, frowned down at her tightly clasped hands, and said in a low, almost apologetic voice, "it seemed to me that I was called."

"What do you mean?"

"Our minister was reading from Scripture, and the passage he chose seemed to be directed straight at me. As if the Lord were chiding me for faintheartedness: *Even the youths shall faint and be weary, and . . . utterly fall: But they that wait upon the Lord shall renew their strength . . . they shall walk, and not faint.*"

She broke off and looked up at him, as if she hoped he would confirm or deny her interpretation of the "sign," but Theodore was not willing to do that.

"Have you talked to Mrs. Weld about this project?" he asked instead.

Harriet shook her head.

"She could tell you about the climate, if the school you choose is near Charleston," he said. "And perhaps something about living conditions, as well."

115

"Is Mrs. Weld from Charleston?" Harriet asked.

It took Theodore a moment to realize what the question implied: that the girl knew nothing of Angelina's past connections or achievements! *Sic transit gloria mundi* . . . not of the world of fashion or wealth or power! But the very world in which Harriet herself aspired to play a part!

"She was born in Charleston," he said. "Her family name was Grimké."

Harriet looked as if she might have heard the name but could not put it into any context. "Has Mrs. Weld been in the South recently?" she asked.

"Not for thirty years. She was exiled from it. Forbidden to set foot on the soil of her native state."

Harriet's eyes had gone wide, but the bell that announced the beginning of class was ringing, and there was no time to fill out the details of Angelina's career.

"She has spent all her life, since she was younger than you are now," Theodore finished quietly, "laboring in one way or another for the advancement of your people. She will be glad of the opportunity to be of any help to you that she can."

He had intended to start off this morning, as he often did at the beginning of a week, by reading from Shakespeare. Theodore had developed a trick of using the plays as some ministers did the Bible, opening the volume at random, placing his finger anywhere on the page, and either taking that as his text or—if it offered no special illumination—reading on, aloud, till he came to a passage that did.

But his conversation with Harriet had set his thoughts running along a track for which he could think of no appropriate Shakespearean epigraph. What he wanted to say was simple enough in essence: that one's reach must exceed one's grasp, but not by too much. The girl's fears were probably well founded. If she undertook such a task, it should be under the most favorable conditions. She should set limits ahead of time, and take care not to exceed them. To push one's self past the possible was as great a mistake as to fail to push toward it. But Theodore was teacher enough to know that the lesson of the golden mean is not one that youth learns from sermons on the subject. Not the sort of youth that sees visions and hears calls!

He did not want to violate Harriet's confidence or to embarrass her. He must speak in a way that would have meaning for all his pupils, whether or not they had occasion to make a personal application. He began, therefore, with an apparently aimless and rambling discussion of "signs and wonders" and the difficulty of interpreting them.

"It is not only that most of us are no Daniels, and cannot read our *mene, mene, tekels* when they appear. We are not even sure that they do appear. The letters we see are not afire. Or the fire we see does not form letters.

"So it usually happens that we must ask ourselves such questions as this: If the Lord chooses to speak to us—to exhort us to do this or to leave off doing that—and if He who created us knows our limitations of understanding—is it possible that He will speak so ambiguously that His intent is lost?"

Some of the girls looked disappointed or puzzled at this long didactic prologue. Some apparently suspected him of putting them off their guard in order to spring some intellectual trap. These sat very straight in their chairs and listened with attention. Harriet sat with her hands folded and her eyes down, the corners of her mouth upturned in a smile.

"Let me give you an instance from my own life," he said. "I'll relate the occurrence in detail, exactly as it happened. Then I'll ask each of you to give me her interpretation. If I am not greatly mistaken, all they will have in common is agreement that the coincidences were 'miraculous'!

"Are you willing to make the test?"

The heads of all who were listening nodded vigorously. All except Harriet, who sat quite still and would not raise her eyes to meet his.

"It was the winter of 1835 or '36. February was the month, and there had been a sudden early thaw. I was traveling up and down what was then called the Western Reserve of Ohio on a one-man crusade to win the territory for Abolition.

"I spoke at least once a day, sometimes more. Sometimes in well-heated rooms, but more often in barns or the open air, in cold so intense that vegetables and eggs which were hurled at me were frozen and felt like stones. That is, they did when they hit. Fortunately, most of my critics were poor shots."

The girls clucked their retrospective sympathy. He had everyone's attention now.

"This incident occurred late one night when I was approaching the city of Columbus. The stage in which I was traveling came to the banks of Alum Creek, an insignificant little stream with a good hard-surfaced ford. The thaw had sent it roaring out of its banks, and it appeared to me—and to the only other passenger, who was a Negro man—too dangerous to attempt a crossing.

"The drivers—there were two of them, both experienced and familiar with the terrain—got down off the box and examined the stream and the bank as well as they could with only a lantern. They both decided that it was safe to send the team of horses across the flood so long as they kept to the paved surface of the ford. We started, lurching and jolting down the slippery clay slope.

"My companion was nervous. He apologized for it by explaining that he had never learned to swim. I made some poor excuse for a joke—something about the stage being as good a place as any for a first lesson—and suddenly, to our amazement and horror, water began to flood in upon us from both sides!"

Theodore explained in meticulous detail how the horses lost the hard surface because the water was so deep that it buoyed them up. As soon as they began to swim, the current swept them downstream into water deep enough to cover the coach if it should sink.

"My companion and I were barely able, by using our combined

118

strength, to force one door open and escape from what would otherwise have been our common coffin!"

A dozen pairs of shirtwaisted shoulders shuddered, and there were audible sighs.

Theodore went on to explain how he tried to help the Negro get a hold on the top rail that held the baggage, and how—just as he thought he had succeeded—the lead horse suddenly wheeled and started to swim back toward the bank from which they had come. "The coach overturned, toppling drivers, baggage, and all into the water. I lost my hold on the man who could not swim, and I never saw him or either of the drivers again."

There was another collective shudder and sigh. Harriet was looking at him too, now. The secret smile was gone.

"I was sucked under for a moment or two and came up gasping. The water was melted snow, so cold that it seemed to paralyze whatever it touched. My rib case was protected by my heavy woolen clothing, or I should not have been able to breathe at all till I grew accustomed to it.

"Meanwhile I had a new danger to face, for I was directly in the path of the terrified horses. I caught the bridle of the nearest one, to keep it from swimming over me, but I was forced down in a tangle of harness and hooves from which I thought I should never extricate myself.

"When I did come up again, I was far enough downstream to be out of danger. I managed to pull off my overshoes and heavy surtout, but by now I was numb and exhausted. I tried to swim toward the nearer of the two banks, but my strokes were feeble, and the water was running very swift on that side. The bank was so steep that there was no foot- or hand-hold that I could see.

"I made one desperate dash across the current to the far side. It was shallow there, and not as swift. There was a large tree, one of whose limbs stretched out close enough to the surface of the water for me to grasp it. I actually did, but my hand was so stiff that I could not close my fingers around the branch, and I was swept past it."

What saved him was a clump of low bushes a few rods farther on. His body caught in them like a piece of flotsam. His feet touched bottom, and if he could have used either his arms or his legs, he could have crawled or pulled himself up on the bank. But he was able to use nothing but his voice, and that only faintly.

There seemed little to be gained by crying out, for there was no light to be seen, no sign of human habitation. But he made the effort anyway.

"Help, oh, help!"

The bank on the other side sent back an echo, but that was the only sound, except for the rushing water. His strength was ebbing fast and he could hardly hold his head up and away from the water. But at least he was beginning to be free of pain, as he lost all feeling in his freezing extremities. He tried to pray, "Father, Thy will be done," and absolved of the obligation to struggle against fate any longer, he let himself sink into the soft blackness that welled up around him.

But something forbade surrender.

Each time he sank below the surface of consciousness, it would send him back up, force him to cry out again. "Help, oh, help!" Sight and hearing were going too, but his mind was clear, and the command that rang in it was to endure.

After sinking and rising, he had no idea how many times, he was aware of a dim and flickering vision of lights and moving forms . . . voices . . . then the vision vanished.

Time passed in darkness and silence.

He opened his eyes once and saw a woman's face bending close to his. But before he could bring the features into focus, before he could tell whether she was real or another vision, friend or stranger, she too vanished, and the blackness cradled him again.

Who the woman was, and all that had happened, he learned only after he had come through forty-eight hours of excruciating agony as feeling came slowly back into his legs and arms, fingers and feet.

"It chanced—or perhaps you will think it was no chance—that the bend of the stream where I came to rest was the only place for miles where there were inhabited houses." Theodore ticked off the coincidences as he came to them, but made no other comment. "In one of these houses, about eighty rods downstream and on the far side, a woman happened to be lying awake—though it was after midnight—listening for just such a cry for help."

Earlier in the day, before the stream rose, a young man of their acquaintance had crossed over in a crude dugout canoe, which he left tied on the far side for use on his return. The whole family was anxious lest, not realizing how the creek had swollen, he attempt the crossing in his clumsy craft, and be swamped. The woman's sons had waited for hours on the bank to warn him, and had come home only a short while before Theodore's first cry.

It came so faintly to the woman's ears that she was not sure she had really heard. She woke her husband and he listened for a while, but hearing nothing, dozed off again. The woman could not sleep. Several times she thought she heard a call, and at last she woke her husband again.

He went to the door of the cabin and stood there listening till he was chilled to the bone. Just as he was about to close the door, the call came. Only a single word, but clearly audible—

"Help . . ."

The man roused his sons, and the three of them went out and searched the bank on their own side for a hundred yards in both directions. They found nothing, and they did not hear another call.

"Under ordinary circumstances, there would have been no way for them to cross the stream to the place where I lay." Theodore ticked off another coincidence. "For they had no boat but the dugout, which was on the wrong side. But it happened that that very morning a canoe had come drifting down, and they had pulled it to their side and tied it up. Without oars or paddles, they managed now to pole it across the freshet. Only a few steps from where they landed, they found what seemed to be the lifeless corpse of a stranger—not their missing friend."

It was hard work to pull the inert body out of the bushes and up the slippery bank, but they succeeded in doing it. They debated whether it was too risky to try to convey it back across the stream to their own cabin, where they could make some effort to revive the drowned man—at least a token effort, for none of them had much hope.

But the canoe which had so fortuitously appeared had now disappeared!

In this extremity, it occurred to one of the sons that in the nearest cabin on that side—about a quarter of a mile away, through thick woods—lived a woman who was the daughter of a physician. She might know better than they whether it was any use to work on the man, and if so, how to go about it.

So they dragged him the whole distance—he bore the bruise marks for weeks—and arrived just as the husband and wife were retiring. By another providence, there was a kettle of water steaming on the stove, and the children had warmed a bed into which he was now placed.

Herb tea was brewed, and Theodore was stripped of his wet clothes and covered with blankets, weighted down with hot stones taken from the hearth. While the men took turns rubbing his arms and legs, the woman worked at the muscles of his jaw till she was able to pry it open and force down the hot mixture of herb tea and camphor she had prepared.

"It was during one of these moments that I opened my eyes. I lapsed back into unconsciousness at once, but now all efforts were redoubled, for my rescuers knew that I lived.

"By morning I was breathing regularly, enough restored to sleep. By noon I waked. . . ."

Theodore paused. The class stirred, readying themselves for the question he had promised to put to them.

"There were one or two other remarkable circumstances," he

recalled. "After I had left the vicinity to continue on my tour, my lost luggage was found. It had been thrown into the stream when the coach overturned. So far as I know, nothing else was ever recovered. But my satchel with all my papers and letters and books was found about a mile downstream from the site of my rescue, and lodged next to it the mysteriously appearing and disappearing canoe!

"The man who found the satchel and sent the contents on to me—the same man in whose house I had recuperated—expressed the opinion that all those involved in my rescue had been sent— like the canoe—by a divine Protector who spared my life because I was about His work. The accident he blamed on human error. The stage drivers were stupid or careless and paid with their own lives, and the life of the innocent Negro man. My life was too precious to lose—according to my friend, Patch—and the laws of nature were suspended on my account."

Theodore had weighted his presentation with enough bits of irony to offset this opinion, but he wanted to make even more certain of the direction the girls would follow in their thinking, so he added one more point.

"I must tell you that my friends in the Anti-Slavery Office in New York also accepted the incident as a sign and a wonder. Henry Stanton wrote me that it was an awful admonition from the throne of the Eternal. But his reading was different from Patch's. In his opinion I had been flung deliberately into the jaws of death—and then ripped loose—to teach me that I was mortal! That if I wanted to accomplish the great work in which I was then engaged, I must take greater care, fewer risks—"

The bell rang to signal the end of the first class.

"I have talked too long! As usual!" Theodore apologized. "But perhaps it is as well. You have more time to weigh the evidence and work out your own exegesis."

Reluctantly, the girls picked up their books and started for the door. Some were already beginning to argue in whispers. Others were silent and thoughtful.

Harriet got as far as the hall, and then came back.

"May I ask you one question?"

"Of course."

"How did *you* read your sign?"

"Then?" Theodore asked. "Or with the wisdom of hindsight?"

"Then."

"I read it as my friend Patch did. As proof that I was under the direction and protection of the Most High, that as long as I dedicated myself entirely to the work I had in hand, I was more than mortal."

"And . . . ?"

"And I learned that I was not."

At the supper table that evening, Harriet seated herself next to Nina in the place that was usually his. Theodore took a seat directly across from them, so that he could share in their talk.

It was a long time since he had looked at his wife at such close range and in such ruthless light. What he saw shocked him. The lamp that hung over the table threw a cone of brightness that caught her on the forehead, made black circles of her eye sockets, whitened the ridges of her skull bones and shadowed the hollows between them. It drained all color from her hair and skin, so that she looked—the words formed like ice crystals in his mind—haggard! deathly! like a soul whose light had failed!

If Angelina marries you, she will hide her light.

It was a second and worse shock to recall the words of Garrison's gloomy prophecy, spoken on their wedding day! Theodore had not thought of it in years. Why did he now? Was this its fulfillment? And was he, Theodore, to blame?

Even the framing of such questions shook him profoundly. He was not used to thinking of himself and Angelina as separate enough for one to act for or against the other. From the day they revealed their love to each other, both of them had spoken and thought of themselves as halves of a sundered being, united—or reunited—by the will of the Creator. Never from that moment to this had his love faltered or diminished. Nor had hers.

Yet the face of the woman across the table—animated with interest in what she was hearing and saying to the girl beside her—was not the face of one beloved and fulfilled. It was the face of a martyr on the rack.

The questions Harriet was asking were direct and practical, indications to Theodore that his parable had accomplished its end, had brought the young woman down to earth without discouraging her. He had not had a moment to discuss Harriet's project with Angelina, but she was doing very well without knowing the special circumstances. And since he had no role to play in their discussion, it was hard to keep his mind on it. It kept straying back (guiltily, as if in search of a clue to a crime he had committed unknowingly) to Garrison and the wedding feast, and the rivalry that had led up to it.

* * *

It was Garrison who first introduced Theodore and Angelina to each other at the Agents' Convention where Theodore was using the last of his failing voice to "combustionize" a new generation of Abolition evangelists to replace him in the field. He was engaged in imparting the "secret" that the gospel they were called upon to preach was a religious, not a political, one; that what was needed was passion, moral passion, kept at the melting point, so that all they said and did would flow like lava from that burning core— when his eyes fell upon two women sitting at the back of the room.

They were dressed in Quaker gray with white linen caps conspicuous as beacons in the sea of uncovered male manes. One was a sweet-faced, motherly matron. The other—

Was Angelina Grimké!

The name rose to Theodore's lips, and he almost spoke it aloud.

She looked exactly as he had imagined her, and he had imagined her many times. She had been in his thoughts since the day—over a year before—when he read her letter to Garrison in the *Liberator*. It had been like a hand stretched out to caress and support him, the hand of an angel, a guardian spirit.

Theodore was on the point of writing to open a correspondence with her when he recalled that she was a lady, presumably unapproachable without some introduction or intermediary. All through the turmoil of the intervening months, he had hoped for some chance encounter. He made discreet inquiries of co-workers in the cause who knew Miss Grimké, and the answers he got indicated that she was unapproachable on more than one score. She was a convert to Quakerism, said to be so strict in her practice that she did not associate with members of other faiths. Yet she had stretched out her hand in fellowship to Garrison, who was no Quaker. Theodore believed she would do as much for him, if she knew his need. He laid the words of her letter like a talisman to his courage when it flagged. He loved her before he knew.

And now here she was! listening to him as if enraptured, her whole being concentrated on the words that grated out of his aching throat! He lost the train of his argument and could not recover it. He let his voice excuse him and called the session to a close.

Garrison brought the two sisters up to meet him. "There is a plan for them to speak to groups of ladies here in the city," he explained. "If you have no objection, they feel they will profit much by attending your lectures."

Theodore said he had no objection, but it sounded so ungracious that it was almost a rebuff. It was impossible to speak naturally with Angelina's eyes fixed on him at this range. They were blue steel augurs, boring into his soul, exposing the image he carried there in idolatry that had been unconscious till now.

Sarah was chiding him gently and he tried to listen. "Sister and and I are both mortified by the state of thy voice," she said in a husky southern drawl. "We fear thee may injure thyself if thee continues to speak with such an affliction."

"The injury was done long ago," he said, and again it sounded like a rebuff. He floundered about for some way to atone for his rudeness without admitting to it, prolonging the conversation, although others were waiting to speak to him on matters of some urgency. He talked too long and to little point, aware that the effort to control himself was distorting his face into a mask of cold disdain that must surely repel her; remembering that he had vowed —not a month ago—in the hearing of all his close friends, never to marry, never to fall in love, till the slave—all slaves everywhere!— were free.

Angelina attended every one of the sessions of the Agents' Convention. Whenever he was speaking, her eyes were fixed on him with the same unbearable intensity. The only respite came when Garrison or someone else took the rostrum. Then, from his seat on the platform, Theodore could watch her, could follow every reflection of thought and feeling on that marvelous face.

Only one thing marred his pleasure: her apparent acceptance as gospel of everything that fell from Garrison's lips. Garrison was in one of his extravagant veins, denouncing his opposition in the most intemperate of Old Testament invective, drawing naïvely egotistical parallels between his own career and Christ's passion, mixing sound Abolitionist doctrine with samplings of a dozen others, from perfectionism to "no human government." Was Angelina so awed by his strength of purpose that she was blind to the flaws in his thinking?

Theodore was usually more tolerant of Garrison's weaknesses than most of his friends were. For one thing, he knew himself guilty of the worst of them. He, too, was vainglorious, or had been before his fall. Theodore had a reputation for an almost fanatical aversion to any sort of personal acclaim, but this was only because of the extraordinary measures he took to fight his devil. The measures did not exorcise it; they only covered it from public view.

Also, he gave Garrison credit for one supreme virtue that he himself lacked: the absolute refusal to accept defeat. Stubborn, sectarian, capable of smallness and even of stupidity, Garrison was nevertheless the stone against which the spark of a moral revolution had been struck, not once, but again and again.

For both these reasons, although Theodore's close friends were allied with the emerging anti-Garrison faction in the movement, he had refused to take sides, insisting that all need not be unison in the swelling chorus of Abolition. But he could not sit by now and see Angelina's mind enthralled by error!

It dawned on him—just before he rose to speak a rebuttal—that he was consumed by jealousy.

In the days that followed the Agents' Convention, Theodore strove to root his feeling for Angelina out of his heart, or to bury it under so deep a silence that no one would ever suspect its existence. He had more than one reason for such a course. He had just suffered a physical breakdown that was at once the cause and the effect of the failure of his personal crusade. He had neither money nor possessions, no skill or calling that promised any sort of security, nothing to offer a wife, least of all a woman like Angelina. He was a fallen lion, a man with nothing to his name except his name, and that fast fading into obscurity. And besides, there was his vow, made half in jest, but before witnesses who had believed him serious.

If he could have avoided the sisters' society completely, he would have done so. But they sought him out and asked for help that he could not refuse. They asked his advice when their first meeting was denounced before it had been held. He urged them to go on with their plan, and they asked his help with their presentation. He gave it. He stood by them in the last tense hour before the event, and joined briefly in the rejoicing after it. Then he escaped back to his office tasks: pamphlets to be edited or written from scratch; funds to be raised and allocated; correspondence to be answered to agents in the field. There was enough to keep him safely occupied. But as the prospect of a series of large public lectures opened for the sisters, they returned to ask his help again.

With Sarah he worked easily but to little purpose. She would never make a speaker. She thought clearly and wrote well, but her voice flattened out into a deadly monotone when she faced any audience. Her long, frustrated struggle to achieve a Quaker ministry explained this, but explaining did not cure. Neither did his most discreet criticism. Indeed, criticism undermined what little self-confidence Sarah had, and lack of confidence was at the heart of her trouble. All Theodore could do was argue questions of fact, and try to steer her out of the sloughs into which she was constantly steaming (and quoting Garrison to bolster her own conviction that they were the main channel of reform).

With Angelina nothing was easy, but everything bore fruit. Her natural gifts were complete ones. She needed no training as a speaker. Her power of feeling, once unleashed, simply swept all before it. She needed no help in arriving at a conviction. She trusted her own instincts implicitly. He had never known anyone so morally self-sufficient, so serenely indifferent to the opinions of others. But she was willing—even eager—to learn how to argue the position for the benefit of those who needed their faith buttressed by fact. It was to Theodore she turned for such buttressing. She accepted his authority for any disputed point, his opinion in almost all matters of controverted theory, strategy, or tactics. It flattered and it frightened him. But in those rare cases where she differed from him and persisted in it, he became even more frightened, and forgot all caution as he rushed in to berate her. (By letter, now, for they were parted by the distance between New England and New York.)

The sharpest of these differences was on the subject of women's right to speak in public. Theodore did not question this. He had urged not only Sarah and Angelina, but other women Abolitionists as well, to exercise it from the moment of their first opportunity. What he objected to was the sisters' taking time from their real work to debate this principle.

"I know this temptation, for I have wrestled with it," he wrote to them both. "I let half a dozen causes turn me from my first object, which was to prepare myself for the ministry. I broke off my studies to become a lecturer on temperance; to assist Finney, the evangelist; to survey the country for Manual Labor Education. But I came at last to see that for one committed to *this* cause—which is *the* cause of our time—to deviate one degree from a straight course is downright wickedness!

"When you have won liberty and equality for the *most* oppressed brothers and sisters, your own liberty will be easy enough to win. You are establishing the rights you claim by practicing them, by doing your duty as a moral being, the equal of any other. Do not, I beg of you, permit yourselves to be drawn into the controversy on the abstract question."

But the New England Congregational clergy was attacking, and Garrison was urging the sisters to answer the attack. Under his prodding, Sarah had already stirred up new hornets of clerical wrath by a series of letters to the newspapers on "Equality of Rights and the Position of Women."

"You put the cart before the horse," Theodore wrote her, when he had read the first of them. "You drag the tree by the top when you push your women's rights before human rights have broken the path.

"What is done for the slave and human rights must be done now, now, now! Delay is madness! Ruin! Whereas women's rights are not a life-and-death matter, now or ever! Why can't you have eyes to see this? What will you run atilt at next?"

And having worked himself up to this dangerous pitch, he went on to take Angelina to task for faults he had been observing in her. "You are liable from the structure of your mind to form your opinions on too slight data," he wrote. "You are dazzled by the glare of analogies, not led on by cause and effect. You are liable at every moment to turn short from the main point, and spend your whole force upon some little side annoyance.

"Add to this great pride of character and a passion for adventure and novel achievements, and you have an amount of temptation that can be mastered only by a strong effort and a strong faith."

Sarah replied with humility, thanking him for the faithfulness that had dictated his criticism, but Angelina flared angrily.

"Such a lecture I never before had from anyone!" she wrote. "What is the matter with thee? One would really suppose we had abandoned the anti-slavery cause, and were roving around the country preaching nothing but women's rights!

"When I speak, I forget everything but the slave.

"If Sister chooses to write letters to the *Spectator,* am I to be scolded? Please let every woman bear her own burden!"

And she revenged herself with a jab at some of his friends whose "anti-Garrisonism" had interfered with the arrangements for her New England meetings.

Theodore rushed to his friends' defense, not because they needed defending, but because he could not bear the idea that she was ranging herself with Garrison and against him. He dismissed her complaint as "unjust and unloving," totally without justification, and warned her, in what seemed to him afterward a piece of consummate recklessness, that she was in danger of becoming a queen on Garrison's chessboard.

This time he had gone too far.

Angelina did not answer him at all for some time. Then she wrote in a tone that froze his heart.

> *I accept thy strictures as faithful, but I do not understand them. I fear it is impossible that we shall ever understand each other now. I should be grateful therefore if you would return to me all my letters, except those which contain the accusations you find blameworthy. Perhaps if we ever meet again, you will need them in order to point out my errors to me.*

He had wounded her.

It was unpardonable! To explain, to punish himself, he had to write it all out: confess his love and his jealousy, the battle he had waged and lost behind the false front of the disinterested friend and counselor. It not only humbled what was left of his pride; it trampled the last of his hopes. For it had always been beyond his imagining that Angelina could love him. And he did not see how she could honor him with her friendship after this. She might pity, even forgive him, but she must despise him as well.

He braced himself for her reply. He worked more and more frenetically in his office, hoping exhaustion would dull the edge of feeling. He played little malicious games with himself, refusing to take any notice of the mail when it was delivered, waiting for the *coup de grâce* to be dealt by some unknowing friend. He even faced the possibility that there would be no *coup,* that Angelina would never reply to his declaration, that his suffering would prolong itself interminably.

When her letter came at last, he put it into his desk drawer and forced himself to continue with what he was doing. Not till all the others in the office had gone out for their midday meal did he pull it out and break the seal.

> *Your letter was indeed a great surprise, my brother, and yet it was no surprise at all. It was a surprise because you have so mastered your feelings as never to betray them. It was no surprise because in the depth of my own heart, there was found a response. . . .*

His eyes jumped down the page, looking for some certain clue to the ambiguity of Angelina's opening.

> *You say that my letter to you revealed that you had inflicted abiding pain. Yes, you did. And it was love for you that caused reproof to sink so deep into my heart. I thought with such views of my character, it was impossible that you could love me. . . .*

Theodore felt a physical shock, as if he had run on a reef.

He thrust the letter, still mostly unread, into a side pocket and went out into the streets. He walked for hours, like a dazed inebriate. Once he heard a child cry out, and looked down to see him staring up in terror, clutching at his mother's skirt. Theodore saw himself reflected in the mirror of a dark windowpane, and understood the child's terror. His hair was wild as a mane, his eyes staring, his expression demonic.

And yet she loved him! Angelina loved him!

It was a month before he trusted himself near her.

She was in Boston, preparing for a series of public lectures to follow up her success with the Legislature. He made a short trip on some pretext connected with business of the Anti-Slavery Society. Garrison received him coldly, as an outrider for the New York faction. Unfortunately, Theodore could not plead innocent without revealing the real reason for his presence, and he and Angelina had determined to keep their secret from everyone but Sarah.

The tremendous notoriety that resulted from Angelina's addresses to the Legislature made her for the time being the most talked-about woman in America. It was generally agreed, even by her most fervent supporters, that the public role she had played unfitted her forever for married life. (One close friend confided to Theodore that he pitied the man who should attempt to make a wife of her.) There seemed little doubt that if it became known she was engaged to be married, her audiences would be swelled by a great influx of curiosity seekers, and she felt she could not speak to such a public. The only way to keep the secret was to keep it from everyone. Neither Whittier, with whom Theodore shared an office, nor Henry Stanton, with whom he lived, had the slightest suspicion of what was afoot, till they were bidden to the wedding.

Garrison was hurt by Angelina's failure to confide in him, but—to give him his due—he had better reasons than that for his reservations about the match. He and Theodore had come to differ on some points of doctrine, and to Garrison those who were not for him were against him; and those who were against him were against the slave. (This was the logic that was driving him on the one side, and the New York leaders on the other, to an open, ugly break.) Garrison had sponsored Angelina and Sarah from the time of their first effort, with more and more passionate partisanship as the attacks against them grew sharper. He had paid for it with new enemies among the conservative anti-slavery groups. He had come to consider Angelina his Galatea. Beset as he was by many sorts of trouble: financial and physical as well as organizational, it was no wonder he took her "defection" hard.

But when Angelina asked him to perform the one official act in the ceremony she and Theodore had planned for their wedding, Garrison accepted. Theodore was sure he would not have done so if he could not act with a good heart.

The wedding was an extraordinary occasion, unique in ways that impressed themselves deeply on all who took part. Sarah and Angelina were at that time still members of the Society of Friends, which disapproved of a paid clergy. They expected to be disowned by their Meeting (as indeed they soon were)—Angelina for marrying out of the Society, and Sarah for witnessing the marriage. But Angelina wanted to dispense with the services of an ordained minister because on this score she felt herself in unity with her fellow Friends. Theodore, for his part, was offended by the intervention of secular authority, humiliated to be the beneficiary of laws that stripped Angelina of all rights to her person and inherited property at the moment she became his wife. They confided all this to each other and determined to have no prescribed ritual and no figure of civil and religious authority officiating.

They were to be married in Philadelphia, in the home of Nina's widowed sister, Anna Frost, and under Pennsylvania law a marriage was legal if the couple did no more than announce their intention to live together henceforward as man and wife, in the presence of a dozen witnesses. (If none of these was a magistrate, the marriage could not be registered, but that was important only in case of a dispute at some later date, over matters concerning property, a circumstance that could hardly arise in their case.) Many of their friends would be gathering in Philadelphia in early May for the dedication of Pennsylvania Hall and the convention of several anti-slavery societies, so Angelina and Theodore decided to invite them—and all the members of their own two families who could do so without inconvenience or great expense—to gather in Mrs. Frost's parlor one evening and hear them speak the promises they felt called upon to make.

The bride and groom would themselves ask the blessing of God on their union, and each guest would be given the opportunity to speak or to pray or to keep silent, as the spirit moved him. Only one official act was required by the law: the reading aloud of their certificate of marriage. This was the office Angelina (and Sarah, also) wanted Garrison to perform. And perform it he did, with such cordial enthusiasm that Theodore believed his reservations must have dissolved in the warm glow of the event.

For it was a love feast in the real sense of the term. The élite of the whole anti-slavery movement was present (except for poor Whittier, who had to sit outside till the ceremony was over, lest he too be disowned by his Meeting). Both the pro- and the anti-Garrison factions were represented, but there was truce between them. Both races were represented, and the poor as well as the comfortably circumstanced. Two former Grimké slaves whom Mrs. Frost had brought north with her were among the guests. One of them was the baker who supplied the wedding cake, confected of "free," not of slave-produced, sugar. There were two Presbyterian ministers, one Negro and one white, who prayed and blessed the couple after their vows.

Those vows were spoken extempore, but Angelina and Theodore had thought long and hard before deciding what to promise and what not to. He renounced all authority over his beloved except that given him by love itself. She vowed to honor her husband, not to obey him, but to love him "before myself." Each of them promised never to hold the other back from any call of duty, however dangerous, painful, or prolonged.

"If our marriage is truly blessed," Theodore said in the hearing of all, "it will bear fruit in greater usefulness to the cause of the slave."

When the formal proceedings were over and the guests were clustering around the table where Angelina cut and served the cake, Garrison drew Theodore aside. In the tone of a father grudgingly giving his daughter's hand to a man whose qualifications as a husband are open to question, he began to state his misgivings about the match.

"I must warn you, Brother Weld, that if Angelina is removed from the place she now occupies in the movement, all the momentum it has gained in the last twelve months will be lost," he said. "It was a blow to us when your voice was stilled, but to some extent Angelina has replaced you in the public arena. There is no one who can replace her."

Theodore assured him that he had no intention of removing Angelina from her place. "She is exhausted and in need of rest. There will be much to do for a while, as we settle into a new home and a new way of life. I plan, as you know, to make my living as a farmer, and Angelina is determined to prove herself as a farmer's wife.

"But when a call comes to her, she will answer it. I will sustain and support her, as she will sustain and support my answer, if a call comes for me."

"I am glad to hear it," Garrison said (as if he had not just heard it solemnly pledged). "I must confess to you that I have been fearful that if Angelina marries you, she will hide her light."

Theodore's promise was tested—and in the cruelest manner imaginable—by the events of the very next day, by the great public meeting that ended in the destruction of Pennsylvania Hall.

This temple of "free discussion" was the answer of Philadelphia's reform groups to the continued denial of meeting places. Partisans of a dozen beleaguered causes had banded together to raise the sum needed to build a place of their own. The result was a handsome, neoclassical edifice with pillars and pediments, occupying a desirable corner in the heart of the city, and calling attention to itself by its size, as well as by the elegance of its form. The main auditorium was on the second floor, and seated three thousand. The ground floor held a library and several rooms large enough for ordinary meetings of the member groups.

The formal dedication took place on the morning of the wedding day. Theodore had been invited to speak, and excused himself on account of his throat, but he went to hear his own and other greetings read, and to listen to the main address, which was delivered by a moderate anti-slavery man named David Paul Brown. This gentleman's willingness to associate himself with the radicals on the platform that morning was regarded by some as a great concession on his part, but to Garrison, who spoke after him, freedom of discussion meant freedom to denounce anyone with whom he differed. Brown's gradualism sickened him, and he said so.

"Some will consider the remarks of that gentleman as adapted to please all parties. These are your men of caution and prudence and judiciousness. I have learned to hate those words!"

He went on to warn the shocked citizens of Philadelphia that there was "too much quietude" in their city: that slavery would not be overthrown without "a most tremendous excitement." It seemed to Theodore that he was deliberately inviting violence when he bragged of the "popular tumult" the Abolitionists had weathered in Boston, the showers of brickbats and rotten eggs and the threats of tar and feathers. But he could not deny the force of Garrison's argument that only under such conditions would Abolition begin to make "swift progress like that of Christianity in apostolic and martyr times."

The excitement Garrison asked for was stirring the audience as

137

he finished speaking. It grew from ripples of indignation to a strong chop of conflicting sentiments, expressed in bursts of applause or dissent through the speeches that followed his. But the climax was not reached until a full day after the dedication was over.

It had been decided—rather hastily—to hold a public meeting the next night, in order to take advantage of the presence of many out-of-town celebrities, particularly the women Abolitionists, who had been holding their national convention behind closed doors. Philadelphians were curious about these "advanced females," most of all about Angelina, who was fresh from her astonishing triumphs in Boston, and a bride as well.

An hour after the announcement that she would speak, the neighborhood of Pennsylvania Hall was pockmarked with placards warning of violence if the meeting took place. It was like the first time in New York. Neither Angelina nor any of the other speakers was dismayed. Those responsible for the hall took the precaution of calling on the mayor, but he was shocked by the suggestion that police protection be extended. They could, he assured them, depend on the "good manners and good sense" of their fellow citizens.

Theodore was inclined to agree. Being unknown in Philadelphia, he had been able to canvas the docks from which, presumably, any mob would be recruited. He kept eyes and ears open for signs of trouble, but he heard and saw nothing out of the ordinary. He mingled with the crowd that began to gather outside the hall hours before its doors were opened, and caught no hint of anything but the most respectful interest. There was a larger proportion of men in the crowd than he would have predicted in view of the prominence of women on the program. But they seemed to be quiet, mannerly fellows, well—or at least respectably—dressed.

When he went back to wish Angelina well, he found her the calmest of all concerned, her only anxiety whether or not she would fulfill his expectations. (He had never yet heard her on a platform!) He kissed her and blessed her and went out to find that there was

138

not a single seat vacant in the whole enormous expanse of the auditorium.

People were being turned away, loyal members of local anti-slavery societies who protested that they had never missed a meeting on this subject in their lives. Some consoled others by arguing that it was better that the seats be taken by those "still in need of light." But Theodore could not resign himself. He hunted till he found a side entrance and worked his way up through passageways and stairs, till he stood in the farthest corner of the hall, wedged so tightly into a group of standing men that he had no more chance of moving than if he had been bound to a stake.

There was a smattering of applause, then silence, as the speakers filed out. Only one man among them: Garrison! And it was he who came forward to make the opening remarks.

He had asked for this privilege, he explained, because many of his friends had admonished him for his attack on David Paul Brown. He did not wish to leave Philadelphia without apologizing for the unfortunate tone of his remarks.

There was another smattering of applause, but over it, and much louder, a hissing and groaning that did not seem to come from any one part of the room. Theodore had the impression that the dissenters were spread evenly through the crowd. It was ominous, if true.

Garrison ignored the warning and went on, not to elaborate his apology, but to justify the attack on Brown, larding his speech with inflammatory quotations from Scripture. In a voice more like Jupiter Tonans' than Jesus', he reminded his hearers that the latter had also lost his temper and unbridled his wrath when he regarded "this adulterous and perverse generation, a brood of vipers and hypocrites."

There was another volley of hisses, so loud and so prompt that Theodore knew, for a certainty that it was made by men who had come there for that and no other purpose. His heart tightened with fear. Garrison's face tightened with anger. He counterattacked with new intensity, and was answered with more intense hostility from the crowd.

It was impossible not to admire the vigor with which the man fought, but Theodore knew that the tempest would break, not on his head, but on the heads of the women who were to follow him. He wanted to interrupt, to stop Garrison, to warn Angelina, to avert the omen. But he held himself in check, even when Garrison had finished and turned back to his seat, and there was a clamor of booing and catcalls and a stamping of feet on the sounding board of the floor.

Maria Chapman came to the podium and raised her hands for quiet. Some of the audience obeyed her, but soon they were quarreling noisily with those who did not. The result was a tumult over which it was impossible to hear what she was saying or what was going on in the street outside.

Something was certainly going on there. The glow of torches was beginning to brighten the tall windows along that side of the hall. Mrs. Chapman had just stepped away from the podium when a shower of stones rattled against the windows closest to the platform. There was a sharp, tinkling sound, as glass broke and fell. Some pieces landed in the aisle, and some on the stage. As far as Theodore could tell, no one was hit. But the real danger was not flying glass, nor even arson. It was a fear, which might send the crowd surging up those narrow aisles to the even narrower exit doors.

For a moment the issue hung in the balance. There was a stirring in some of the chairs along the far aisle, but no one rose. Inside the hall everything was quiet. Outside, the noise of the rabble broke in wave after wave, like a surf.

Angelina stood up and stepped forward.

A curious rustling sound swept across the room. Her voice rang out over it, clear and sweet as a chime.

"Men! Brothers and fathers! Mothers and daughters and sisters! What came ye out for to see? A reed shaken in the wind?"

More stones struck the windows and more panes shattered. A

howl of brute rage from the mob cut the quiet like a scythe. But still no one moved. Angelina seemed to have mesmerized the whole audience, friend and foe alike.

"What is a mob?" she asked. "Would the breaking of every window here be any proof that we are wrong and they are right? That slavery is a good and wholesome institution?"

There were murmurs of agreement, none of dissent.

"What if those deluded beings out there were to burst in upon us? Break up our meeting and commit violence upon our persons? Would this be anything compared to what the slave suffers?"

There was another howl of rage so loud that it drowned out her voice, but she went on speaking, and people strained forward to hear.

"There is nothing to fear from those who would stop our mouths. It is they themselves who should tremble," she was saying when next she could be heard. "For the current is setting fast against them. If the arm of the North had not already caused the Bastille of slavery to totter, you would not hear those cries!

"A few years ago, the South felt secure and could ask with a contemptuous sneer, 'Who are the Abolitionists? They are nothing!' Aye, and in one sense we are nothing still. But in this we rejoice, that God has chosen things that are as nought to bring about things that are!"

From this improvised beginning, Angelina went on to give the whole of the address she had planned. She spoke for an hour. When the noise outside grew too loud, she waited for it to subside, and went on. When stones flew through the open sashes, she made references to them if it suited her point, ignored them if it did not. As the mob grew wilder, her calm hardened. It was a shield behind which all were safe. So long as she stood there and spoke, fear could not begin its work.

But she could not stand there forever!

Theodore's mind ran ahead to the moment when the spell would be broken, when the meeting would end and those inside would have to run the gauntlet of the bedlamites in the street. What shield would be proof against them?

There were men enough in the hall to protect the women, if they formed themselves into a guard. But would they? Most of them, Theodore now suspected, had come to attack, not to defend, the Abolitionists. Looking around him, he could not see a single familiar or friendly face. They had fallen into a trap! They had let the hall be packed with blood brothers to the mob!

From what seemed a great distance, he heard Angelina's voice. She was addressing herself to the women, rallying them like a general on the eve of battle. She was planning to lead the women out first! Unprotected! And let them make a path through the mob!

It was the sort of inspired recklessness that might succeed. But it also might not. It depended not only on Angelina's courage but also on her control over those who followed her. For at the moment of confrontation, if any lost heart and tried to turn back, or to escape into the crowd, there would be a mêlée in which people could be trampled, possibly to death!

Theodore heard Angelina come to the end of her address. If he had been standing beside her at this moment, he could have faced it without flinching, could have given his life to save hers, could even have released her to martyrdom, so long as he met it at the same instant. But separated from her, an impotent witness to her danger, he was unmanned. His eyes blurred as she made her way down the steps that led from the platform to the center aisle.

She passed close to him without seeing him. Calm, regal, rapt, she seemed to glow like a pillar of fire. The other women from the platform had fallen in behind her; women from the audience followed after them. Up the aisle the procession moved, and through the doors at the back. Angelina was out of sight now. She must be on the stairs, or in the foyer, approaching the doors that opened to the street.

He counted the seconds, straining for the shout that would tell him the mob had seen and recognized her.

Quiet fell instead.

A quiet so profound that he thought of the waters of the Red Sea, stilled and parted for Moses to lead the Israelites across. Just so Nina was leading her column of women through the stilled and parted tide of human rage. He prayed for the calm to hold.

And it did.

The outward calm held longer than the calm in Angelina's heart. There was time for the whole audience to disperse without molestation. There was quiet for the whole of that night and the next day. It was not till the following evening that the mob regained the pitch of frenzy required for its appointed task: the demolition of the beautiful temple of free speech.

Angelina's light had been snuffed long before that awful pyre was lit. By the time Theodore had made his way back to the home in which they were staying, she was hysterical with anxiety for him, behaving as any other bride of two days might be expected to behave if her husband was separated from her by an angry crowd. The heroic figure of the platform Theodore never saw again. She had, like Milton in his blindness, spent her light,

> E're half my days in this dark world and wide,
> And that one Talent which is death to hide,
> Lodg'd with me useless . . .

But why? He had never told her what it cost him to stand by and witness her ordeal, never asked her to spare herself (and him) another. Why had she never returned to the arena? Had she never been called?

Theodore tried conscientiously to recall the early years of their marriage. The first year was easy. They had both worked as many hours as they could spare from the essential tasks of house and farm on the preparation of *American Slavery As It Is,* the awesome bill of particulars that condemned slavery out of its own mouth. Angelina spent endless hours reading and clipping southern newspapers, composing questionnaires and collating answers, soliciting

143

the testimony of qualified observers. True, the task had been Theodore's both in the original conception and the final responsibility. But Angelina's light shone more brilliantly than his in the final text, for she and Sarah contributed signed "testimonies" of great effectiveness, while his name appeared nowhere. He believed at the time—and could not disbelieve now—that Angelina felt the same sense of achievement that he did, for an important and difficult task well done.

The year after that—and part of the next—he was away in Washington for months at a time, working behind the scenes of the great congressional battle. If calls came to Angelina in those days, she refused them without telling him of them. She would have had no choice but to refuse on grounds of health, for the children were born so close to each other that she had not recovered from the effects of the first labor when she was pregnant again, forced by the threat of miscarriage to spend most of her time in bed.

No, it was not the hiding of her light that had wrought the havoc on her physical self. It was the other way around. "That one Talent" had been buried in the ruin of her health, brought on by some other cause or causes.

He was not to blame!

And yet, his love for her had not done for Angelina what hers had done for him. The miracle of loving and being loved by her had restored his soul, and eventually his health and strength; while he—if he had not hidden his beloved's light—had not helped her to fight the fate that did.

*　　*　　*

"Tell me, Thoda, is there not one of your old Lane colleagues teaching in any of the freedmen's schools?" Angelina asked him from across the table. "Harriet ought to have some firsthand report of the state of affairs down there."

"I know of none," he answered. And then a notion came to him that he wondered he had not had before. "What about the young man at Lincoln University? It's possible he attended such a school himself!"

Angelina stared at him in dismay. Only for a moment. Then she recovered herself and said to Harriet: "It is certainly possible. We can ask him, if we have occasion to write him again."

Theodore knew he had blundered, but he did not know how.

Was it possible that Angelina shrank from the exposure of the fact that her family had been slaveholders, which would certainly follow from any contact between Harriet and the young freedman? He knew how deeply she had grieved when her mother and most of her brothers died unrepentant of the sin, and their sons continued in it till the verdict of the War went against them. But she had never tried to hide the truth. On the contrary, she had proclaimed it in her speeches. She had written in *American Slavery As It Is* an account of its effect on the character of the master class that most readers took for a reference to her own kin. If Angelina's courage had flagged in the years since then, if she were no longer brave enough to face up to the evil when it showed itself too close, she would not have written to the boy at Lincoln University, and would not now be anxiously awaiting his answer.

No. His sin was of some other sort. Angelina would tell him when she was ready to. Meanwhile it lay heavy on Theodore's heart that he could no longer look into hers and read it as his own.

VIII

Angelina saw the letter on the mantel the moment she and Theo entered the room.

Stuart had opened the front door to them, and the two Sarahs were coming from the kitchen to greet them. The whole family was there to witness!

If she could have chosen, Angelina would have opened the letter in private, and absorbed the contents herself before sharing it with any of them. But that was impossible now. She crossed quickly to the fireplace and picked up the envelope. Her heart was pounding, and she breathed deeply a few times to quiet it.

"He writes a very good hand, doesn't he, Sarah?" she asked.

There was no answer, and she looked to see why. Sarah was settling herself into her favorite stiff wooden rocker, her back against its back, braced for the shock to come.

But Sarah was the only one who was braced. Young Sarah was

watching her mother, interested and curious, but unwarned—vulnerable! Stuart was helping his father pull off his boots, paying no attention to anything else. Theo was looking at her with that loving, puzzled look that said, "I have sinned against my beloved, and she will not tell me my sin."

He had been waiting all week for her to confide, to tell him his fault and that she forgave it. She had not spoken, but it was not because she was angry. She was frightened, and too weak to put herself to another test.

(When Theo spoke before Harriet about the young freedman, Angelina realized he had no inkling of what she and Sarah expected. She had assumed till then that his mind followed the logic that guided theirs, forgetting how little he knew at first hand of the realities of life in the slave South. The support she had counted on from him was given in ignorance of the possible price!

If she told him, and he regretted her action in writing—if he tried to dissuade her from the course she was determined to follow—she did not know how she could bear it. So she had not told him; she had hoped against hope and all reason that the test might never have to be made.)

Tension was now palpable. It made itself felt even in Stuart's corner. He looked up, first at her, then at his aunt. In a moment he would ask a question.

Angelina slipped her finger quickly under the flap of the envelope and broke the wax seal. From inside she drew out a slab of folded sheets, and as she did so, a small, stiff oblong dropped to the floor. Stuart came to retrieve it for her.

"It's a photograph," he said in surprise.

Angelina took it from him and held it to the light. It was of two boys, posed in almost comic formality against the painted background of a photographer's studio. Their grave young faces were as expressionless as statues, but they were handsome, and held themselves with a dignity that triumphed over the ill-fitting, ill-matched garments they wore. The color of their skin was neither dark nor

148

fair enough to draw attention, and there was nothing in their features to suggest a mixture of racial strains.

"Let your Aunt Sai look at it," Angelina said, as she gave it back to Stuart. She unfolded the letter and began to read it aloud, keeping her voice even and her back straight:

> "Mrs. A. G. Weld,
> Dear Madam:
>   I was somewhat surprised to be receiving yours of the 15th instant. I never expected to hear through the medium of a letter from Miss Angelina Grimké of Anti-Slavery—

"Now this is interesting!" she broke off and looked at Theo, making herself smile and receiving his smile in answer. "The young man wrote *notoriety*, then crossed it out and wrote *celebrity* instead. *Anti-Slavery celebrity* . . ."

"Who is he?" Stuart asked, but no one answered him.

Angelina went back to the letter and read on:

> "I thank you, madam, for your kindness and concern for me. I shall proceed to give you a simple sketch of my history and my connections. . . ."

That was the last line of the first sheet. She slipped it behind the last and began at the top of the second:

> "I am the son of Henry Grimké—"

Not Henry! No! Of all of them . . . !

Angelina closed her eyes. Selina's face swam in the darkness, sweet and sad and bewildered. . . . She heard her own voice, faint and far away, saying, *I stay here to protect you, Henry. From the violence you do yourself!*

"Don't try to go on, my dear, if it's too painful," Theo said gently. There was not a hint of anything in his voice but concern for her.

She opened her eyes and found her place on the page and went on:

"Of course you know more about my father than I do. Suffice to say he was a lawyer and was married to a Miss Selina Simons. She died, leaving three children, viz: Henrietta, Montague, and Thomas.

"After her death, he took my mother, who was his slave, and his children's nurse. Her name was Nancy Weston . . ."

There were no children in the house when Angelina left it, and no nurse. Nancy Weston must have been bought soon afterward, or brought from the Bellemont place. . . . Nancy Weston . . . As she said the name over in silence, an image began to form itself . . . the unknown Black Sister.

Angelina opened her eyes to drive it away.

"Would you like me to read the rest of it for you?" Theo asked.

She handed him the pages. He moved close to the lamp that stood on the parlor table, cleared his throat, and began aloud:

"By my mother he had three children also, Archibald, which is my name, and Francis and John. . . ."

"Three sons!" Sarah spoke for the first time. "Three sons by a slave mistress. And we knew nothing. . . ."

Theo waited a moment, but she said no more. He went back to the letter:

"He—that is, the father—died about fifteen years ago, leaving my mother with two children and in a pregnant state, for John was born about two months after he died. . . ."

Theo read on in silence for a moment, and then said, "I really think you ought not to listen to all of this just now. I know what you are suffering, and—I'm afraid it gets worse as it goes on."

"Read it all, please," Angelina said.

She saw him look at Sarah, as if she too had a right to object, but Sarah had not moved since she spoke. If her eyes had not been open, one might have thought she slept.

And so the tale unwound, coil after coil, like a hideous serpent: Henry's sin of lust . . . his sin of deceit . . . his deathbed promise and Montague's betrayal of it . . . Eliza and Mary's complicity in the enslavement of children they must have known to be their nephews . . . No wonder Eliza had never spoken their names!

Theo was not reading all that was written. She saw that he skipped a detail here, censored a word there. But what could be worse than what he did read? The incredible ordeal of the mother as seen through the eyes of her son! A black woman in a white man's world! Laboring to the limit of her strength all the years of their childhood! Suffering hunger and cold and illness—not only her own, but theirs! And then, when she had scaled the mountain of adversity at last, to be confronted with a new valley of sorrow! To have her sons taken from her, one after another, till all were lost!

"Earth became a blank. She saw nothing, she thought of no one but her sons, who were groaning from the severity of their hard taskmasters, and when she remonstrated their unjust treatment, she was thrown into a loathsome cell and kept there till sickness prostrated her. . . ."

The Black Sister loomed like an ebony statue of anguish. Nameless no longer!

There was only one way to appease her. Angelina must go herself, find Nancy Weston, kneel to her and beg forgiveness, beg to be given a task—or many tasks—that would constitute at least a beginning of amends. . . .

Theo had finished reading, and the others were speaking now. Stuart and his sister. They were asking questions. Sarah was answering. Life was beginning to flow on. Each was working off the numbness in his own fashion. It was good that they could. . . .

As for Angelina, she could say nothing . . . see nothing but Nancy. . . . She was going to be ill if she did not lie down for a little while. The door to her chamber and Theo's was only a few steps from where she was standing. She thought she might be able

151

to take them without calling attention to herself. But as she moved from the mantelpiece, a dizziness came over her. Her head was full of sounds and lights and then darkness. She was falling.

Someone cried out to her, but it was too late to stop herself.

She struck her head against the corner of something wooden and sharp as she fell.

Theodore gathered her into his arms, a frail, limp bundle of a good deal of fabric and very little flesh. Young Sarah ran ahead of him to turn down the bed, and Sarah went to the medicine chest for salts and Nina's carefully hoarded bottle of laudanum.

Stuart was left alone in the parlor. He picked up the photograph and studied it again. The boys did not look much like brothers. But neither did his mother and aunt look much like sisters. He had heard it said that there were two distinct types of Grimké physiognomy, and he could see that one of the boys resembled Aunt Sai, and the other . . . yes, he was something like Mother.

Which, he wondered unhappily, was Archy, the writer of the letter that had already done so much hurt?

IX

Mrs. Weld's letter was addressed to Archibald and Francis Grimké. Frank must have been in the hall while the mail was being sorted, for there was nothing in their pigeonhole when Archy passed it on his way to the kitchen, but when he came back to the room with a pail of wash water, the letter was open on his desk, and Frank was nowhere to be seen.

Mrs. Weld had taken his letter more kindly than he had expected:

> . . . *your deeply interesting and touching letter. The facts it disclosed were no surprise to me. Indeed, had I not suspected that you might be my nephew I should probably not have addressed you.* . . .

The word "nephew" gave him a queer twinge. He read on quickly, skipping the homiletics and a long account of the exemplary life of Thomas Grimké, who—she said—had been a convert to Abolitionism at the time of his death. (Was Archy supposed to interest himself in the ancient history of all the white Grimkés now?) Then came the questions—most of them about Mauma: in what street she dwelt, whether John was still with her, whether he helped to support her, required support from her, the state of her health, and so on and on.

Do you think Montague knows that you are his half-brothers? —Of course, he will not own it. . . .

He would like to answer that, if nothing else. And perhaps the one about their finances that followed:

Are you able whilst in college to do anything to earn money yourselves?

The last paragraph was an invitation to come to Boston and visit the Welds, in June, when the vacation term began. If he answered the lady at all, he must accept or refuse.

It was not an alluring prospect. And yet, there had been a time when he teetered on the brink of making such a visit uninvited . . . a time—just about two years ago, it was—when he had looked in that direction, desperate for help.

*   *   *

He and Frank were standing in the doorway of the office of the Freedman's Relief Society on the second floor of the building on Tremont Street in Boston. They had been standing there for what seemed a very long time. They had cleared their throats and shuffled their feet, but the lady had taken no notice of them. She was standing at the far end of the room, staring out the window toward the churchyard across the way, where a raw autumn wind was whipping leaves from the vines and splashing them like blood on the gray headstones.

"Beg pardon, ma'am," he said politely.

She turned, and Archy was surprised to see that she was colored. Darker than either he or Frank. But dressed like a white school-marm, with a starched shirtwaist and a tightly belted skirt. She was not old. No more than twenty. Pretty, too, in spite of her put-on severity.

"What may I do for you?" she asked as she crossed to take her place in the high-backed official chair behind the reception desk. "Be seated, if you please."

Archy glanced at Frank as they slid into chairs facing her across the table. Frank was not apt to take kindly to a tone of condescension coming from a female of his own race only a few years older than he. Like as not he'd start sassing her back. Archy spoke quickly to head him off.

"We were to ask for a gentleman," he said. "We have a letter—"

"A white gentleman," Frank said.

Archy dug his elbow into his brother's ribs as he pulled the envelope out of his pocket and read the name on it. "Reverend Josiah Wentworth. Is that right?"

"That's right," said the young lady. "He's in charge of the office here, but he's been called away for a few days. I'm taking his place."

She held out her hand for the letter, and, when Archy had surrendered it, tore it open and began to read.

Archy examined the office, or as much of it as he could see without turning his head, which he felt might be considered unmannerly. The room was large, and the walls were lined, floor to ceiling, with shelves on which were piled books, leaflets, old periodicals, and files of correspondence. In one corner near the windows stood a massive rolltop desk, darkened by time and stained with ink, just the sort of desk at which he could imagine some fire-eating Abolitionist sitting to compose a jeremiad. In the opposite corner stood a large packing box with a sign that requested:

APPAREL FOR NEEDY FREEDMEN
CLEAN AND MENDED GARMENTS ONLY

155

Archy caught Frank's eye and they both grinned, wriggling their shoulders self-consciously in their clean and mended jackets.

"My!" said the young lady without looking up. "You certainly are embarked on a great enterprise, aren't you?"

Archy mumbled an answer and felt himself blush as the young lady ignored it, continuing to read. He lowered his eyes to the neutral territory of the tabletop. Directly in front of him stood two stacks of periodicals he had seen in Mrs. Pillsbury's office back in Charleston: *The American Freedman* and *The Anti-Slavery Standard*. Archy had never looked into a copy of either, but it gave him a comforting sense of continuity to recognize the titles. Any link between the world he had left and the one into which he had been set down so abruptly was something to be grasped and held.

Also on the reception table was a set of small alms boxes, each carefully labeled with the name of a particular school in the South that would be benefited by a coin dropped through the slot. There was no box for the Morris Street School, and the omission disturbed him. He looked to see whether Frank was noticing it too.

"Tell me," said the young lady, putting down the letter. "Are you two the first to be sent north? The first from Charleston?"

"Yes, ma'am," Archy said.

"Well!" She pronounced the monosyllable with a prim emphasis that left her uncommitted either to approval or disapproval of the choice. "Great things must be expected of you."

"Yes, ma'am," Archy said, and started to blush all over again. What was he supposed to say? No? Or nothing?

"It's both an honor and an obligation," the young lady went on, talking down to them as if she were up on a platform or in a pulpit, instead of so close they could reach out and pinch her or pull her hair.

Frank was fidgeting like a fly-bitten horse, and he just might try some such impudent trick, or bust out with some sass that would be just as bad. Then where would they be? Besides, Archy thought with a pang of sympathy, all the young lady was doing was trying to make up for her youth and her lack of authority by imitating the Reverend whose place she was taking.

"Please, ma'am," he interjected. "If you don't mind . . ."

The young lady stopped and sat up even stiffer, waiting for him to go on.

"The thing is—we shouldn't ought to be taking up your time— but Frank, he—" Archy floundered to a stop, pulled the loose ends of his thoughts and needs together, and made another start. "I reckon you read there in the letter, I'm to stay here in Boston with a Mr. Sewell, but Frank, he's to go on to a place called Stoneham."

"Stone-ham." The young lady made it sound like two separate words (which was enough to make a body crack his sides!). "And you want to know how to get there. Is that it?"

It was part of it, and Archy was willing to settle for that much as a start.

"You have to take the train," she said. "The depot is down on Causeway Street. I can make a map to help you find your way."

She had already begun to draw when Frank asked, "Is it far to walk?"

"To Stoneham?" she looked up in surprise. "It must be nearly twenty miles. Why would you . . . Oh!" The young lady caught on, then. "Is it that you don't have the money for a railroad ticket?"

"Yes, ma'am," Archy said. "That's right."

"Tell me: Did you come all the way from Charleston with no money in your pockets?"

"Yes, ma'am," Archy said, and then, lest she start to pity them, he added, "But we didn't want for money. We come on a government ship, all the way to New York City. We took our meals with the soldiers."

Frank forgot his grudge against the young lady in his eagerness to relive the experience. "And in New York City the folks that came down to the ship to meet us, they took us to their house to eat and stay the night, and to a museum where they have wax statues of famous people, done so fine you can't tell them from live."

"Those were the folks that bought us our tickets and put us on the cars for Springfield," Archy explained, "and when we got there—"

"Yesterday that was. And they—"

"No, Frank, it was day before yesterday, because we went to bed after supper that night—remember?—and last night they took us to the play."

"That's right. It was last night we went to see the play. On a stage! It was a wonder to us!"

"You'd never been to a theatre before?" the young lady asked.

"No, ma'am."

"It was by Shakespeare," Archy said. "It was about an old king, and there was a storm in it. A real one, with real rain and thunder and lightning. And this king's voice—that was the wonder!—it was louder than the thunder. It got inside you and shook you till you couldn't help yourself but cry for him."

"I didn't cry for him," Frank said, "except a little at the end when he was ready to die. I didn't like it the way he wanted everybody to bow down and sweet-talk him, no matter how evil-tempered he be to them.

"The one I liked was the little fellow. The one they called the fool. He had more sense than any of the rest of them. And he was brave, too. He told them straight out to their faces whatever was true, even the king."

As Frank went on, his gray eyes began to glow as if they had swamp fire in them, and the skin along his cheekbones flushed. The young lady was looking at him the way Mauma did sometimes, as if she was between wanting to shake him and wanting to put her arms around him and hug him good.

"You came here directly from Springfield?" she asked when he had finally run out of things to tell her about the play.

Archy answered: "Yes, ma'am. Mrs. Church made a lunch for us to carry, and Dr. Church bought us our tickets and wrote down the address here, in case there was no one at the depot to meet us."

The young lady frowned and bit her underlip. "Of course, it's only a matter of a single fare to Stoneham. . . ." she murmured.

"No, ma'am," Archy corrected her quickly. "I got to go too. I got to see Frank settled."

The young lady bit deeper on her lip. "The trouble is, I'm not supposed to disburse funds without an authorization. I was thinking that I might be able to manage one fare out of my own purse, but I'm afraid I haven't enough for two."

"We wouldn't want to use your money," Frank said. "We don't think anything of walking that far."

But the young lady wouldn't hear of such a thing. She went to fussbudgeting around all over the big desk, looking in drawers and under piles of papers, talking all the time about how it was queer that in other cities the Freedman's Society had been notified to expect them, so why not here in Boston, too?

"Of course, Reverend Wentworth may have been expecting you and forgotten to tell me in his haste to get away. But there ought to be some correspondence on file, letters between him and whoever it is you're to stay with in Stoneham."

"Dr. Brown. Dr. James Brown."

"Yes. The name was in the letter, wasn't it? Well now, I wonder if I oughtn't to get off a note to Dr. Brown this very moment. You're quite sure he's expecting you *at this time?*" She turned long enough to get a nod in answer. "But then he might have been called away, too! I wouldn't want you to go all the way out there only to find no one at home."

Behind the young lady's back, Frank was making impatient little signs to indicate that all this was a waste of good daylight. He was in a hurry to be on the way. Archy was too, but he wasn't sure but what the young lady had a point: that it might be better to stay over in Boston till a letter could go to Stoneham and a reply come back. He was about to say so, when the young lady broke off in the middle of a sentence and turned to them.

"Grimké!" she said. "Isn't your name Grimké?"

The boys nodded.

"I don't know why that didn't strike me right off! And you come from Charleston! You must have belonged to someone in the same family! Sarah and Angelina Grimké! They live just outside Boston in a little town called Fairmount. Did you know that?"

Archy said nothing. Frank said nothing. Neither looked at each other or at the young lady.

"The Grimké sisters," she said more slowly, as if she supposed that would make the matter more clear. "The famous Abolitionists."

Archy had found a worn place in the turkey carpet and was counting the threads, warp and woof.

"You don't mean you've never heard of them?"

Archy shook his head.

"I can't believe it!" the young lady said, more to herself than to them. "I suppose they did try to keep the news from the North from spreading among slaves. But you'd think that *after* the War, someone would at least have *mentioned* . . ." She paused to give them a final chance to affirm or deny knowledge. Neither did, and she gave up. "At any rate, I'm certain the sisters would welcome you. They're on the Executive Board of our society, though they haven't been active for several years. I've never met them personally, but I'd be glad to give you an introduction—"

"We got an introduction," Frank snapped irritably. "All the introduction we need. And I mean to go on to Stoneham like it say I'm to do."

The young lady looked as if she was trying to make up her mind whether to take offense or not. Archy held his breath. He knew what made Frank cantankerous, but what if the young lady got cantankerous too? What if she took a mind to tell them to get along and stop bothering her? What would they do for the fare to Stoneham? Or directions? Or supper and a place to spend the night?

"Very well," she said at last, "I'll have to take the responsibility myself."

160

She opened a drawer in the big desk and took out a cashbox, which she opened with a key from another drawer. She counted out an exact amount in bills and silver, made out a voucher, put that in the cashbox, and locked it. All very businesslike and brisk.

"Now, I'll make that map for you," she said. "Here is Boston Common. Here's where you are now, on Tremont Street opposite the Old Burying Ground. Here's Scollay Square down here, and over here is Haymarket. Now: you follow this line of arrows I've drawn, turn left into Causeway Street, and the depot is right here."

She stopped drawing, and surveyed the result.

"It's really a shame to walk through this part of Boston without a guide," she said sadly. "There are so many interesting historical landmarks along your way. I'd offer to go with you and point them out, but I don't feel I ought to leave the office untended."

"No, ma'am, we wouldn't want you to do that," Archy said. "Maybe you could just tell us a few things to look out for."

The young lady was delighted to be asked. "You could begin right across the street. There are quite a few of the Signers buried there, as well as victims of the Boston Massacre. I don't know that the graves are interesting in themselves, but . . ." A glance at Frank seemed to convince her that they were not. "Well, then you could go down Cornhill and see the office where Mr. Garrison used to publish the *Liberator*. It's a little off the route I've marked. You'd have to go this way instead." She drew a curved detour on her map. "Or if you want to go out of your way to the right instead of the left, you could pass by the Old State House. I'll make an X to show you where it is. You'll recognize it when you see it by the weather-vane. It's made in the shape of a grasshopper. And there's a balcony that juts out on this side, where the Declaration of Independence was read to the citizens of Boston.

"And just one short block down the street this way is the site of the Boston Massacre. I'll make a circle for it, because there's a real circle of stones in the pavement."

"What's a massacre?" Frank asked Archy.

"When a lot of people get killed."

"The Boston Massacre was the first battle in the War for Independence," the young lady said, very much the schoolteacher again. "Our citizens were protesting the quartering of British troops in their homes. They were shot down in cold blood, right there in the street. And there was Negro blood along with the white! Some people say that Crispus Attucks was the first to fall!

"If you were only to visit one spot in all Boston, perhaps it ought to be this one: to pay your respects to a hero of your own race."

Archy said they would do that.

The young lady was about to go on and make more suggestions, but he cut her off as tactfully as he could. "We certainly want to thank you for all you've told us and done for us too."

He gave Frank a nudge, and Frank said his thanks.

"Well," said the young lady, reluctantly, "I wish you the very best of luck." And to Archy she added, "I hope after you're settled in Boston, you'll come by sometimes and tell us how you're both getting on."

As the boys emerged from the building, they were assaulted by a bitter wind that cut through their thin clothes. They pulled up their collars, and pulled their hatbrims down, and headed into it. The going was hard.

The sidewalks were narrow and crowded with people, all hurrying in some direction or other, cutting across streets whenever the notion took them, with determined disregard of all other traffic. It was a marvel to Archy that they never collided with one another or any of the wheeled vehicles in the thoroughfares. It was almost as much of a marvel how they found their way through the maze of crooked streets and five- or six-pointed intersections. It was more than he could do, even with a map. Or perhaps the map was making things harder, for the young lady had left out all (to her) irrelevant details.

Before they knew it, the boys were lost.

162

Archy accosted a gentleman and asked directions, but he got an answer so curt as to be incomprehensible. He tried another and got only a grunt. A third gave them directions that were obviously wrong.

"How long you mean to keep it up like this?" Frank asked.

"We got to find the way, don't we?"

"You ain't finding it. 'Please, sar . . . Axin' yo' pardon, cap'n . . . Effen you be so kin', c'nel!'" Frank mocked him with a parody of the sort of talk they had scorned even as children in slavery times.

Archy was annoyed. "You want to give up right now and go on back home?"

"Who said anything 'bout giving up?"

"I'll say this: If you can't make out with the folks up here better than you're doing so far, you ain't going to stay and study to be a doctor. That's certain!"

They walked on, and after a minute or so Archy put his question to a more likely looking informant. This time he was answered. They had gone only a little out of the way. Two turns would bring them back to the route on the young lady's map. Archy thanked the gentleman, and they went on.

"Lookee here, Archy!" Frank stopped and pointed to the pavement at his feet. "Ain't this here the place she was telling us the people got shot? This here circle?"

Sure enough. There it was. And up to their left was the red brick State House with its green grasshopper vane and its square balcony.

"You ever hear tell of this colored man she was talking about?" Frank asked.

"No," Archy said. "But I expect it's true, all the same."

They stood in reverent silence, trying to imagine what it had been like that day when the first patriots fell here, how it came that a black man was among them, what he felt as he faced and defied the white-skinned, red-coated soldiers of the English king.

"Look what ye're doin', damn ye!"

Frank staggered, nearly fell, caught his balance and whirled to face the man who had jostled him. It all happened so quickly that Archy had no time to think and moved in response to a habit ingrained like a reflex. As the old war cry ripped out of Frank's throat and his head dropped, Archy's foot pulled back to aim a kick at the man's groin.

"What's going on?"

The voice of an anonymous pedestrian brought Archy to his senses. He checked himself, yanked Frank back, away from his target, out of the crowd that was already forming around them.

"Jasus! Did ye see that? The yellow-skinned devil! Goin' for me throat, he was!"

The jostler had lost his voice in astonishment at the sudden ferocity of Frank's reaction, but he found it now. It followed them as Archy pulled Frank into the stream of foot traffic flowing down the side street, around the corner and into the first alley. Not till they were safe in a recessed back entryway did Archy stop. Frank was struggling to wrench himself free, and when Archy released his grip he lurched hard against the wall.

"You want to get us arrested?" Archy demanded. "Starting a fight like that right in the street!"

"It was my fault, I guess! He come up from behind and tried to knock me down!"

"He did no such thing. He didn't even know you was there. It's like Mauma used to say: Everybody that don't reach out to take your hand don't mean he's fixin' to slap your jaw."

"I didn't do a—"

"You were haulin' off to butt him. And you would have, if I hadn't got you away. You would have struck the first blow, just like you promised Mauma you—"

"I don't want to hear all the time what Mauma say and what I promised!"

"All right, then," Archy said harshly. "Go on and pick you a fight.

Ever since we got up north you been asking for something. Maybe you just got to have it. Go on back!"

Frank looked at him in amazement that turned slowly into pain. They had quarreled before many times, over big things and small, but never in their lives had Archy threatened to let Frank fight alone, and against a white man too! It was a measure of his desperation.

"Well?" he said after a whole minute had gone by. "What you want to do?"

Frank's eyes dropped and his thin shoulders hunched defensively. "Let's get on to the depot," he said.

The train ride, which Archy had been dreading, turned out fine. It could have been that in the dim light of the car they were taken for white. (That had happened more than once, Archy was sure, since their arrival in New York.) But the pleasures of the trip were not only negative. It was fine to get warm clear through, to rest and look out the windows at a landscape as beautiful as it was varied.

The wind had shifted and was clearing the sky of its clouds. Through the openings, the afternoon sun shone slantwise, making a series of illuminations, like framed engravings, too handsome to be real. Here was a stand of dark, long-needled evergreens around a tiny pond that reflected the sky. Yonder a hillside ablaze with scarlet sumac. Closer to the tracks, a solitary farmhouse at the apex of a long avenue of yellow maples, the house so white you could almost smell the paint, and behind it a great sonorously red barn. In the distance there, a village: a cluster of houses set around a square of green common, the church steeple rising like a benign ghost out of the haze of shadow and interlaced branches.

It was all so different from the South. No scars of war, no slatternly debris of poverty and servitude. And no great contrast between rich and poor. Large and small alike, the houses were better kept than any but the finest mansions at home. Wealth—

even a modest degree of it—had always been associated in Archy's mind with slaveholding, and since no one up here held slaves even before the War, he had imagined most folks as living like the slaveless Charleston poor whites, or back-country rednecks. But it was not so. Not so at all.

It set him thinking about other differences he had noticed since they landed. One of them—one he felt most persistently—had to do with the way people treated one another in crowds, like in the theatre in Springfield, or the wax museum in New York. Perhaps because it was on his mind, it presented itself now in a small but significant incident.

They had changed from the train to a horse-drawn car, that ran uphill and down dale on tracks laid out in a stern, unswerving line. Near the top of a particularly steep grade the horse grew balky, and the driver reined him to a halt.

"Everybody that can walk better get down and do so," he called in a loud voice.

It was a tone that would have been considered impudent in Carolina, coming from one of the laboring class and addressed to those who were his betters. The man did not ask their cooperation or their pardon, did not explain his difficulty or apologize for it. He simply drew the general attention to a fact.

Archy watched to see which of the ladies and gentlemen passengers would comply and which would make a fuss. To his amazement, everyone—except two elderly ladies—obeyed. Without umbrage or condescension or apparent loss of face! Yet—and this was the most puzzling thing!—there was no lessening of the distance between driver and passengers, or between any of the latter who were not already acquainted. None of the breaking down of barriers under a common inconvenience, the pleasantries or grumblings that would have resulted at home. It was as if all these folks wore invisible glass cloaks to protect them from unwanted contact with their kind.

As the boys stepped down from the car in Stoneham, the sun was sinking into banked horizon clouds. The flames of maple and sumac were snuffed, and the cold wind resumed its assault on their inadequate clothing.

They had no idea which way to start walking, but another passenger had got off the car just ahead of them, and they hurried after him to ask directions to Dr. Brown's.

"Walk up this street to the church square. He lives just a few doors off it on Tidd. Ask anyone around there which house is his."

It was the same tone the driver had used. No questions about what they wanted with the doctor, no offer to walk along with them (though the man was heading in that direction himself). He showed neither hostility nor warmth, merely gave them the facts they asked for and set off at a pace that soon left them behind.

Archy and Frank walked in silence.

Most of the trees along this street were elms that had already been stripped of their leaves. There were a few oaks that still held their foliage, great tufts of it, the color of dried blood. But the strongest impression was that of bareness, as if the whole place were a front parlor swept and dusted for a funeral. The houses were sharp-cornered, rectangular boxes, each set in an emptiness of lawn. There were no hedges or walls. Picket or post-and-rail fences marked an occasional property line, but offered no shield of privacy.

"We haven't seen another colored the whole day," Frank observed.

"What about the young lady in the office?"

"I mean on the streets."

It was true, and it made one feel set apart, stared at, like one of the wax figures in the museum, made one feel there were eyes behind all the windows. Archy had to push against a surge of panic that made him want to break into a run.

"This is the church square," he said aloud. "Which you reckon is Tidd Street?"

There was no one in sight of whom to ask.

"I expect we got to knock at one of the houses," Frank said.

Archy looked from one to the other, the knowledge gathering like a cramp in his belly that in one of these tomorrow he would have to leave Frank to dwell among strangers—tomorrow!—and go to dwell among other strangers himself! . . . They had been so close as children that people made jokes about it: *Like them freak calves you hear 'bout sometimes, born yoked.* Although Archy always reminded the joker that he was older by a whole year, and bigger than Frank, too, the truth was that one of his earliest memories was of himself and Frank yoked: coming back from the pump with water for Mauma's wash kettle, each of them carrying a small bucket in his outside hand, the big one swung between them, so they had to be careful to keep in step or they'd slosh.

They slept together, played together, fought together in self-defense against the white bullies that used to lie in wait for them on Calhoun Street, hoping to beat them into giving up the money they were carrying home. They ate together out of the same dish, dividing the hoppin'-john Mauma spooned into it, not always amicably, but resigned to the fact that they must come to agreement in the end. Their brother John figured in Archy's memories of those days, but as a separate being, like Mauma. All four were close, but only Archy and Frank were yoked. . . .

"You studyin' 'bout something, Archy?"

Frank's voice had gone high like a small boy's. Looking at him, Archy saw he was afraid. Nothing could have cured his own cowardice so quickly as this proof that it was communicable. He smiled and shook his head and started up the nearest walk.

"What is it you want?"

The voice that answered his knock was sharply suspicious, and the door did not open. Archy could see the shape of a woman silhouetted on the frosted glass of the door pane. She was only a few feet away, but he felt he was hallooing across a vast distance as he explained his need.

"Doc Brown? Why, he's right around the corner there on Tidd."

"Yes, ma'am, but we don't know which is Tidd Street."

The door opened a crack, and light fell in a beam that caught Archy in the eyes, blinding him.

"The first one you come to. All you have to do is turn. It's three houses down, and yellow. You can't miss it. The only one in the whole row that isn't white."

"Thank you, ma'am. I'm much obliged."

As he started back down the walk, the words caught at him: *Yellow . . . the only one that isn't white. . . .*

He whirled round to see if the woman was making game of him, but she was gone. The door was closed. The pane was dark again.

They were admitted to the yellow house by a white servant girl (the first they had ever seen), who showed them into a parlor where three patients were waiting on stiff chairs. Dr. Brown was in his consulting room, she said, and would see them in their turn.

They could hear his voice behind the thin door. A heavy voice, dry and warm, at once mocking and reassuring. Archy liked the man it implied, and looked to see if Frank did. But Frank's face was locked up tight, giving out no secrets.

"All right, then," the voice drawled humorously. "We'll give him a tonic."

The patient said something that did not penetrate the door.

"No, not sulphur and molasses," the doctor said. "Only give that in the spring. Price of sulphur gets too low this time of year. Folks don't feel it does them the same good." He chuckled audibly at his own joke.

A few minutes later the door opened and a fat, motherly-looking lady came out and beckoned to her fat son, the occupant of one of the stiff chairs. As they left, the doctor appeared, and nodded to the pair who were waiting. Just before he closed the door again, he looked back at Archy and Frank.

"Don't believe I know you boys, do I? You waiting to be seen?"

169

Archy stood up, crushing his hat with fingers that were damp and shaky. "Yes, sir," he said. "We're the ones Mrs. Pillsbury wrote you about. That is, *he* is. He's Frank. I'm Archy. Frank's the one is to stay with you."

The doctor looked like a man who had just received news of a long-dreaded catastrophe. He groped for a chair, muttering to himself, "I don't know what to say. I declare I don't!" He motioned the boys to take chairs, got up from his own to close the door to the consulting room, and came back.

Archy handed him the envelope with Mrs. Pillsbury's letter. The doctor took it, slipped it into his pocket, got out his spectacles and polished them absentmindedly, and at last with a deep sigh, leaned forward and spoke.

"There's been a misunderstanding."

The suspense snapped, and Archy heard the crash of the whole complex and delicate structure of their hopes.

"I'm partly to blame," the doctor said earnestly. "I'll own it. But the way the thing was put to me was: Could we give a place to a young freedman. That was the word—*place!* Nothing said about schooling, least of all in medicine!

"Well now, my wife and I talked it over and concluded we could find work enough to keep a pair of extra hands busy. We had a spare room in the ell at the time. I've always been kindly disposed toward colored people. Matter of fact I was surgeon to a colored regiment in the War. The 55th Massachusetts."

Archy quit listening. He felt the slight separate sting of each word, rattling on the surface of his consciousness, but that was all.

". . . my wife came down sick and we had to hire a girl . . . ought to have notified whoever it was . . . slipped my mind . . . letter from this Pillsbury woman . . . boy to study medicine."

The doctor interrupted himself to look Frank over more carefully.

"It's you want to be a doctor?"

"Yes, sir."

"Well, I wish you luck, but I'll tell you the truth: it's a long haul for one who starts where you do."

"I don't mind working," Frank said.

"I should hope not," said the doctor with a trace of irritation. "But the point is, you don't teach medicine by apprenticeship like blacksmithing or carpentry. Any sensible woman ought to know as much. But then no sensible woman would send a boy a thousand miles without so much as an exchange of letters! I wrote her the very day I heard from her, told her how things here had changed, told her she was going about it wrong in any case if what she was looking to do was to make a doctor out of an ex-slave boy. But she didn't wait to hear! And never bothered to answer me! Not to this day!"

He had run out of words and remorse. The silence had the quality of a verdict from which no appeal could be taken. Frank got to his feet.

"We might as well be getting along," he said.

"Wait now," said the doctor defensively. "I didn't mean you to think I was turning you away. You can stay the night. Sleep in the hayloft. It's not too cold for that yet. We'll talk this thing over and . . ." He paused, pulled the envelope from his pocket, and frowned at it, still without opening it. "Tell you what. You hungry?"

Archy said Yes. Frank shook his head.

"Well, you go out to the kitchen and tell the girl to give you a good hot supper. Take your time. Rest up. I'll be out there to talk to you when I've seen those two patients and had a word with Mrs. Brown."

As soon as the consulting room door had closed, Frank spoke in a grating whisper. "Let's go out the way we come."

"We're not going out," Archy whispered back. "We're going to do like he said. Eat supper and—"

"Not me!"

"Yes, you!" He wanted to take and shake Frank, or slap him across the jaw the way he had seen Mauma do to a woman who was going into a fit. But Frank was too near Archy's size now to be managed by violence. "You can't walk back to Boston tonight," he said, "any more than I can. You can't sleep out or go up to just any old door and beg supper. You seen how it is here. Folks don't even open up to tell you to get on along. You may as well make up your mind—"

"You may as well make up yours that I ain't going to eat dirt! You can if you want! But I didn't come all this far to be a house nigger and wear brass buttons!"

Archy clenched his fists till the nails bent, but he kept his temper and outstared Frank.

"We're going to listen to what this here doctor has to say after he's talked to his wife," Archy said when he knew he had won.

He led the way toward the kitchen, and Frank followed.

They sat through the meal without speaking. The servant girl poked plates at them as if through bars, withdrawing her hand quickly lest they snap. Hungry as he was, Archy couldn't make his jaws and throat work together. His mouth had gone dry. No matter how long he chewed it, he couldn't get his food wet enough to swallow. His plate was still almost full when Dr. Brown came into the kitchen.

He seemed much more cheerful. In the first place, he had to apologize to Mrs. Pillsbury, whose letter he had finally got round to reading. His letter to her must have gone astray, for she had waited quite a reasonable time before sending the boys on. Secondly, Mrs. Brown felt as bad as he did about how all this had worked out, and she had made a very practical suggestion.

"There's plenty of yard work to be done before winter. If you want to stay on, we could fix up some sort of place for you in the loft, or if it gets too cold, in one of the sheds. It wouldn't be permanent, you understand. Wouldn't work out at all when the real cold sets in. But by then you should have found something else. Matter of fact, there's one possibility come up already."

Frank looked up from his plate.

"There's a patient of mine staying here in the house, name of Harrower. Comes up from Peacedale, Rhode Island, where the woolen mills are. Her husband is superintendent, and they have a big place. She was saying she could maybe use a hand."

Frank's eyes went back to his plate, but the doctor did not notice.

"Mrs. Harrower doesn't feel up to talking to you this evening," he went on, "but some time tomorrow she will. You see what she has in mind and tell her what you do. See if you can work something out."

"That'll be fine," said Archy. "We'll do that."

Dr. Brown looked from Frank to Archy and back at Frank. "I'll show you the way to the barn," he said quietly. "I expect you want to have some talk before you turn in."

He got a lantern and led the way through a series of storage rooms and sheds, each colder than the one before, all contained under the single roof of the ell. At the end, set at right angles to it was the barn, large and well kept. There was only one stall, its occupant a fine gelding.

"By the bye," said the doctor, "Mrs. Harrower was asking me just now if you know anything about horses."

Again the remark was addressed to Frank, but it was Archy who answered. "Yes, sir. We took service with some cavalry officers at the end of the War, and looked after their horses for them."

"Union officers or Confederates?"

"Union."

Archy saw that Frank was itching to say he had also served a Confederate, and a good deal longer, too! But he couldn't bring himself to address the white man directly, even to antagonize him.

"You'll sleep warm in the hay," Dr. Brown said. "Many's the time I did it at your age. But there are blankets in the crib here, if you want them."

He showed them where to hang the lantern, told them to let it burn itself out, and said a brusque good night.

"These blankets been used on the horse," Frank said in loud disgust. "They stink, and we'll stink if we lie under them."

"We don't need blankets. Not if we dig in."

They climbed the ladder to the loft and dug a tunnel into the cold, dusty, prickly hay, folded their jackets for pillows, and settled down back-to-back for warmth.

"It puts me in mind of how we used to sleep," Archy said softly, "you and me at the foot of the bed and John up with Mauma."

He felt Frank stiffen, and knew it was to resist tears. His own throat closed and his eyes began to smart, as the wave of homesickness rolled out of his brother's heart and across his own. They were still as close as ever, held together like burrs in anger and sorrow as well as in love.

Not long after that, Frank was asleep. Archy knew by the little running movements and whimpering sounds he made in the first stages of dream. (*Sign 'e dreamin' some mischief,* Mauma used to say.) It meant that the battle over what to do would have to be postponed till morning, but maybe that was just as well. Frank might wake in a better mood. . . .

Archy was waked by a strange voice.

It took a long time to penetrate the double wall of sleep and hay, and even longer for him to recognize it as that of Dr. Brown.

"Hey, up there! Can't you come down and give me a hand with the harnessing? I'm late on my rounds."

Archy reached over to wake Frank and could not find him. He flailed about in the hay for a minute, but there was another summons from below. Brushing the dust from his hair and clothes, he scrambled down the ladder and did as he was asked. When the doctor's gig rolled out the barn door, he climbed back to the loft, bringing a pitchfork to prod till he found in which corner of the hay Frank was pretending to sleep.

But Frank was not anywhere.

It was possible that he had waked early and slipped out to have a look around the town, that he would turn up when he got hungry. Archy tried to suspend anxiety as well as resentment, to go about his business, eat his breakfast under the goggle-eyed stare of the servant girl, perform the simple chores that were asked of him. But the certainty was growing in him all the while that Frank had run off.

It would be just like him. Never thinking about anyone but himself. The moment Frank saw the yoke descending, he dodged out from under, never mind who else might get caught. Archy was pinned down so he couldn't move. Couldn't go to his own place at the Sewells'. Couldn't go anywhere or plan anything till Frank came back.

"If he comes back . . ."

The "if" chilled his indignation before it had time to grow hot, and set him imagining all the direful accidents that might intervene between "if" and "when." For this was not like running off in Charleston, where every house and yard and alley was as familiar as one's mother's face; where half the inhabitants might be born enemies, but where the other half were, by the same logic, blood brothers. Here Frank could be crushed underfoot and brushed out of the way like an insect, without anyone's intending him harm. Anyone but Frank would have understood that, or been intimidated without understanding. But Frank was both ignorant and brave.

There was nothing to do but wait. No telling how long.

When Dr. Brown came back from his rounds, Archy met him at the barn door and told him what had happened. He asked permission to stay on in the loft and work for his board at the yard chores that had been offered Frank. Dr. Brown nodded and made no comment, except to say that since Mrs. Harrower expected to meet Frank today, Archy had better have a talk with her.

Archy had many talks with Mrs. Harrower in the days that followed. The weather had turned warm, and he spent the mornings raking fallen leaves into piles to be burned, or up onto the flower beds that bordered the house. Mrs. Harrower brought a chair out and sat near him for an hour or so most mornings, chatting away as if they were old acquaintances, while she took the sun.

She was an easy person to get on with, cheerful and friendly, so taken up with her own concerns—health and family obligations for the most part—that she had no energy left with which to be inquisitive. She assumed Archy's interest in everything she said, and gave no evidence of interest in him except as a token auditor, a human presence that gave her the right to speak her thoughts aloud.

Archy was glad to fill even so small a need. It was an antidote to his daily breakfast with the hired girl. To have Mrs. Harrower seek him out, move her chair to follow him when his work took him out of range, gave him back his identity. Also, since her monologue demanded no response from him, he was free to pursue his own thoughts, freer in some way he did not understand than when he was really alone.

One morning near the end of the first week, Mrs. Harrower came out to the barn, which Archy had been asked to sweep.

"Well!" she said. "I don't think I want to sit in all that dust. But if you'll set my chair in the door here, I'll finish this length of tatting before it's time for my treatment."

Archy got the chair and settled her in it, and let her ramble on as usual, while his mind nibbled around the edges of his most urgent problem: What was happening to his place at the Sewells'? Had they written Mrs. Pillsbury to say he had not arrived? Would she send another boy to take advantage of the opportunity? How much of an opportunity was it? Was it what he was promised: a place to live and schooling to prepare him for college? Or when he got there —if he ever did—would he encounter the same disappointment Frank had had here?

Behind a barrel in a dark corner, he saw a new-laid hen's egg, picked it up, and tapped it against his front teeth.

"What in the world are you doing?" Mrs. Harrower asked. "Fixing to eat that egg raw?"

"No, ma'am," Archy said. "That's the way to tell how strong the shell is. That's how I used to tell if I wanted to match my hen's egg against somebody else's. You only get to tap once, you see; then you say if you're willing to venture, and which way."

Mrs. Harrower was so interested that Archy had to explain all about egg-popping, the sport that had been his and his friends' substitute for cockfighting and that measured the difference between the adult world and theirs. Instead of angry rooster against angry rooster, it was egg against egg. The one that cracked first was forfeit. There were many gambits, the commonest being point versus point.

"The point is the strongest place," he told Mrs. Harrower, "And the butt next strongest, and the side's the weakest. My old hen laid eggs that would crack others side to point!" And he told her about the time he had made himself sick eating all the eggs he had won that way.

Mrs. Harrower declared she had never heard anything so funny in all her born days. (Archy had an uncomfortable feeling that she laughed because she had no way of knowing what would make a boy eat too many eggs: because he knew that in another month— or two or six—there would come a time when he hungered hopelessly for a single one.)

"You know, I've been thinking," she said, when she had stopped, "why don't you come on back to Peacedale with me? I'll see you have all the eggs you want."

"Thank you kindly, but I have a place promised me in Boston." And then, as a tactful reminder of her original offer, he added, "Besides, Frank can't stay on here after the weather turns."

"It's nice the way you look out for your brother," she said. "But he may not come back at all, you know, and you have yourself to think about." She went on to list inducements: a room of his own, right in the main house; all the warm clothes he would need for a

Rhode Island winter; and the run of her husband's library. "Mr. Harrower is a great one for reading. At least he was when he had the time. I don't know how many books he's got on the shelves! You're welcome to read all you care to, so long as you're careful not to do them hurt."

Archy was growing uneasy, seeing no way to refuse without giving offense, when the hired girl came out to call Mrs. Harrower in for her treatment.

"You think it over," Mrs. Harrower said as she gathered up her paraphernalia and started toward the house. "A bird in the hand is worth two in the bush, as they say."

It was another week before Frank came back.

Archy came out to the hayloft one night and found him waiting there. No explanations, no excuses! But there! Alive and unharmed!

Relief flooded through Archy so suddenly that it threatened to tear him from his moorings, set him laughing or crying or talking foolishly, losing him his precarious authority just when he needed to exert it. He groped for the spar of his anger and clung to it in silence, planning what he would say when it was safe for him to speak.

First he would tell Frank about the letter to Mrs. Pillsbury, already composed and copied out, a good letter that told just what had happened, and asked her please to find Frank another place, one with schooling. Next, calmly and logically, he would lay out the choices available to Frank while he waited for Mrs. Pillsbury's answer: to go to Peacedale with Mrs. Harrower (if she could be persuaded to take Frank instead of Archy); or to go back to Boston and consult with the Reverend Wentworth (who must surely have come back to the Freedom Office by now); or to go to the Misses Grimké. None of these alternatives was going to please Frank much, but it was only for a few weeks, and he would just have to . . .

"I found me a place." Frank cut Archy's rehearsal short. "I'm working in a shoe factory."

"I didn't know there was any sort of factory hereabouts."

"It's nothing much of a factory," Frank admitted. "There's this man on the road to Wakefield has his barn fitted out for making shoes in the winter when he can't work his farm. Man name of Dykes."

"How come he to take you on? You don't know nothing 'bout shoemaking."

Frank laughed. There was something queer in the sound of it, something limp and played out, as if a spring had gone slack somewhere inside him.

"Do you get wages?" Archy asked.

"Not yet. I get my board and room, that's all. But next month I'm to get wages. That is, if we stay on."

"Why wouldn't we stay on?"

Frank looked directly at Archy for the first time. "We ought to go on back home," he said, "before the cold weather sets in and we can't walk it. Otherwise we got to wait till next spring."

"I don't know why you talking 'bout 'we,' " Archy said coldly. "I'm not studying 'bout going back. You better write ahead, if you are, and make sure you got a job waiting for you. Lieutenant Miller mighta found somebody else by now to look after his horse."

Frank looked mad enough to fight, but anger seemed to tighten the spring that had gone slack. "Listen here," he said. "I been all over; I talked to all sorts of folks. Over in Woburn there's a colored man was even born up here. And he says the same."

"The same as what?"

"As everybody! Everybody but you! There ain't no schools take colored up here! None at all!"

Archy was shaken. "If that was so, why would Mrs. Pillsbury send us?"

Frank shrugged. "How do I know? Maybe she thought things would have changed by now."

"What about Mr. Sewell? He ought to know what there is here, and he wrote and said he'd see to it I got schooling. I saw the letter myself."

"Go on and see Mr. Sewell if you want," Frank said. "But I got something to tell you 'bout him. He's friends with Miss Sarah and Miss Angelina."

"What if he is? I'm in no more of a hurry than you are to ask favors of them, but that don't mean they're the same as Miss Eliza or Montague."

Frank laughed his new unhappy laugh again. "Guess who's living in their house now! Miss Angelina's and Miss Sarah's house. Old Miss Eliza herself!"

This time Archy was staggered.

"Isn't that something?" Frank went on. "You remember how she used to carry on 'bout them being Sabbath-breakers and all sorts of other things? 'Bout how she prayed for God to punish them so's He could change their wicked hearts? Well, I guess He must have did, or else changed Miss Eliza's. For she's come up to stay with them."

"For good?"

"Don't ask me. If you go to stay with Mr. Sewell, you can ask Miss Eliza. You're bound to meet up with her sooner or later."

Then Archy was not going to Mr. Sewell's! He had not come north to entangle himself with Eliza Grimké or anyone connected with her. But he was not going back home. "I got to write Mrs. Pillsbury 'bout *both* of us," he said slowly, thinking it out. "And while we're waiting to hear, you can stay on with your shoemaking, and I'll go with Mrs. Harrower. Give Mrs. Pillsbury time to find us both other places."

Frank had very little confidence in Mrs. Pillsbury, but he had no objection to Archy's writing her. "She might could send us the fare home, seeing it was her got us up here."

Archy was willing to let it go at that. "The thing is, we mustn't get lost from each other again. Peacedale's a whole day's journey from here. We can write back and forth, but we got to make some sort of plan, in case something goes wrong."

They sat up most of the night refining and elaborating the plan. They were to write to each other every seven or eight days. If either failed to get a letter at the expected time, he was to write and say so. The first letter might go astray, but unless something was really wrong, the second would not. If there was no response to it—if sixteen days had gone by without word—both were to head for an agreed-upon rendezvous. The first to arrive was to wait for the other a minimum of a week.

"But it's got to be some place we *can* wait," Archy said.

"How 'bout the office in Boston?"

"I reckon that's all right. And I'll tell Mrs. Pillsbury to write us in care of the Reverend."

The more elaborate the arrangement became, the less assurance it gave. When Archy bade Frank goodbye in the morning, he had a premonition that they were parting forever.

In one sense, it proved true.

*　　*　　*

Archy was writing out his Greek lesson when Frank came back to the room.

"You didn't tell me you been to see Dr. Randall 'bout changing our name," he said indignantly. "You had no business to go 'thout me."

"I didn't go to do it," Archy apologized. "It just happened. And anyway all I did was ask him if we could, if we had a mind to."

"Dr. Randall stopped me just now and wanted to know if we decided what we want to be called. I didn't know what to say to him!"

There was a pause.

Frank expected him to go on, to explain, to say what he had decided and for what reason. But Archy had decided nothing, could explain nothing. . . . Neither could he bear the silence.

"How you like Miss Angelina asking us to Boston?" he said, pointing to the open letter.

"I told you not to answer her back," Frank said.

"You don't want to go?"

"I don't care. It was you didn't want to when we were right there."

"It was not. It was you. You said Miss Eliza was living with them."

"That was at the beginning, when we were out in Stoneham. But later on, when you came back from Mrs. Harrower's, and we were in Boston—don't you remember? Reverend Wentworth wanted to take us out to see Miss Sarah and Miss Angelina, and he said Miss Eliza was gone back to Charleston, so there was no reason we couldn't have gone, except you were so dead set against it."

"If you'd wanted to go, you could have," Archy said irritably. "I wasn't stopping you."

It was degenerating into a pointless squabble. Neither had any heart for it. But it was better than silence and the admission that communication was no longer possible.

Suddenly Frank spoke in a quite different tone. "You mad at me 'bout something, Archy?" he asked.

"You know I ain't."

Archy wasn't mad at anybody anymore. He had lost the power to feel anything—except despair. Lost the power to explain himself to himself. He felt like a driverless wagon, rolling slowly down a long hill.

X

The house looked dark and quiet, as if it were un-
inhabited, as Theodore turned up the path from the street. He
opened the front door and stood listening. There was no sound from
anywhere but the kitchen. The voices there were Stuart's and young
Sarah's, and they seemed muted, as if they were speaking in the
shadow of illness . . . or of death.

The anxiety that had been growing like a weed in him all
week bloomed into terror.

He walked quickly to the door of his and Angelina's chamber.
No light showed under it. His hand touched the knob, but he was
afraid to look in, afraid to call, lest there be no answer.

Forcing himself to act with a reasonableness he did not feel, he
went back to the vestibule, hung up his greatcoat, pulled off his
boots, and then walked to the kitchen and opened the door.

The room was warm and bright and smelled deliciously of something spicy—beans baking in molasses, or Indian pudding—a scene that was in such reassuring contrast to what he had imagined that Theodore felt himself mocked. Both Sarahs were seated at the round table, on either side of Stuart, who had his books and papers spread out as if he had been trying to work. But he was at the moment engaged in an earnest debate with his sister. Theodore caught the name of Mrs. Hamilton, the mother of Sarah's fiancé, before the girl broke off to come and greet him with a kiss.

"Father! How I wish you'd been with me today," she said. "I went into Boston to see William's mother, and you won't believe the stupid, cruel things she said! You would have answered her properly. I didn't think of half what I should have said till I was nearly home."

"Sarah's not being entirely fair," Stuart dissented. "The point Mrs. Hamilton was trying to make—Sarah told her about the two young men in Pennsylvania—was that it would be kinder to them to claim no relationship because—"

"That's what she said," his sister broke in, "but that's not what she meant at all. Father, let me tell you exactly how the conversation went."

"I want to hear first how your mother is," Theodore interrupted her gently. "I've been very anxious."

Sarah's report was not all bad.

"Nina's still supposed to lie quiet and not use her eyes," she said. "But the swelling has gone down, where the blow was on her head. The doctor has been by twice, and he's to come again Monday. She's been very patient about following his orders, but—"

"But you know what she's talking about doing?" young Sarah burst out. "Going to Charleston! As soon as she can be up!"

Theodore looked to her aunt for confirmation of this.

Old Sarah nodded gloomily. "She's taken a notion that she must talk to . . ." She hesitated. ". . . to the mother of the boys."

"But she can't undertake such a trip as that in midwinter! Didn't the doctor tell her so?"

184

"Yes, he did. But when Nina has her mind set on the path of duty . . ." Sarah sighed. "I haven't seen her like this for years."

"Is she sleeping now?" Theodore asked.

"I don't believe she really sleeps at all. But she asked to be quiet till suppertime. She's coming to the table."

It was best to wait, to collect his thoughts and calm the turbulence in his heart, before he talked to Nina. Best to recall once more the promises they made each other and how they had been kept, to be sure in his own mind that he had the right to oppose her decision . . . as well as whether there was any use in doing so.

"Aunt Sai needs a good talking to, just as much as Mother does," Stuart said as Theodore pulled a chair up to the table. "She's been threatening to go back to teaching, so she can earn extra money."

"Not real teaching in school," his aunt explained. "I've only been thinking I might find a few pupils who could come here to the house. I'm alone a good deal during the week. And I should like to have a few pennies to put toward Nina's trip, if she makes it. Or to send to the boys."

"It's their mother that needs it," young Sarah said. "It seems to me if we send money to anyone, it ought to go to her."

Stuart shook his head. "There's no point in going to college at all, if you haven't got the books you need. Archibald's letter said they hadn't enough to buy books."

"One could buy a good many with what it would cost to go and come from Charleston," said Theodore softly.

Young Sarah frowned. "Do you know, this is the first time in my whole life I ever heard us fret about money!"

"What we fret about is that we have spent our inheritance on others, so that we find ourselves with nothing—or almost nothing—to meet such a claim as this!"

"I understand, Aunt Sai," the girl answered, "But it still sounds strange. I always thought you felt—and Father, you too!—that there was something disgraceful about having money."

Theodore drew her down to his knee, rumpling her hair with a loving hand. "It's true. I've gone all my life on the assumption that it's a sin to be heaping up riches. It's a poor time to discover I've been wrong, isn't it?"

"You're not serious, are you?" Stuart's tone implied that he considered this also a poor time for persiflage.

Theodore felt a stab of irritation and quick remorse for it, a combination of feelings his son stirred in him far too frequently of late. Until Stuart's decision to resist the draft, Theodore had believed he was molding the boy's character, as well as his mind, in the image of human perfection that was his goal as a teacher. His disillusion was the more bitter because he could not accept Stuart's objections as anything but cowardice, dressed in the fig leaf of pacifism.

"Do you really wish you had worked for money instead of what you believe in?"

"No, Stuart, I don't suppose I do. I wouldn't choose a different life work—or works, for I have been a jack of more than one trade, as you know. And yet I was not joking just now. I often wonder if it was not a wrong I did all of you, a luxury I bought at your expense."

"Amen," said Sarah.

"Amen to what?" Theodore turned toward her, smiling. "That it was a luxury? Or that it was bought at your expense?"

"To both. You know how I complained of the disorder you left to be picked up by me or by Nina, the rush and confusion of your goings and comings—"

"But I reformed, did I not? I took your censure to heart and mended my ways."

"As well as you were able, I expect," Sarah conceded affectionately. "In any case, I agree that there is no greater privilege than to wear one's self out in the service of the Lord. It doesn't matter in the end whether it be in the arena or behind the scenes—picking up the gage of battle or the soiled shirts and socks of the soldiers."

"Now I'm sure you're both teasing," said young Sarah. "Aunt Sai may believe that *they also serve who only stand and wait,* but she certainly isn't content to spend her light doing the laundry."

"Or making supper," said Theodore. "But the beans smell wonderful. Shall I take them out of the oven for you?"

"No. They must have at least another three-quarters of an hour." Old Sarah got to her feet. "Let us see what else there is to be done. The milk is poured and the table is laid. Sarah, you may fill a bowl of stewed apples from the crock in the pantry. I'll slice the bread."

"Is there any possibility that these—that Archibald and Francis are not what they claim to be?" Stuart asked.

Both Sarahs stopped in their tracks and looked at him in astonishment.

"I think not, Stuart," said his aunt.

"But you're not sure?"

"Not absolutely sure."

"Do you mean to try to find out about them from anyone? Someone back in Charleston, for instance?"

"My dearest boy," Sarah rebuked him mildly, "to question their truthfulness would be to add insult to the terrible injury already done them."

"I don't mean to question their truthfulness, exactly. But mightn't their mother . . ."

"You sound just like Mrs. Hamilton!" young Sarah broke in indignantly. "That was one of her notions! She says slave women sometimes pretended to be misused by their masters, when it wasn't so at all."

"Well, it's possible," Stuart insisted. "And you must admit it's odd no one told us about them. Archibald's letter said Mrs. Pillsbury was the one who helped them. She and her husband are old friends of yours, aren't they, Father?"

"It is Parker Pillsbury—Gilbert's brother—who is my friend," Theodore said. He too had wondered at the apparent bypassing of him and the sisters, but what concerned him at this moment was Stuart's raising the question in the way he did. Was he, who had affected to despise public opinion, feeling its horns at last? "Perhaps the Pillsburys kept silent out of friendship for us," he suggested to Stuart. "To spare us the disgrace."

"But how is it disgraceful?" Stuart asked. "Not to *us*, certainly."

"Father's being ironic," said young Sarah loyally. "He knows that as well as you."

But Theodore did not.

He felt disgraced. The effect of the letter had been overlaid by his anxiety for Angelina. But that was in abeyance now, and in probing for his son's weakness he had laid bare his own.

Stuart and young Sarah went back to the argument Theodore had interrupted by his arrival. Every word they said increased his discomfiture. The girl was dissecting the pious hypocrisies of her mother-in-law-to-be. Many of the things the lady had said to Sarah, and more that Sarah suspected her of feeling but lacking the courage to say, were not unlike his own secret thoughts.

". . . what she really means! What she said was that we ought to keep it quiet because it sullies the honor of the anti-slavery cause!"

"I didn't know Mrs. Hamilton was an adherent of the cause," said old Sarah dryly.

"She's not! And William will see right through all this!"

Theodore had never felt that he had much in common with Mrs. Hamilton, but was she not in this instance at least partly in the right? Were there not two sides to the question? Reasons against, as well as reasons for, making public the relationship between these boys and two women whose name was associated with the Abolitionist movement in its most glorious apostolic days? For there was still work for the old Abolitionists. Theodore had already been asked to speak out against corruptions and compromises that threatened the fruits of victory. Angelina and Sarah had begun to use their pens to protest small betrayals that might well be tokens of greater ones to come. How could they presume to teach others their duty under such a cloud as this?

And yet—as Stuart said—the disgrace was not to them, as radicals and reformers. They had not failed in their practice, nor were their preachments proved false. . . .

Then what was really at the bottom of the reluctance Theodore felt? Was he no better than any Massachusetts Brahmin who felt himself polluted by contact with one of the Untouchables?

He was sure he was not guilty of that.

Theodore had been raised by a mother whose conscience was so tender on the point of prejudice that he was militant against it by the time he went to school. When the lone colored boy in his class was treated with rudeness by the teacher and with cruelty by the other children, Theodore moved to sit next to Jerry, and befriended the black boy so openly and so consistently that soon it was he who became the target.

"Theodore Weld is a nigger lover," was chanted at his heels for days. When the text was amended to "Theodore Weld is a nigger," he did not remember that it had disturbed him in the least.

In adult life when he had to find living quarters in a strange city, he made it a point to seek out the home of a Negro family that would take him as a lodger or even as a boarder at their table. Sometimes the company was congenial; sometimes not. Sometimes his room was warm and clean and comfortable; sometimes it was none of these things. But he persisted in the practice till he married and had a home of his own. He still felt himself linked in something close to kinship with friends he had made in this way. To be linked still more closely would not have shamed him, if it had not been that the link, in this case, was shameful in itself.

The relationship that had produced the boys was vile: That was what stuck in his throat and would not swallow down. To acknowledge their existence and the truth of their story was to acknowledge unspeakable vileness in the bosom of his own family. For the pitch that defiled Angelina's brother defiled her and, through her, him. . . .

" 'Let the innocent armor themselves in their innocence'!"

Theodore was brought back to the present by his daughter's voice. "I remember your saying that once, Father, about something that happened when you were at the seminary, and I think it fits this case just as well. The two boys must feel that way, or they would never have answered the letter Mother wrote. Don't you think?"

"I'm not sure what I think," Theodore answered candidly. "My head is in a tangle I shall never straighten out sitting here. Is there time for me to walk before supper?"

Sarah said he could be gone for fifteen or twenty minutes. He slipped on his overshoes, but left his coat open so the cold air could hit him full on the chest. Where the front path reached the street, he paused, choosing between the down- and the up-hill stretch. In his young days he would have started down, taken the long slope at full speed, jumped the ice-covered stream at the foot, run along the far bank to the big hemlock tree, climbed till its thin top bent under his weight, and ridden it like a horse. Alone, out of the sight and hearing of the neighbors, he would have whooped and hopped and screamed like a loon till his breath was gone, thrown stones till his arms were tired, cut capers till his demons were exorcised and he was calm enough to think. But he was an old man now, white-bearded and balding, stiff-jointed and spindle-shanked. The best he could do was to face up the hill, into the wind, and keep his strides long and swift.

It was better than nothing.

Before he was at the top of the grade, his head felt clearer and his spirit more quiet. He could begin to look into himself without flinching or finding excuses, although what he saw was not good.

He was shamed by his own shame.

For in it he discerned the features of his oldest besetting sin: pride, so overweening that he must not only demand absolute moral perfection from himself, but from all those about him. Must constantly prove his authority to speak against evil by incarnating the good!

*   *   *

It was a weed that had sunk roots into the soil of his character at a period in his life when he was too busy to have much time for self-examination. He was warned of his weakness, but by opponents who had other reasons for finding fault. His friends and followers were blinded by a battlefield loyalty that would admit no blemish in their champion. For that was what he was—a *chevalier sans peur et sans reproche*—to an élite corps of young radicals.

Most of them had followed him out from New England to make up the first class at Lane Theological Seminary, a new institution, financed by two New York philanthropists of strong Abolitionist persuasion, Arthur and Lewis Tappan. Theodore was older than most of his fellow students, already the veteran of a number of reform campaigns. He had been consulted by the Tappans on everything from the selection of the site and the plan of study, to the choice of Dr. Lyman Beecher as president. It was Beecher's intention—and the Tappans' as well at the start—that Lane should serve as a seedbed for a whole crop of evangelists who would carry the great religious and moral upsurge of the 1830's across the heartland of the nation, preaching all sorts of gospels from temperance to emancipationism. It was partly Theodore's leadership, partly the geography of the situation that altered the plan and made one cause predominate.

Abolitionism was endemic to the soil on which the seminary was built, near Cincinnati, on the north bank of the Ohio River, only one watery mile from slave territory. The city was a dispatching point on the Underground Railroad, and the public mind was kept in a constant state of ferment by escapes and pursuits of fugitives from the South. Inevitably, Lane students found themselves faced with a choice between giving and refusing illegal aid to men and women— and frequently to children—whose lives depended on it. If that did not make Abolitionists of them, there was the experience of contact with free Negroes, of whom there was a large colony in the town. Most of them lived in poverty, laboring to earn the money to free a wife or husband or parent or child, before pushing on to a haven beyond the reach of the Fugitive Slave Law. When Lane's apprentice ministers went on charitable visits to the dwellings of "God's poor," it was apt to be into this sort of household, and they got a new view of the being whose humanity was denied by the apologists of slavery, a new view of the "peculiar institution" about which they heard such conflicting opinions.

That conflict was sharpened in the mind of the community by the memory of ugly race riots only a year and a few months past, and in the mind of the college by the presence of New Englanders and Southerners, "immediatists" and "gradualists" and "colonizationists"; some who expected one day to inherit property in the form of slaves, some who already had, and one manumitted slave. Extreme positions were taken in the discussions (which began almost as soon as the term did), and while the controversy was still in its first stages something happened that altered the quality of every student's attitude toward it.

An epidemic of cholera broke out. Half the student body and many of the faculty were stricken suddenly and simultaneously. There was no time to go into town for help. Besides, Cincinnati had not enough doctors to deal with its own victims. There was nothing to do but endure: nurse the sick, comfort the dying, cook and clean and struggle to stay awake at one's post, night after nightmarish night.

Then it was over.

The dead were buried. The living gave thanks for their deliverance. Classes resumed. But nothing was the same as it had been before. Those who survived felt different toward one another and toward themselves, knit in a closer kinship, bound by a new loyalty, more deeply dedicated, "chosen."

Because he had been able to endure more than most of his fellows, to stay on his feet for forty-eight hours without relief at the worst of the crisis, Theodore had tightened his hold on the hearts of his devotés, and he had won new converts from the ranks of the southern students. One of these was a young man named William Allan, who sat the long watches of the night with him, debating the rights and wrongs of "colonization"—the proposal to resolve the vexing problems of slavery and the free Negro by sending all blacks not held in bondage to settle the west coast of Africa. When Allan was finally persuaded that this position (which had become respectable in religious circles, north and south) was so impractical as to be essentially hypocrisy, he decided to attack it head on.

He went to Lane's president, Dr. Beecher, and asked permission to organize a series of debates. President Beecher gave permission, and offered to come and expound his own view, which was that "Abolition and Colonization were not mutually exclusive, but that both could dwell peaceably together in the blessed country of Reform." He was later persuaded by conservatives on the faculty that his offer had been rash and that public discussion of such controversial issues was unwise. He advised Allan that it might be better to postpone, if not to drop, the debate, but Allan and his fellow enthusiasts chose to ignore the advice, and went on with their plans.

The audience attracted by the announced topic was too large to be comfortably seated in the largest assembly hall on the campus. Theodore made the opening presentation, but Allan and other Southerners—including the lone freedman—played the leading roles, both as speakers and as organizers of the Abolition Society that resulted from the debates. News spread into Cincinnati, and across the river into Kentucky and beyond, that Lane Seminary was making the sons of slaveholders into Abolitionists, and the pillars of the Establishment trembled.

Heady with success, the young reformers at Lane declared that "faith without works was a dead thing," and set about following up their resolution—that slavery ought to be immediately abolished—with a program of action designed to speed the day. Theodore, who was more widely acquainted in the Negro community than most of his fellows, made the suggestion of a lyceum—a free evening school where any Negro, child or adult, could come to study grammar, geography, arithmetic, or any other subject on which he desired light that some Lane student could shed.

The project caught on. Within a few weeks there were more students than the volunteer faculty could handle. Applicants had to be turned away with a promise that they would be admitted as soon as new classes could be organized. Two Lane students asked for leaves of absence to devote themselves full time to the lyceum, but even that did not fill the need. The Tappans in New York were appealed to; they recruited four young white ladies and sent them out to hold classes for Negro women and girls. The lyceum was becoming almost as much of an institution as Lane itself.

Cincinnati was forced to take notice, to form an opinion, pro and con.

One opinion was voiced by a newspaper editor who charged the *Lane rebels* with *raising malignant passions and rancorous party spirit.* His editorial was so blatant an overstatement of the case that it really required no answer. But Theodore indulged himself in the pleasure of rebuttal. He wrote a letter that the editor printed:

> *Sir:*
> *You have mistaken alike the cause, the age and the men, if you think to intimidate by threats, to silence by clamors, or to shame by sneers, those who have put their hands to this work.*
> *By the grace of God, the history of the next five years will teach this lesson to the most reluctant learner.*

But the opinion that counted in the long run was less clearly articulated, and more difficult to move by such appeals. There were a good many Cincinnatians—by no means pro-slavery men—who were uneasy at this sudden epidemic of self-improvement in a group they were accustomed to regarding as the mudsill of society. They would have been glad to look the other way if the Lane rebels had left them any way to look. But the young zealots were convinced that the cleansing of the white community of its sins as oppressor was as urgent a task as the raising up of the oppressed. And the shortest route to both good ends was Christian fellowship, without reservation or qualification.

It was, therefore, no accident that Lane students began to be seen on Sunday mornings, walking up the rickety steps of Negro churches, while Dr. Beecher preached to smaller and smaller assemblages in the chapel at Lane. The four young lady teachers from New York were seen coming and going in the most wretched neighborhoods at all hours and without escort, hurrying to perform some errand of mercy, to ease the pains of birth, or to pray with the dying. The young ministers were seen taking part in the celebration of Negro weddings and christenings, walking in the procession that followed a Negro's coffin to the grave. They were seen on the streets, deep in converse with young Negro men, and even on occasion with young Negro women. Students from the lyceum were seen driving on the road that led out to Lane, and eventually seen walking about on that campus, with or without white hosts.

All this was reported, distorted, interpreted, and brought to the ears of the trustees of the seminary, a body of solid citizens, charged with the duty of making decisions "regarding the general welfare of the institution." Theodore had had enough experience with well-fed, churchgoing "pillars of the community" to predict their behavior when confronted by a challenge to the mores to which they conformed. He was not surprised when Dr. Beecher called him into his study to inform him that the trustees were convinced that the seminary had become a station on the Underground Railroad and that the students were neglecting their studies to engage in illegal activities as Conductors.

Dr. Beecher's deprecating smile assumed that the charge was false and that he and Theodore shared a common view of the problem, the objective, and the obstacles in the way. All that needed to be agreed upon between them was the tactic best suited to the situation of the moment.

"The mistake you have made is not the doing of wrong," he told Theodore. "Doing right too soon can be an even more serious error in some circumstances."

He smiled again to test the concord before venturing further.

Theodore let his own face set in an expression of stony disapproval that he had often been told was enough to strike terror into the heart of an innocent. Dr. Beecher did not look terror-stricken, but his own smile was extinguished, and for good.

"If what you want is to raise up the free colored people through teaching, I can get you all sorts and amounts of help," he said. "But if what you want is to encourage the public mingling of the races, I can promise you only one result: you and your school will be overwhelmed."

"Why?"

Dr. Beecher's handsome and genial face went red. "Because the community is not yet ready to accept such a state of affairs," he said curtly.

"It is because the public conscience is sluggish that ministers and evangelists are needed." Theodore had held himself back as long as he could, aware that preaching to a preacher was fatally undiplomatic. But the compulsion was upon him now. He reminded Dr. Beecher of his own statement of the purpose for which Lane had been founded: "to light a great moral conflagration which will spread like the grass fires of these western prairies, and burn the dross from the nation's soul!"

"You have also said from your pulpit that God created man in his own image—black as well as white—and that it is a sin against His creation to consider the Negro as less than a man. If that is so, it is a sin to discriminate against him in any way. To shun him or to shut him out is to shun or shut out the Word made flesh, the Son of God born as man!"

Dr. Beecher listened longer and with more patience than Theodore expected, but at last he was provoked to wrath. His counterattack was personal and cruel.

"You are guilty of the sin of vaingloriousness! Of exulting in power without responsibility!" He jabbed his finger at Theodore as if to pin him to a spiritual wall. "I have known for some time that you are the uncrowned king of an *imperium in imperio* here. I have not challenged your hold over your subjects because I expected you to exercise authority with judgment, with as much respect for the welfare of the seminary as if you were appointed to the place you have assumed. I see now that I was mistaken in you.

"You are too puffed up with your own importance to listen to any opinion that crosses your own. You will bring down the roof of the temple! betray those who trust you! and do it with a clear conscience, convinced that the adulation of your admirers proves the rightness of your opinion and the purity of your motives."

As he made his way back to his bare, monastic cell of a room, Theodore weighed the president's angry accusations against his own calm conviction of being in the right. He had not demeaned himself by turning the charge of vanity against his accuser, as he might easily have done. But that did not of itself exonerate him. How could he put the question to a test?

"If the work I undertake is of God, it will prosper," he told himself.

The thing to do was carry it forward without delay or compromise, and read the divine verdict in the result.

Not long after Theodore's stormy interview with Dr. Beecher, summer vacation began, and the president beat a strategic retreat to New England where he kept himself busy for the next three months raising funds for a new building in which to house more students more comfortably. Theodore and his élite corps stayed on campus, preparing Abolition pamphlets and lists for mailing, continuing the work of the lyceum and—in some cases—the dispatching of passengers on the Underground.

Next time the alarm of the trustees reached a critical point, there was no figure of authority to whom they could delegate the responsibility of treating with the students. They consulted together—those who were in Cincinnati at the time—and decided that they must take action. They issued an ultimatum, prefaced with a statement of "facts" that was even more appalling than the conclusion drawn from them:

Slavery is a subject to be approached—if at all—with diffi-dence and discretion. Discussion of such a topic is apt to unfit the minds of prospective ministers for genial and useful in-tercourse with mankind . . .

In view of this and more of the same sort of pompous wicked-ness, a ban was decreed forthwith on all student societies at Lane, and on all public statements on controversial issues. Discussion of such issues was forbidden not only at meetings but at meals! Of-fenders against these new commandments were subject to expul-sion.

Theodore's confidence was weakened. Was this disaster a sign that he had been wrong and Dr. Beecher right? In a mood to take advice and perhaps even direction, he wrote the president and begged him to come back while it was still possible to negotiate some sort of compromise. But Beecher did not respond till too late. By the time he returned, students and trustees faced each other like gladiators in an arena maneuvering for a hold. The faculty had chosen sides, except for Professor Stowe who was courting one of Dr. Beecher's daughters and tried to stand on the same dangerous dead center as his prospective father-in-law.

Before the president's trunk was unpacked, he was waited upon by a delegation from the student body, requesting an "interpreta-tion" of the trustees' new rules. Theodore and William Allan were already threatened with expulsion, so they had refused to be part of the delegation; but they sat with the committee of the whole to which it was reported that "nothing either Dr. Beecher or Professor Stowe had to say made the rulings less clear or more acceptable."

Someone rose to ask in irony whether "we are permitted to discuss the rules."

A second delegation waited upon the president with this question and returned to report that the answer was negative.

"Old Beecher is sweating as if he felt the breath of the Devil on his neck," said one of the reporters with the righteous scorn of the radical for the man of moderation, caught in a cross fire.

"Let's send to ask if we are permitted to discuss the question of whether to stay on here at the seminary?" someone suggested.

A third delegation was chosen, went, and returned to report that "the trustees have the right to make rules for the conduct of students, and under their rules no aspect of the present unfortunate situation can be debated or discussed."

There was a rumble like distant thunder in the chapel. Anger, indignation, grief, and confusion combined in a diapason that set up an answering vibration in Theodore's heart. It seemed to him that it had been necessary to push the matter to this absurdity to answer the question Beecher had raised in his mind. He got to his feet. The assemblage grew quiet.

"There is still one privilege left us," he said. "That is to decide whether or not we will submit. For myself, the most solemn conviction of duty to God, to my conscience, to my country, and to the race on whose behalf we have been laboring, all constrain me to say that I can no longer continue here."

As he spoke, all his lost confidence and courage came back. He felt unleashed, as if he had been checked not only for the past weeks or months, but for all the years of his life, from the full use of powers that were now committed to the struggle that lay ahead.

That same evening he drew up a statement of the student position vis-à-vis the trustees' ukase. Fifty-one of his fellow students signed it and withdrew from the seminary. The Lane rebels had earned their soubriquet.

The effect of their declaration of war was felt all over the nation. Student Abolition societies were formed on campuses from Harvard to Indiana. Professors and college presidents spoke out for the first time, and were honored or pilloried for their views. Repression of Abolition sentiments only served to quicken and spread them. New recruits were daily added to the ranks. New societies were springing up in communities where no one had suspected a single partisan. A thousand tasks proliferated from the ferment.

Theodore felt himself compelled to undertake these tasks.

His friends pleaded with him to postpone them long enough to finish his many times interrupted education for the ministry. Oberlin College, which most of the rebels were entering, had offered him a post as professor of theology. He could support himself and do useful work for the cause while he finished his own studies.

"Whereas if you turn down this opportunity, there may never be another like it," Henry Stanton warned him. "You will never be ordained, and your usefulness will never be what it could, if you spoke with the authority of a minister of the gospel."

"True," Theodore replied. "But if I turn down the opportunity this moment offers for Abolition, there may never be another."

This time he felt no inner need to prove himself. It was to convince Henry and others who advanced similar arguments that he once again put his "call" to the test of an ordeal by battle. He chose an objective—a formidable one—and promised that his success or failure in achieving it would determine his future course.

The objective was Ripley, a town on the north bank of the Ohio, a bastion of pro-slavery sentiment in the Western Reserve. Theodore had not a single speaking acquaintance in the town or its environs, but he determined to storm it alone. Like Joshua, he would sound his trumpet, and if the will of God powered his lungs the walls of prejudice would fall.

He arrived in the town unheralded, and went to call on the Presbyterian minister, whom he persuaded—not without some difficulty —to lend his church for a public discussion of the topic Abolition, What Does It Propose? Next, he walked through the streets, making his announcement wherever he saw men gathered. By this means, with no other assistance, he drew a crowd of some fifty persons to hear his first lecture.

Although he spoke in as calm and dispassionate a manner as he could, his message seemed to explode like an overheated stove, setting fires all over the community. He was informed next day that the church would not be available for the second lecture, which he had already announced. But by then he had his first converts. Not many, but enough to provide him with a place to sleep and help him secure a room in the courthouse for his meeting. Later, when that too was withdrawn, a store was offered; then a private home. Once he spoke from the back of a wagon, and several times in barns. There were hecklers at all his meetings. Eggs were hurled at him. Some broke and covered his clothes with evil-smelling filth that was impossible to clean off. But he went on speaking, and eventually the opposition ran out of ammunition and breath.

Then he got down to his task in good earnest.

He challenged those who disagreed with him to come forward and share the platform. No one accepted. But the minister who had first given and then withdrawn his church rose to make a public confession of error. Theodore invited him to bear witness to his change of heart by sitting on the platform. At the next lecture other clergymen also took seats; then a lawyer, an editor, a candidate for Congress. Like the evangelists under whom he had served his apprenticeship, Theodore used his first converts to win others. When he had enough, he put the question to a vote: for or against the immediate abolition of slavery; for or against the formation of a local Abolition society. The ayes won on both counts.

He had his answer. This was his destined work. He wrote Henry Stanton that he was determined to win the whole of the Ohio Valley, carrying on alone until and unless others felt free to join him.

It had taken him eleven nights to win in Ripley. In the next town he attacked, it took him fifteen. In the next, less than a week. His reputation preceded him now, making things easier in some places, harder in others.

In one town, his first meeting was invaded by a well-organized band of hecklers who had brought along a bass drum that could be pounded loud enough to drown him out. He came off victor in that encounter by a shift of tactics. Instead of shouting himself hoarse, he dropped his voice and continued to speak, emphasizing his points with dramatic gestures. Whenever there was even a brief pause in the drumming, he got in a phrase heavily weighted with suspense, and watched the front row of hecklers for signs of curiosity.

At last one of them shouted to the drummer: "Keep quiet a minute! I want to hear what it is he's saying the Bible says."

The drummer stopped, but was immediately ordered back to his pounding by others.

"I said to shut up!" the first man yelled angrily, and when he was not obeyed, settled the matter by putting his foot through the drumhead.

But not all victories were won painlessly. As Theodore's conquests mounted, opposition grew more violent. Suits were ripped off his back or otherwise ruined so frequently that he gave up trying to dress properly, and wore rough linsey-woolsey clothes, which were cheap to replace. The damage to his voice (even before the accident in Alum Creek) was harder to repair. But as long as he kept winning battles, he did not count their cost.

Larger fields were opening to him now. Oberlin's winter vacation time released his old confrères to take over the work in Ohio. Theodore was free to move east. The General Assembly of the Presbyterian Church convened in Pittsburgh, and he attended as a lay member. His proselytizing won new adherents in the ranks of active ministers. He was sowing dragon's teeth of truth and reaping a harvest of fighting men.

There were calls for him from Rhode Island, where a bill to gag all Abolition debate was before the Legislature. He was needed to help defeat it. He was needed in Boston. Garrison begged him to come. He was needed in Utica, where delegates to an anti-slavery convention had been driven out of town by a mob led by a member of Congress and a local judge.

He chose Utica because it seemed to offer the greatest challenge. But it took him only a week to draw such crowds that no hall could hold them. He decided to test the sincerity of these rapid conversions by warning away "mere signers of a pledge."

"If you join us out of a sense of duty, let us alone," he told his audience. "We have millstones enough swinging at our necks. Give place to those who leap into our ranks because they cannot keep themselves out. Who, instead of whining *duty,* shout *privilege! delight!* as they give their names to execration and their bodies to buffeting!"

Recruits crowded forward in even greater numbers than before.

And so it went, a triumphal procession across upper New York State, against towns that offered no resistance at all to his message, and towns that threatened much but mustered little.

Until he came to Troy.

Many times in the years that followed, he asked himself why that city proved his nemesis, but he could never find the answer. The mayor and the town council were not friendly, but neither had they been in Utica or Syracuse. He had long since learned not to expect support from the "respectables" of a community or to lean for protection on the law.

He was not dismayed when his first meeting in Troy was broken up by a gang of roughs who tried to drag him physically from the platform. A band of loyal supporters came to his defense, and from that night on formed a guard that went with him wherever he had to go. Stones and cudgels were thrown at him, along with the usual eggs and vegetables, and once he was struck on the side of his head so that he was stunned and could not go on speaking for a moment or two. But he collected himself and did go on. He finished the lecture, if not in his most powerful style, at least in something close to it. The next night he had completely recovered.

The fury of the mob against him was testimony to his effectiveness, part of the familiar pattern of maturing crisis. Soon now the tide would turn, sweep the enemy away and carry him to his objective.

But a week passed, and then another. The crowds did not grow. Neither did the number of his converts. He kept doggedly on: arguing, denouncing, exposing, explaining, reasoning, pleading, exhorting, till all his words sounded hollow in his own ears. It was degenerating into a stalemate, the first he had ever experienced.

He was bone-weary now, and so hoarse that it was painful to speak. A physician to whom he went for relief warned him, "You will lose your voice if you persist."

Very well, he would lose it. He would lose everything except the battle. That he could never lose, for the power that was being tested was not his own!

Friends were writing him anxiously. "Are you courting martyrdom?" one asked.

Perhaps he was. A man who presumed to ask others to commit themselves to his cause must prove himself willing to meet the full consequences of such a commitment.

"Blessed are they that die in harness and are buried—or bleach—on the field of battle!"

But even as he steeled himself to accept that bitter blessing, it was denied him. The mayor announced that Weld was ordered out of Troy on the grounds that his continued presence endangered the city's peace. He was to be dumped like a load of trash at the edge of the town, prevented by the police from reentering it, if he should try.

He woke, as from a dream.

For all practical purposes, he was a mute. He could hardly make himself heard to explain his capitulation, to promise those who had stood by him till this end that he was not deserting them, only stopping to rest and regain his voice, that he would return.

But he was not Joshua. Nor Moses either. The power that had been vouchsafed him was taken away, and he had not only to yield his place at the head of the advancing column but to drop back into the ranks, accept the humblest of tasks and the leadership of those he had trained to be his disciples.

Theodore had plenty of time to ponder his sin and work out his penance during the next twenty years, for it was that long before he spoke from a public platform again. He had come to understand many of the ways in which pride insinuated itself into cracks in his defenses, and he had striven to root it out. But he had failed.

He could see now why. For the story he told the class and Harriet Morgan reminded him that he had once thought of himself as more than mortal. The loss of that luster had been more than he could bear. All the years of his retirement from public life he had consoled himself by hugging in secret the image of the stainless knight. While other men won the victories that would have been his to win if he had not fallen, he measured their purity against his own, and always to their detriment. He had to be perfect because that was all he had left.

*   *   *

Theodore gave his head a shake that sent drops of melting snow in all directions. Then he turned and started back down the hill toward home.

Energy was liberated into his bloodstream so strongly that he tried—timidly at first, but with more and more abandon—to run! He ran a few steps and slid on the packed snow, ran and slid, ran and slid. Breathless with the effort and the delight!

Angelina was up and sitting at the supper table when he came in. She looked better than he had dared to hope, and there was a vibrancy in her voice that matched his own mood.

"I've been waiting for you, Thoda," she said with a warm smile of greeting, "to tell what I've been thinking and what I've decided."

He glanced quickly at Sarah, who was looking even more apprehensive than before, as if the improvement in her sister's condition threatened some sort of rashness that was bound to end in catastrophe.

"I've decided not to attempt the journey to Charleston—much as I should like to make it," Angelina said. "I hope you will think well of what I mean to do instead. That is, to go to the boys. After all, the mother has sacrificed everything to send them to be educated, and the first and best amends we can make to her is to see that they achieve their purpose at the university."

"I agree absolutely," Theodore said. "But you don't mean to go *now*."

"Yes, I do."

Sarah groaned softly.

"I have written and invited them to come here to us," Angelina explained. "But even if they accept, it would not be until June, and perhaps not then. Archibald wrote us, you remember, that they work in the summer to earn money for their tuition. And in any case, I don't feel easy to wait as long as June."

"Would you be willing to wait till Easter?" Theodore asked. "I'm sure Dr. Lewis could spare us for an extra day or two, and I could accompany you—"

"No," Angelina said firmly. "You cannot be spared from school. I'm hoping you will take over some of my classes so that I shan't feel quite so much the truant."

"I can go with you," Sarah said, "but the trip will be too much for you even so."

"You can't be spared from the house any more than Thoda can from school," Angelina said. "I am not indispensable in either sphere. And the trip will not be too much. I can break it twice, if need be; stay one night in New York with the Tappans, and the next with Jane or Sister Anna, in Philadelphia."

"You will have to take a stagecoach from Philadelphia. The railroad does not go to Oxford."

Angelina dismissed this warning with a gentle wave of her hand. She was already showing the strain of this much discussion. Sarah was quite right to be anxious for her, Theodore thought, and wrong to make any effort to dissuade her. . . .

"What I don't understand is why you feel you have to go in person," Stuart said, as if he had read his father's mind and dissented so strongly that he had to intervene.

"Because I want to see the two boys—our nephews—face to face. To know them and their needs."

"You're not talking of material needs, then?"

"Not *only* material needs," Angelina said. "Though I'm not sure Archibald was entirely candid in what he wrote on that score. It may be that there are things he lacks which he does not speak about.

"And there is something else . . . a note of deep bitterness, in his letter . . . and anger. That he has cause for anger we all know. And yet . . . bitterness and anger turn him toward the past. It should be in the other direction that he faces now.

"I shall ask his forgiveness," she finished with more assurance. "If he can grant it, I believe it may relieve both his heart and mine."

"But why can't you ask that in a letter?"

Angelina did not attempt to answer, and Stuart turned to his father.

"Do you think it's sensible, Father? Isn't the risk to Mother's health too great to balance the gain? Whatever that may be."

"No. I think your mother is right."

"You think she ought to go?" Stuart asked in amazement.

"Yes. If she feels she can be of help."

"But that's just my point! What help can she be? Except financially . . ."

Both Sarahs were as puzzled as Stuart, waiting for Theodore to explain.

"I'm remembering a young man I once knew," he said. "A bright, brave, handsome lad—about the same age as Archibald—a student in our lyceum in Cincinnati. I spent more time with him and knew him better than any of my other pupils there. He was full of anger —anger and hatred of the white master from whom he had escaped—of all white men or almost all. I could hear it shrill like the wind whenever he spoke of the future, of what he wanted to be, to do. . . .

"I knew the value of hatred—hatred of evil and of injustice—and how it could be put to use. But the problem with our best students—

the most sensitive and intelligent ones, with the greatest promise as leaders of their people—was to help them steer between the reef of resignation and the rock of revenge. How to blunt the edge of their anger against the oppressor without dulling their courage to combat oppression.

"If someone had been able to reach my young friend—as your mother hopes to reach Archibald now, and I suppose Francis, as well—I believe he would have lived to become another Frederick Douglass or a Charles Lenox Remond."

"What happened to him?" young Sarah asked softly.

"He wanted to come with me when I left Cincinnati, but I persuaded him to stay, to keep on with his studies, and the menial work by which he supported himself," Theodore continued with great reluctance. "Two, or perhaps three months later, word reached me that he had lost his reason. Gone as mad as Nat Turner, driven to the same acts of insane violence. Shot down in the street, like a rabid dog."

The room was still.

"One cynic had warned us when we started the lyceum: 'The best ones go crazy,' he said. My young friend was not the only one, though he was the only one I knew. . . ."

Stuart cleared his throat and pushed his chair back from the table. "Would you like me to go to Oxford with you, Mother?" he asked.

"Why, yes," Angelina answered, uncertainly. "If you would like to, my dear."

"I should. Very much."

It did not sound as if he would really like to. It sounded—to Theodore, at least—as if Stuart had made up his mind at long last to accept the draft. Theodore had been on the point of suggesting that young Sarah accompany her mother, but he did not want to intervene between Stuart and Angelina now. The room seemed to be filled with rips and undercurrents that he could not chart, amid which he must either steer blindly or anchor and wait till the tide had run out.

XI

Dr. Randall stopped the boys as they were coming away from chapel. "I've been meaning to speak with you about the summer," he said. "Have you made application for a position anywhere?"

"Not yet," said Archy. "But we mean to."

"You're not planning on spending the time in Charleston with your mother?"

"No."

"We don't have the fare," Frank explained. "And anyways there's no work there pays enough for us to put anything by for next year."

Dr. Randall hummed approvingly. "I have an offer which may interest you, in that case. There are two places open in the schools in Cumberland County, North Carolina. Would you consider teaching for the summer terms?"

Frank looked at Archy, and grinned.

Dr. Randall went on to explain the offer: all that was guaranteed was the round-trip ticket from Philadelphia to Fayetteville and back, and board and room for the eight weeks. Anything over that was dependent on the number of pupils who showed up. "But whatever you earn, you will be able to put by, because you will have no expenses. And you will have the satisfaction of knowing that you are already putting your hand to the great task for which you are preparing yourselves here."

Archy was in no mood for one of the president's sententious speeches on one's duty to lift the less fortunate.

"Would we be together?" Frank asked.

"I'm afraid not. The schools are at opposite ends of the county. I suppose you might manage to see each other on a Sunday now and then, but it would mean some traveling."

"We could go down and see Mauma at the end, though?"

"No reason why not. I don't know what the fare between Fayetteville and Charleston—"

"Oh, we'd walk," Frank interrupted eagerly. "Or beg rides from wagons. We didn't get home all last summer, and Mauma's getting right anxious to see us."

"I should think so!"

The tone of hearty sympathy set Archy's teeth on edge, and so did Frank's response to it. They were exchanging platitudes like old cronies, Frank and Dr. Randall, too taken up with themselves to notice his silence. Well, that was fine with him! Save him having to pretend to be grateful, to accept this offer or think up a good excuse for refusing it.

"By the way," Dr. Randall addressed himself to Archy, but included both in his question, "have you made up your minds about the change of name?"

Archy's face began to burn. "Not yet. We got to talk a little more."

"Very well. But let me know as soon as you can," Dr. Randall said cheerfully. "I must write the people in Fayetteville, and I ought to give them the name you mean to use when you get there."

Archy mumbled something. Frank thanked the president in a voice from which all enthusiasm had been drained. They made their way out of the building in silence.

It had been snowing when they went in, but the sun was out now, blazing on the white surface of the new fall so bright it made Archy's eyeballs ache. He dropped his head and watched the toes of his boots as they plodded, right, left, right, left, down the narrow pathway trodden into the snow. Frank walked behind him.

"You still studying 'bout changing your name?"

"Maybe," Archy replied.

They came to the place where the path turned left toward the dormitory door. Archy turned right and kicked his way through a small drift to reach the parallel tracks of the carriage road.

They walked abreast now, Archy in the right-hand track, Frank in the left, down the long curve of the driveway, out through the main gates, and up the road in the direction of the Delaware River and far-off Philadelphia. If they had been swinging a bucket between them, Archy thought, it would have been just like the old days. He could almost feel the yoke. It was heavy on him, and hurtful. But to pull loose, that was going to hurt even worse. More than he was yet prepared to endure.

If only he didn't have to. If only he could tell Frank straight out what it was he meant to do, and why, maybe Frank would want to come. It would be easier together. Yoked they were more than twice as strong as either was alone. And there would be only one set of ties to break—those that bound them to home and Mauma. And those were already a little slackened by the time that had passed.

"How would you like to keep on walking?" Archy said suddenly.

"All the way to the river?"

"Farther. Maybe we could find a ship bound out, and get us places on it and go somewhere. Maybe everywhere. Around the whole world."

"You mean it, Archy?"

Frank was looking at him sideways as if he suspected him of playing a crude joke or maybe having a fever high enough to make him foolish. Archy gave up without a struggle.

"No. I was just talking."

It was not right—even if it were possible—to try to persuade Frank. For it seemed as if he was going to make out up here after all. In a way they had changed places, he and Frank. It was Archy who had wanted to come north, who hoped much from the white world; Frank who been hostile, suspicious, blocked by his own hatred from accepting what was offered. Now it was just the other way round. Archy saw it, but he couldn't help himself.

"It seems like you talked 'bout taking a ship before," Frank said after a moment or two. "Wasn't it in Boston? After you come back from those folk in Peacedale. What was their name?"

"Harrower," Archy said.

"You 'member?" Frank persisted. "I believe you meant it, because everything was all fixed up then for us to come here. But you even went down to the wharves one day to see what ships were there."

"Did I? I forget."

But Archy did not forget. Neither what Frank was recalling nor the reasons behind it. It was the worst of all his memories, one he tried never to stir, but Frank had hit against a limb of the ugly submerged thing, jarred it loose from the mud in which Archy had buried it, and now it rose to the surface, whole.

* * *

Mrs. Harrower had decided not to make the trip from Stoneham to Peacedale in one stretch, but to stop for a visit with her sister in Providence. "Be nice for you, too," she told Archy. "You can take in the sights, while Martha and I catch up on the family news. Providence isn't as large a place as Boston, but it's every bit as handsome."

They arrived too late in the afternoon for any sight-seeing that day. But Archy was given a room to himself, and a bed, which was a pleasant change, and urged to get up early and go out for a walk.

"I'll leave something in the kitchen for your breakfast," said Mrs. Harrower's sister. "You do as you please with the forenoon. Only make sure you're back by dinnertime."

Having no guide, Archy wandered aimlessly at first, finding nothing remarkable about the city except the naming of its streets. There was one set that bore such titles as Dollar Street, Pound Street, Shilling, Sovereign, Doubloon, and so on. Then a set of pious alternatives: Benevolent Street, Benefit, Peace, Friendship, and Hope. A candid acknowledgment of divided allegiance that made him smile to himself.

Eventually his walk brought him to the river, fronted with mills and manufactories, all humming like tops, plumed with gray smoke. He wandered along the bank till he came to the docks, where ships of all sizes and flags were being unloaded. Archy had often watched such activity at home; here he had the strange sensation that he had gone deaf. There were no human sounds. No stevedores' songs. No shouts or cries or curses. No slap of the lash. Yet no one was idling. Every man seemed to be working, none to be giving orders. Every man seemed to know what was expected of him and to be about it, moving with an earnest energy, as if he were positively and personally interested in the accomplishment of his task. . . .

Some time late in the morning, Archy stopped to look at a bottled ship model displayed in the window of a shoemaker's shop. It was admirable work, and as he started to turn away after staring at it a good while, he caught the eye of an elderly brown man, sitting close to the window to get light for his work. He smiled at Archy, and suggested by a gesture that the boy come in.

Archy hesitated. He ought to be getting back for dinner, which was served at two. But he would like to get warm, and he did need new soles on his shoes. They were soaked through from the slushy pavements. He decided to go in and ask the cost.

"These shoes ain't worth putting soles to," the old man said. "Besides, they too wet to work on now. Reckon you got no others to wear while you leave them here. Just come up from the South, ain't you?"

Archy confessed to being a newcomer, and endured a sermon on the perils of getting one's feet wet in a northern climate.

"I recollect my first winter up here," the shoemaker said. "I took cold and like to died. Next winter the same thing happened to my wife. Same reason, too. Let her feet get wet and stay that way. There's nothing you got to pay more mind to than your feet, son. If you aim to stay on them, and work."

What Archy needed, he said, was a new pair of boots, but no doubt he lacked money to buy them. (The old man didn't put it as a question. He stated it as a fact.) "I come here same as you, without two coins to rub together. Yes, indeed, old Bailey knew slavery times! Ran off from as mean a master as you'd find in the whole state of Maryland!"

That was ten years ago, before the War. He had worked hard, and prospered. He had married a wife, a "born-free" woman who had taught him to read and to cipher. Between them they had saved enough to buy a "right smart of a house" to which, in a gush of hospitality and pride, Bailey invited Archy.

"It's near about dinnertime anyway," he said. "I'll lock up here, and we'll go see what she's got in the pot. You can finish drying your feet, and give us all the news."

It would have been hard to refuse such an invitation without giving offense, and Archy did not really want to refuse. He liked the old man, and was curious about his house. He was expected, but not required, to take his dinner at Mrs. Harrower's sister's. After all, he was free!

"The right smart of a house" was not new, but it was freshly painted, in good repair outside, so neat and clean inside that it was hard to believe Mrs. Bailey had not been forewarned of a visitor.

She was as cordial as her husband, though not as voluble, and she set another place at the table as if it gave her real pleasure, accepting Archy's compliments on one or another aspect of the establishment with unaffected grace.

Neither she nor Archy got a chance to speak more than a sentence at a time till well along in the meal. For Bailey had been hungering and thirsting after such an audience as Archy, and he was determined to satisfy himself while he could. He would ask a question, answer it himself, and change the subject, jumping from trade to politics, from local to national or even international matters, with frequent references to Scripture, Old Testament as well as New.

"Bailey's just showing off," said his wife with an affectionate smile. "He preaches on Sundays, but seems like he don't get enough listening to, just one day out of seven."

Showing off he certainly was—his house and his possessions, his achievements and his knowledge—but there was no malice in it. He was not trying to make Archy small and himself big. Just the opposite. "What you got to keep in your mind," he said several times, "is that this here's a new heaven and a new earth! Young fellow like you got to stretch forth your hand and gather in its fruits."

"Have you come north for a visit or to stay?" Mrs. Bailey asked, when her husband interrupted himself to give some attention to his dinner plate.

Archy said to stay, and then—because he did feel so completely at home—he began to tell the story of his hopes and their frustration. When he got to where Frank told him that there were no schools in New England that would admit them, Bailey stopped him.

"Nothing of the sort! Plenty of schools take colored hereabouts. Must be some up Boston way, too."

"Not the sort of school he's thinking about," said Mrs. Bailey. "He already knows reading and writing and ciphering, don't you, son?"

Archy said he did.

"Then what's the sort of schooling you want?" Bailey asked.

Archy spoke first of Frank's ambition because it was easy to define and immediately acceptable. His own was not. Sometimes he thought of being a preacher, sometimes a teacher, but neither profession was an end in itself. What he wanted was to fill the need Mrs. Pillsbury had spoken of, when she asked her pupils to prepare themselves to take offices of all kinds, even the highest.

Bailey was enraptured. He raised his hands over Archy's head in a gesture like a benediction. "The Lord done right to direct you here," he said solemnly. "To the city of His Providence! There's a college here, fine as any in the land! He's directed you to enter its gates, and us to stand behind you and see you through!"

"You sure they take colored up to the college?" asked Mrs. Bailey a little anxiously.

"Why wouldn't they? Calls itself Brown College, don't it?" The old man's delight in this play on words and the one about Providence had a naïve charm. It was as if he had fought a long war in which words and the letters that made them were his adversaries. He bent them, this way and that, to show who had been victorious.

"Might be there's a requirement of permanent residence," he went on, relishing the polysyllables. "But all you got to do is answer Yes. Don't concern them none how long you been permanent here."

"Can I live in Peacedale and go to the college?" Archy asked.

"'Course you can't. You got to live here with us!"

Bailey looked to his wife for confirmation, and got it. They would be honored to have Archy as their guest. There was a spare room upstairs that could be made comfortable. Mrs. Bailey was already mentally shifting the furniture. Bailey was anticipating Archy's financial needs and planning ways to meet them. The congregation to which he ministered on Sundays would help. They would contribute clothing, shoes, paper and writing materials, money to buy books and pay fees. Archy could work in Bailey's shop to earn pocket money.

No more implausible than Archy's own daydreams, this one had the added power of hundreds—even thousands—of other dreamers:

men too old, too far away, or yet unborn, whose deputy he would be as he moved to fulfill it. Launched like a dove from the Ark, he would pluck the olive branch of opportunity on behalf of all, the manifest sign of the new heaven and earth that Bailey proclaimed. . . .

The wind blew cold in his face as Archy climbed the steep hill, but he hardly felt it. Behind him marched the unseen hundreds, all pressing their faces into the same wind.

The houses on either side fell away, and he was crossing an open space, threaded by many paths. The center one led to a large brick building, four stories high, its façade laced with many-paned white-trimmed windows. Archy followed the path straight to the main doorway, and went in.

There were warmth and quiet inside, and a door marked with a brass plate that said REGISTRAR. Archy opened without knocking. A pale young man, prematurely balding, came to meet him at the high counter that divided the room. For some reason Archy disliked him on sight.

"What can I do for you?" the man asked, courteously enough.

"I come for the—" What was the word?

The pale man cleared his throat, and waited. The stopper was pulled from the barrel of Archy's confidence, and in an instant it had drained dry.

"I come for the papers to fill out," he mumbled.

"For yourself?"

Archy nodded.

"You are a resident of Providence?"

He nodded again, on guard now, careful not to speak any word that might trail southern moss.

"What is your address?"

Archy had no idea! He had neglected to take Bailey's street number or its name! At the moment he couldn't even recall the address of Mrs. Harrower's sister, which would have done in a pinch. And he could not explain his predicament. Could not let himself be drawn into any sort of conversation! Bailey had warned him about that. "Just request the application blank . . ."

That was the word!

"Just let me have the application blank, if you please!"

He rattled it off so briskly that it came near doing the trick. The man's hand reached toward a pile of printed forms—then drew away.

"Excuse me a moment," he said, and disappeared through the door of a side office, which shut behind him.

Through it, Archy could hear two voices. His heart began to race and his skin to prickle. He could guess what was being said. The pale young man had been examining him closely the whole time, looking at his red-brown hair, his light skin and gray-blue eyes, weighing the evidence. . . .

Evidence of what? Of his residence in this city of God's providence? Or of his race? Did he suspect Archy of trying to pass himself off as white? Denying that part of him that stretched back into time, a rope of love and hate that grew stronger as it grew blacker, in favor of something else that was not a line at all, but a series of disconnected actions, some of them accidents, all of them shameful?

The door of the inner office opened, and Archy looked defiantly into the eyes of an older man, who was coming toward him, followed by the pale one.

Let them ask him straight out what they wanted to know!

"You were inquiring about matriculation to the college?" the older man asked mildly.

"Yes," Archy said.

The man drew a paper from the pile and reached into a drawer below the counter for another. He laid both so that Archy could read them, and began to explain, pointing with his pencil to relevant paragraphs as he went along.

"These are your prerequisites," he said. "They are much the same as you would find anywhere. Examinations are both oral and written. You are expected to be prepared in arithmetic and algebra as far as quadratic equations. Ancient and modern geography, English grammar and the use of language. Greek grammar, the first four books of Xenophon's *Anabasis* or an equivalent portion of some classical Greek author, and the writing of Greek. Latin grammar, Caesar's *Commentaries,* the *Aeneid* of Virgil, six orations of Cicero, Latin prosody, and the writing of Latin.

"We also require testimonials of good moral character and—if you come from another college or academy—a certificate of good standing and of regular dismission."

He moved on to the second sheet.

"Here you will find the charges listed. And on the reverse side, the application form itself. References may be attached. I believe that's all. Unless you have questions?"

Archy groped his way out of the office, out of the building.

It had taken only a minute for his illusion to explode. It took longer for the dust to settle so that he could see the depth and the breadth of the crater in his soul. There was the almost comical disparity between the image of himself he had carried up the hill and the figure he cut in the Registrar's office. There were his hopes, shattered to shapelessness, never to be repaired.

It would be the same anywhere! The man in the office said so. Frank said so. Dr. Brown tried to say so when he told Frank, "It's a long haul for anyone who starts where you do." Long! Just as long as all the years of your life, that was how long! Latin and Greek, prosody and quadratics and what all, before you could even begin!

Worst of all was the simple stark fact of his ignorance, so abysmal that he had not even known how much there was to know. Only an equally ignorant fool, like old Bailey, could have tricked him into this shameful exposure. Archy hated Bailey for it. He would not go back to his house, not even to tell him so.

He would not go back to Mrs. Harrower and her sister, either. Nor to Stoneham and Frank. Nor to Mauma.

He would run off. He would go back down to the docks and seek out a captain who would take him on. He would sail out into the darkness of this snowy night and lose himself from all the separate shames that waited for him. He could see the river gleaming like oil at the foot of the street. The docks must be to the left. Houses cut off his view in that direction, but if he kept walking till he came to the river and then turned downstream, he was sure to come to them.

He walked on and on, wrapped in the snow's soft cloak, shielded from eyes that might have mocked him, soothed by the silence till he felt nothing but a great tiredness.

He had come to the tattered ends of the city before he realized that he was lost. He would have to retrace his steps, walk all the way back and farther still, find a bridge and try the other bank of the river. There was a hard, hot lump in his throat that made swallowing difficult, but otherwise he was fine. Only a little sleepy.

He rested a while and then started back. The wind was colder facing this way, and the lump put out fingers that clutched deep into his chest. His feet moved more slowly. Near the center of the city, he took shelter in the entrance of a building, dropped his head to his knees and hunched his shoulders against the wind that was driving the snow into his place of refuge, driving the cold into his bones, and the hot fingers toward his heart. He slept. . . .

Some time before morning he was taken up, carried to a large room with a hot stove and bright light. Questions were asked, but he could not wake himself enough to answer. His head ached and his cheeks burned. Everything else was numb. Somebody made him drink something that got past the lump in his throat and set his whole chest and belly afire.

Then it seemed he knew the person who was talking to him . . . talking, talking, talking, . . . creaking like a wheel, clopping like a horse's hooves . . . joggling him up and down till his very skin was sore. It was dark, and he could have slept but for the woman's talking, and the creaking and joggling . . . on and on. . . .

He woke at last with his head clear. He was in a stage. There had been other passengers till a moment ago. Now there was only Mrs. Harrower and himself. It was daylight, cloudy, but not dark.

"We're almost there," Mrs. Harrower said. "We'll get you right into bed and have the doctor to see you."

"It's the chills and fever," Archy said apologetically. "I'll be all right for a while now. Maybe till evening."

The effort of speaking started his head aching, and he would have gone back to sleep, but Mrs. Harrower was asking questions that required answers. What was chills and fever? Was it the same as the ague? What did doctors do for it in the South? Had Archy ever had it before?

"Yes, ma'am. Last time I had it was at the Coles. We couldn't have the doctor in, so Aunt Cole cured me with bark brew."

"Why couldn't you have the doctor?"

"It was when I was hiding."

"Oh! The time you ran away." She recalled the incident, but none of the details. "How long was it you said you had to hide?"

"Near about two years."

"Two years! But didn't you tell me you never went out of the house?"

"Yes, ma'am."

"Except at night, you said, and then only into the backyard?"

"Yes, ma'am." If she remembered all this, why did she have to ask?

"It doesn't seem possible. How in the world could they manage to keep everyone out of their house for that long? Of course, your mother must have been allowed to come and see you?"

"Yes, ma'am."

"But no one else?"

"Not to see me. Sometimes folks came to see Aunt Cole. While she was unlocking the door, I had to run upstairs and get into the closet."

"I suppose they kept the window blinds closed?"

"No, ma'am. Not in the daytime. Folks would have noticed, and wondered why. I kept back from the windows. Or, if I had to come near, I stooped down."

"I notice you have a sort of stoop," Mrs. Harrower said. "I suppose that's what it's from."

There was no need to answer, and Archy started to doze.

"I don't suppose anyone ever dies of chills and fever?"

"Yes, ma'am."

"They do?" Her voice prodded him awake. "People actually die of it?"

"Lots of times," Archy said irritably. "Uncle Cole thought I was going to. We had to do some figuring to know what to do with me, if I did."

Mrs. Harrower was shocked. "They talked about things like that in front of you?"

"Yes, ma'am. You see, they couldn't bury me in the backyard on account of the land being so marshy out that way. You can't dig down more than a foot without the hole filling up at high water. But we happened to think of a place not far off where there was a pond with palmetto scrub around it. It was a shortcut to the brickyards.

"What we could do—what *they* could do, I mean to say—was carry me out at night and lay me there by one of the paths. Folks that worked at the brickyard would be sure to find me in the morning, before the day got too hot or the buzzards came."

Mrs. Harrower asked no more questions after that.

But now Archy couldn't fall asleep. The fever had gone down some, but he wasn't sweating. That was a bad sign. Aunt Cole said it was worse when the fever didn't leave you before the next chill took hold.

222

Mrs. Harrower put Archy to bed in a small, clean room over the kitchen, called her own doctor, and nursed him to the letter of the instructions she received. She seemed to enjoy it, as if it restored some lost sense of authority.

She also enjoyed his company as she had before, sitting for hours on end in a chair near his window, chatting and tatting. Gradually, the history of the household began to emerge from her talk, the past contrasted with the present and her dreams of the future. For the house had not always been as empty as it was now. It had been filled with children. Some had died. The three who survived were all grown and gone away. The youngest son was in college. The other was away at sea. The only daughter was married and living in Boston. She had one child and was expecting another.

"They'll all be down for Christmas, and the house will be a bustle and a bother," Mrs. Harrower would say, frowning and smiling at the same time. "You've got to wrestle with your weakness, Archy, so you can be on your feet to help me get ready."

Then she would drift off into a detailed rehearsal, not of the event itself, but of the preparations for it, listing errands and tasks, debating the order in which they should be accomplished, planning and revising menus, amending old recipes, talking more and more for herself, less and less for him. Archy wondered how soon she would have noticed if he had got out of bed and gone away—or died right there.

Yet she was very kind. She brought him his medicine and a bowl of porridge made of sweet, white cornmeal each morning; another dose of medicine and a fine chowder in the afternoon; a tall glass of milk and a few slices of buttered bread in the evening, after she and Mr. Harrower had finished their own meal.

And there were special touches of thoughtfulness, like the new suspenders she bought for him. "I want you to wear these and see if they don't break you of the habit of stooping," she said.

Archy tried them the first day he got up and dressed, and found that they forced him to square his shoulders and carry himself erect.

223

But grateful as he was, the gift reminded him of the suit Miss Julia had ordered for him. Was he once again being turned into a white woman's pet, washed and groomed like a dog, or caged like a bird?

This was a different sort of cage from the Grimkés, but in some ways more confining. There was no hour of the day when he was free to leave it, no other human contact but with his captor. Not being able to hate her made it no easier. But the situation was at least bearable until Frank's letter came.

It apologized for being overdue (Archy had completely forgotten the promise to write on schedule), asked if there was word from Mrs. Pillsbury (it was still too early for that), and enclosed a clipping from a Boston newspaper, reporting that *Ashmun Institute in Oxford, Pennsylvania, being dedicated to the higher education of youth of the Negro and other races,* had recently changed its name to Lincoln University *to honor the memory of the martyred President.* Mr. Dykes, Frank's employer, thought the clipping ought to be sent on to Mrs. Pillsbury. Frank left it up to Archy to do so, if he saw fit.

"Mr. Dykes look up where it is and say it near about halfway to home," Frank wrote. "But I already put money aside, and I reckon I could pay the fare, if Mrs. P. was to get our fees paid some other way."

Archy shook with weak laughter. As if fees had anything to do with it! As if you could pay for not knowing quadratic equations and ancient geography! Poor Frank! He had dropped his shield of cynicism too soon.

But Frank was putting money by!

Archy was not. The subject of money had never been mentioned between him and Mrs. Harrower. He had not been concerned with money when their agreement was reached, only with a place to stay till he was ready to—what was the fearsome word?—matriculate! It was hardly the time to raise the question of wages now, when he was just able to be up and around, already beholden not only

224

for sustenance and shelter but for doctor's fees and medicine. An unknown debt he must work off before he could start earning money for his own needs! But how could he work it off, if no rate of pay was set? It was slavery all over again.

Not long after that, Archy was sent on an errand that took him past the woolen mill, a large building of yellow-gray stone, set in a hollow beside the little stream. Its iron gates stood open, and there was a sign on one of them that advertised:

HANDS WANTED

He was tempted to go in and ask what the pay was. It would hardly do to apply for work at Mr. Harrower's own mill, but Archy would like to know what to expect if he sought work elsewhere.

"Looking for the hiring window?" A man who was just coming out of the yard put a hand on Archy's shoulder, spun him around, and gave him a shove that started him through the gates. "Right there between the doors. See it now?"

Well, why not ask? To ask was not to commit himself. Archy squared his shoulders against the braces, approached the wicket, and put his question.

The man behind the window pushed a roster at him and told him to sign it, rattling off a bewildering set of statistics about hours, wages, and prospects for advancement. "Be here tomorrow morning at six-thirty sharp," he said, and slammed the window shut.

Archy walked away in a daze.

He was hired. And if he had understood the man's jabber, at more than double what Frank was earning! Enough to pay Mrs. Harrower back in installments, and still put away a sizable amount each week. Especially if she would let him stay on in his room, working nights and holidays to pay his keep. He ought to have given her some warning, but he would explain how it had come about, assure her that he was not ungrateful nor unmindful of his

225

obligation. He did not anticipate anything worse than embarrassment on his part, irritation on hers.

But his announcement loosed a tempest of self-pity, lashed by winds of what sounded—incredibly!—like fear.

"I'm a sick woman," Mrs. Harrower wailed. "I don't show it, but it's the truth. Ask Dr. Brown. He told me straight out: my constitution is undermined. My nerves are ready to give way. I keep a cheerful countenance and try to carry on the best I can. But there's a limit, and I've just about come to it. I don't know what's to become of me if you do me a trick like this. I just don't know."

Her anguish was real, but it made no sense. There were so many simple and obvious remedies. If it was help with the housework that she needed, all she had to do was to hire it.

Mrs. Harrower's hysteria was still running at the flood when Mr. Harrower came home, and to Archy's amazement seemed neither surprised nor much moved. He greeted Archy with his usual nod (a gesture that had nothing as personal as hostility in it), indicated that he would prefer to be alone with his wife, and shut the door behind Archy as he started up the back stairs to his room.

What if he found himself caught between two sets of closed doors? Archy wondered. Forced to leave the shelter of this house and barred from the mill by order of the superintendent himself! He was still weak enough to feel instantly and physically the effects of fear. He broke into a sweat, his bowels knotted, and he had to sit down where he was on the stairs. He had not intended to eavesdrop, but every word spoken in the kitchen came clearly to his ears.

"If you had nothing to do with it, how is it they took on a colored boy?" Mrs. Harrower was demanding. "I never heard of them hiring one before."

"They'd hire a bear cub if he could hold a broom or a hammer these days," Mr. Harrower said in a voice that was tired, but not angry. "You know I don't meddle in the hiring of hands, and I don't mean to start now, and that's all there is of it, Myra."

There was a fit of loud sobbing. Mr. Harrower waited for it to subside.

"I warned you what would happen when you brought the fellow down. No man, young or old, black or white, or anything in between, will be bound as a servant when he can earn what we're paying hands. And there won't be many women, either, if this goes on. You'd better settle while you can for one of those green Irish—"

"I'll do no such thing! Not if we have to write the children and tell them there's no home for them to come to! Not if we have to close the house and take lodgings in Kingston! I'll have no more of your hussies in my house!"

"Stop it, Myra!"

"That's all you can think of! Some brassy, bright-cheeked, common young thing!"

"If you were yourself, you'd be ashamed."

"I was ashamed! Ashamed to ask decent people into the parlor! The way she looked at you every time she passed. As if she owned you!"

"There was nothing except in your mind."

"Don't tell me that! It may be I got rid of her before things had gone as far as she meant them to, but no credit to you! Talk of *me* being ashamed!"

Mr. Harrower's voice rose in exasperation. "All right! Have it your own way! Get a woman to suit you. Blind, deaf, dumb, toothless, shapeless, maimed! There must be some female so low you can't bring yourself to be jealous of her!"

There was a gasp, a high trickling whine, and then more sobs.

"Before you start in again, let me ask you this," Mr. Harrower said. "Have you stopped to consider which is more apt to cause the kind of talk you fear: a young immigrant girl who goes home to her parents at night or a handsome young mulatto man who sleeps here in the house?"

Archy started to his feet. He wanted to run to his room, but he was afraid to make a sound that would betray his presence. He was forced to listen to the woman's terrible weeping, till it brought tears to his own eyes.

He had never thought of white people as capable of suffering—only of causing it. Secure as fortresses, they had presented nothing but blank walls to him. He had never really looked past those surfaces. He could not, for instance, have described Mrs. Harrower except as white—and heavy—and old. She had been nothing but an answer—a rather inadequate one, but still an answer—to his need of the moment. He had been, he saw now, an answer to several quite different needs of hers, some real, some illusory.

The strange thing was that at this moment he felt even the illusory ones as keenly as his own. It would pass. Tomorrow would insulate him from her humiliation and self-inflicted torment, but for this moment the wall between them was down.

About an hour later, Mr. Harrower came up to Archy's room.

"Have you found a place to lodge?" he asked abruptly. "Because if not, you may as well stay on here till after Christmas."

Archy understood that his job at the mill was secure. This relieved the worst of his anxieties, but it didn't make him want to stay in the house. He hesitated only because he didn't know how to excuse himself.

"You can make yourself useful in your spare time. Your room and meals will cost you nothing."

It would cost him a good deal to have to work here under the lash of reproach, spoken or unspoken, to be wrung with pity and to feel guilt.

"I may as well tell you that you won't find many in Peacedale who'll rent to you," said Mr. Harrower impatiently.

Archy had, then, no choice. He thanked Mr. Harrower, and said he would do his best to earn his keep and to pay back his debt. The man nodded, unimpressed, and went away.

For days it seemed to Archy that a silence encircled him wherever he went. In the Harrowers' kitchen. In the streets of the village. In the mill.

At first the people there stared at him. The women who tended the looms, pale and thin as plucked chickens, jerked nervously away as he swept the ravelings and lint from under their machines. But little by little they stopped. They stopped even turning their dark-circled eyes in his direction. Archy felt he was fading from sight, as a swamp bird fades into matching colors of plant-stem and leaf, moss, wood, and water.

Invisibility and silence made a shell, protecting him. The bad times were when the shell cracked and he stood exposed. When the looms stopped, and the women and girls gathered to eat the lunches they had brought in pails or baskets, or when he stood in line with the men at the paymaster's window. At such times his senses sharpened till he could see and hear what was just beyond sight and hearing, feel a weight of hostility that made him long for a wall to set his back against. But nothing happened to justify the terror that possessed him at those times. After a month he was persuaded that the security was real, the danger unreal.

He was off guard at the moment when doom cracked.

"I was down at the South before the War, and I know a thing or two about them high-yellow bastards."

The voice came from a knot of men lounging in a sheltered corner of the mill yard, smoking their pipes and waiting for the line at the paymaster's window to shorten. Archy was one of the first today. In another moment he would have his pay envelope in his hand.

"How come they to be that color?"

That was a different voice. The first had a nasal whine that placed it in some other part of New England. Rhode Islanders spoke a crisp, clipped speech whose rhythm reminded Archy a little of Gullah talk.

There was a crash of sniggering laughter.

229

The first voice took up again.

". . . son of a yellow whore, born of a brown whore, born of a black whore, as you might say."

Archy turned away from the window and started for the gate, determined to make his way out of the trap before it was sprung. The snarling voice curled out like a whip as he approached the knot of men, but did not break his stride.

Then a foot kicked out.

He stumbled, and the pay envelope flew from his hand. He heard it hit the pavement, but didn't turn his head.

"What's the matter, boy? Don't you care for your money?"

"Most likely he can't bend down to pick it up for fear he'll split his britches. Them white niggers is all too big for their britches, and that's a fact!"

There was another crash of laughter.

"Wall, now, if he don't care enough to bend down for it, reckon he won't care if he loses it."

A man stepped out of the group and retrieved the little envelope, a short, thick-necked, thick-bodied man whom Archy had seen many times and hated from the first. He stood facing Archy now, tossing the envelope in his hand, leering provocatively, daring him to fight for what was his.

Archy's foot arced up and caught the man's wrist. The envelope flew a second time. There was a howl of pain. A drawing-in of breath. A shuffling of feet, as the group drew back, leaving the aggressor isolated. Archy crouched till his head was on a level with the man's crotch. Then he butted hard. The man grunted and fell, and Archy was on top of him, staring down into his watery green eyes, beating the astonishment out of them.

He saw himself and Frank and John fighting together, fighting like a single, furious fiend, a terrible triple monster with six legs, six arms and hands, three heads, three sets of teeth, and thirty tearing nails. So long as he committed himself wholly, Archy had the strength of three. It was a magic that would endure so long as

230

nothing restrained or distracted him from the single objective of destroying his enemy.

Hands snatched at him and he snapped at them. His own hands slipped on the man's face, and he dug in with his nails. Once he was on his feet, stamping and kicking, butting with his head as the barrel-chested thing rose from the ground. Then he was astride it again, and there was a stench of urine and excrement.

Something whistled close to his head. A club had been swung or a brick thrown. It grazed his cheek and hit the man lying on the ground, who grunted and went limp. Archy looked over his shoulder to see if his new assailant was going to strike again.

It was only a thin sliver of time, but it was enough to break the spell.

"There! Get him!"

Someone caught him from behind. Strong arms pinned his arms to his sides.

"Got him!"

"Sure you can hold him?"

"Get him off Sam."

He was yanked up and back. There was a babble of voices. Heads closed in between him and the man on the ground.

"By God, he's killed him!"

"No!"

"It was the brick done it!"

"Somebody get water. We can bring him to."

"Somebody call the constable."

"To hell with the constable. We ought to string him up ourselves. The dirty little coon!"

Archy was pulled back another step, and a voice hissed in his ear. "Hear that? Run!"

The arms released him, and he ran.

He darted out the mill gates, turned in the direction of the North Road as if he were going to the Harrowers', ran a short distance, and ducked into a lane, jumped a fence, and made his way through backyards, in a circle that took him back to the stream that powered the mill. He worked his way into a thicket of bushes that lined its bank just a hundred yards from the building, and stopped.

There was no sound of pursuit. Nothing but the humming of machinery, the booming of the blood in his own ears, and the groan of his own breath. But he waited till darkness fell before he left the thicket and made a wide circle around the village, crashing through bogs and stumbling over dry stone dikes and oak scrub, till at last he saw the lights of the Harrowers' kitchen.

He hid in the barn and watched to be sure no one was lying in wait for him at the back door. He was filthy and disheveled. His feet were caked with mud, his clothes ripped, first by live hands and later by dead branches. He felt dried blood on his cheek where the brick had taken the skin with it. No doubt his hands were bloody, too. There was nothing in the barn with which to clean himself.

He approached the house warily, hoping to slip in by the back door, and get up to his room so that he could wash and change clothes before he had to face the Harrowers. He waited for a minute or so on the back stoop, listening for voices, and at last—having heard none—he opened the door.

Mr. Harrower was leaning over the kitchen table, speaking to his wife in a low, intense whisper.

"The foreman told me he fought like an animal! Gouging and kicking and biting! He said he'd never in his whole life seen—"

He broke off as he saw Archy. Mrs. Harrower turned, and screamed. Her husband came to stand between them, as if to protect her from assault. There were anger and disgust on the face where Archy had never seen anything but indifference.

"You'll have to leave," Mr. Harrower said. "You can't go back to the mill after what happened this afternoon, and we don't want you here."

"Whatever made you do such a thing?" Mrs. Harrower asked in a quavery voice. "You never showed temper around here."

"No one would have blamed you for defending yourself," Mr. Harrower said. "Sam Cotton's not well liked hereabouts. But men fight with their fists."

For one frozen moment Archy thought of leaping on this enemy and felling him as he felled the other, beating the cold, unjust words back into the white throat. Instead he drew his fists tight against his sides.

Without a word or a look at either of the Harrowers, he turned and went up to his room. He tied his ruined clothes in a bundle and put on clean ones, those he had worn when he came here, so that he was taking nothing he had not brought. Then he went back down the stairs to the kitchen, where Mr. Harrower was waiting.

"I've got your money," he said nervously. "You'd better take it. You'll need it."

"You keep it. Put it to what I owe you."

It gave Archy the keenest delight not to stop, but to walk out and shut the door behind him.

Little by little, the furnace heat in his head cooled, till at last, like a fish in its element, he was at one with the cold December night.

He walked the forty-five miles to Boston.

It took him three days. Late in the afternoon of the third, half famished, aching with weariness and cold, he opened the door of the office of the Freedman's Relief Society.

Frank was sitting at the reception desk in the young lady's chair. He looked up at Archy, and grinned.

"Well, you made it pretty fast, I'll say!" Frank said. "I didn't think you'd even get my letter till today." And he went on jabbering nonsense about Mrs. Pillsbury and Mauma and Lincoln and somebody named Randall.

Archy could make neither heads nor tails of it. His mind had to thaw out a little, like the muscles of his jaw and tongue.

"Here! You read the letter, if you don't believe me!"

Frank thrust a letter into his hands. The postmark on it was Charleston. There were two letters inside, one from Mrs. Pillsbury to him and Frank, the other addressed to Mrs. Pillsbury and signed by the Reverend Isaac Randall of Lincoln University. Archy read that one first:

> *. . . Have the young men come here and I will do all I can for them. From what you write I judge they do not qualify as regular first-year students. But we have decided to offer a preparatory course for those whose opportunities have been limited but who possess both the ability and the determination to make up their deficiencies.*
>
> *For admission to this department we ask only that the entrant be able to read, write a fair hand, and know arithmetic through fractions. . . .*

The office door opened, and Frank jumped to his feet, smiling broadly.

"This here is Archy," he said.

The man who had just entered wrung Archy's hand. "My name is Josiah Wentworth. I'm delighted to meet you. I was away from the city when you came through the first time. Most unfortunate! But all's well that ends well, eh? You've seen the letter from Dr. Randall?"

He had hung up his hat and overcoat and was moving toward the big desk, talking about how the offer from Lincoln University was the answer to prayer. "You have both prayed, I'm sure. My wife and I have done so nightly since we were made aware of your plight. The Lord has heard His servants' petition and given the sign of His grace."

"Amen!" said Frank.

Archy thought for a moment that he was jeering, but the expression on Frank's face was serious. In another moment he and Reverend Wentworth were discussing the practical details of the journey: what homes the boys would stay at en route, what clothing they would need, what money . . .

Archy wanted to tell Frank to go on without him; that he had been called the yellow son of a black whore, an animal, something beneath even the hatred of a white man; that he could never forget it, never forgive; that he hated his persecutors so that he could not live in the same world with them; and worst of all, that he hated himself because he was part of that world, bound to it not only by his name but the color of his skin, his hair, his eyes, and perhaps other things he had yet to discover.

But he funked it.

"Archy writes a real fine hand," Frank said, and turned to him, beaming. "You better write the letter to Dr. Randall, Archy, and we'll get it into the mail that goes today."

Later, when he tried to tell Frank what it was he wanted to do, it was too late. His half-made plan sounded foolish even to himself. . . .

*　　*　　*

They had been walking a long time in silence. It was beginning to get dark. Suddenly out of a side road that led to a farmhouse a chicken came strutting. Without a word, without an instant's pause, they both started to chase it.

The chicken ran squawking ahead of them; they followed, slipping and sliding in the snowy tracks, laughter making them awkward, till the farm's gate barred the way. The chicken went under the lowest rail. Archy dived just too late and buried his face in the snow. Frank hauled him out by one leg, howling like a gleeful demon.

"Like when you chased that chicken under that board fence," he gasped. "You 'member that, Archy?"

He had caught it by the tail feathers, and it was making such a fuss he couldn't hear the corporal yelling at him to let go because he had it by the neck on the other side! It was during their days as foragers, when they rode with the Yankees that were scouring the back country for the last of Wheeler's cavalry, looting and pillaging, gorging themselves on the painfully hoarded stores of white households they came upon, killing pigs and chickens they had no time to cook, taking no thought of how the white women and children they were robbing would live till their men came home. Archy had been filled with remorse and regret when the raids were over. But now he regretted only the remorse. If he had it to do over, he would not stop at pigs and chickens! . . .

"That was the same old corporal tried to roast a gander with the feathers on him," Frank was saying.

Relief was welling up like tears under his laughter, and Archy didn't have the heart to warn him against it. Better let it happen "naturally." Without arguments or accusations, or the anguish of a real parting. They would travel together to Fayetteville in June. Frank would go to his school, Archy to his. But when it came to the summer's end . . .

It would be as easy as dying.

Archy would simply not be there. Frank would wait for a while, and then go on to see Mauma, hoping to find Archy there ahead of him. They would wait together—he and Mauma and John—till it was time for Frank to go on back to Oxford, where he would finish his schooling and go on to be what they all wanted.

Archibald Grimké would never be heard of again. Someone else would use the other half of that round-trip ticket north. Someone else would spend the money earned in the black country school to buy passage away from the white world, perhaps to the great black continent of Africa where, if he tried long and hard enough, he might lose the white half of himself.

XII

The trouble must have started before the train stopped at Fairmount. Angelina and Stuart had just found their seats, had not yet presented their tickets, when the conductor's voice was raised somewhere behind them in anger too hot to have been generated on the instant.

"Don't show me yer goddamned pass again. I c'n read, if you can't. The gentleman there told you what it means. Nothin'! Not a goddamned thing in the world!"

The voice that answered him was equally angry, but low, pitched so close to the rumble of the moving car that all the words were lost.

"Half fare me eye!" The conductor's voice went still higher. "You pay like anyone else, m'boy, or off y'go! I don't know as y'ought to be sitting in here anyways, with white ladies on the car."

Angelina and Stuart turned to see the disputants.

The conductor was a thin-faced, thin-shouldered, thin-haired man, his blue serge uniform shiny in some places, patched in others, his shirt collar white but not clean, his manner aggrieved, whatever tolerance he was born with long ago exhausted in the battle not to be pushed lower than he was. The man he was berating was a Negro, dressed in shabby rags that might or might not have once been military issue, and a cap that almost certainly was; very dark, younger, bigger and stronger than the conductor, not averse to settling the point at issue by physical combat if he was pushed to that point.

Several other passengers had also swung round in their seats and some were already entering the fracas. Out of the babel of threats, explanations, advice, and imprecations, Angelina caught enough to understand that the Negro was attempting to use an old army pass for half the fare between Boston and Springfield. The conductor was beside himself with indignation, out of all proportion to the apparent cause.

"Think ye're going to ride free the rest of yer black life?" he demanded. "Jes' because ye rolled a few barrels and dug some latrines? While white men was fightin' yer damn war and winnin' it fer ye! I lost one son and come near losin' another. And fer what?" His voice cracked like an old man's and he seemed near tears. "So's the likes of you c'n ride around like ye owned the earth, expectin' favors yer betters wouldn't think to ask!"

There were cries of "Shame!" but it was not clear to which of the pair they were addressed.

Angelina's head was beginning to roar so that only the visual aspect of the impending violence reached her, as the conductor grabbed for the worthless pass and tore it in the Negro's hand. Rage thundered and lightning licked her with its tongue. She caught Stuart's arm, pulled herself to her feet, and cried out.

"You profane your own sons' sacrifice! You disgrace yourself, your country, and your kind!"

Stuart was tugging at her elbow, but she would not be still. The power was in her, and she must use it! She must put out this brush

238

fire of bigotry! And yet, though her tongue moved with the old pentecostal frenzy, no one seemed to be listening. No head was turned, not even those closest.

Was she speechless?

The roaring in her ears made her deaf. Was she dumb as well? She turned to Stuart and read the answer in his embarrassed smile.

"It's all right, Mother. The gentlemen are separating them."

As she let herself down into the seat, a group of men pushed the Negro up the aisle toward the front of the car.

"They must not . . . do him harm."

Stuart either heard her or read her lips. "They're just going to keep them apart till both sides cool off a little," he said. "I'm sure there's no more to it than that."

"Say . . . we will pay . . . his fare."

She handed Stuart her purse, closed her eyes, leaned back against the sooty green plush of the seat, and began her old ritual against fainting: breathing deeply (though the air of the car left an acrid, metallic smell in her nostrils) and drumming her gloved fingers on her thighs in the rhythm, first of the Lord's Prayer, then of the Twenty-third Psalm.

"How on earth could he?" asked a shrill female voice behind her. "He couldn't just let anyone who happens to have some old piece of paper ride for nothing. That would be the same as stealing from the railroad."

Angelina could hear now, almost too well. Conversation in the car had been stilled while the Negro was being ejected, but it began again, like echoes returning, doubled and redoubled.

"It's the malcontents and misfits that come up here for the most part," a man was saying. "The others are perfectly content to stay down where they belong."

Someone else was talking about military service, debating whether black soldiers had or had not fought well, whether they would have done as well for the Confederacy if Lee had been permitted to arm them when he wanted to.

". . . matter of education, I suppose."

"No, it's not. Nothing to do with it. It's in the blood. Cross them and you get the worst of both. That's a proven fact."

Across the aisle someone laughed.

Angelina felt laughter pushing up in her own throat. She had heard all of this before. She had run away from it in Charleston, only to have it catch up with her here, a few short years after the War that was to have wiped the slate clean of all such ancient obscenities.

". . . don't know any better. They're just like children."

"I'll tell you one thing: I'd hire colored before free Irish, if I had the choice. Don't give you half the trouble, once you let them know who's boss."

Only one thing was missing, and now that came too.

"I got nothing against them, you understand. But what I say is this: somebody's got to draw the line pretty sharp and pretty soon. Or those nigger-loving Abolitionists will have them lording it over the rest of us, marrying themselves white wives. That is, if they take the trouble to marry."

Angelina shuddered.

"It's all right, Mother," Stuart slipped into the seat beside her. "The man is going to ride the rest of the way to Springfield in the baggage car. He had already paid half his fare and he won't have the rest paid for him. I offered. The conductor is willing to let it go at that, provided he stays where he is."

(She was back in the Friends' Meeting in Philadelphia. She and Sarah were brushing past the Friend who stood at the entrance to the black pew, taking their places beside the two Negro women who sat there. She saw the look on their faces as they turned. . . .)

"I shall ride in the baggage car with him," she said aloud.

Stuart looked to see if she meant it. "You can't, Mother. It's very cold in there. And I don't believe you could even make your way to it, with the train swaying as it does."

She heard in his voice the high harmonics of dissent. He spoke

240

to placate her, to calm her. But he was appalled, not so much by the outrage they had witnessed, as the possibility that she might make a scene in protest against it.

Why had he volunteered to come?

"I'll sit with the man if it will make you feel easier," Stuart said. Angelina shook her head.

"You don't want me to?"

She shook her head again. What meaning would there be in such a gesture? It would bring no comfort to the man who had been wounded by hate, for there was no love in it.

She leaned back in her seat, trying to nap, but the clatter of the wheels made it impossible. The quarrel between the Negro veteran and the conductor played itself over in her mind. She had been told that this sort of thing was occurring more and more frequently all over the North, but the forewarning did not make the experience easier to bear.

What was even harder to bear was her own part—or rather, her failure to bear a part in it: the loss of her voice at the very instant she felt the urge to use it in the old way. As she rose to cry out against the injustice to a black brother, she saw the Black Sister, and was frightened into speechlessness. It was almost like the other time . . . the time she lost her gift of tongues, because she cut it off at its source. . . .

*　　*　　*

That was in the first year of her marriage. She and Sarah were helping Thoda with his book. They read southern newspapers for advertisements and news items about runaways. They read private testimonies, eyewitness accounts of atrocities—some written by northern visitors to southern plantations, some by Southerners like themselves who had renounced the evil and were willing to expose their own and others' sins. There was little in all this that Angelina did not already know of, but the tales white ladies had told in her hearing, and even those black women had confided to her, had all been mercifully vague.

Now it was different. Now she knew the reality of physical love and could imagine its opposite: the ultimate intimacy perverted to the ultimate insult. Shorn of her innocence she lived out each violation in all its sickening detail. Sometimes she could not recover herself quickly enough to respond to Thoda in love.

And there was no end to it, no escape. As the weeks went by, the burden of anguish and horror grew. She was already pregnant when she had to copy out the story of a plantation master who offered another white man twenty dollars for every wench he could get in a family way, "in an effort to improve the stock." She was beginning to imagine that awesome moment when she would hold her own baby in her arms, when she came upon an account of a slave auction at which black babies had been torn, sucking, from the nipples of their mothers, who were to be shipped to Louisiana, where an infant detracted from the value of a female hand.

One evening, not long before Stuart was born, she sat after supper reading a letter written by a New York merchant who had toured Carolina and Georgia and had stopped with several of his business connections there. He wrote of one man—the owner of a small general store—who kept two mulatto sisters as clerks, so that one was always available to wait upon his customers if he should be moved by a whim of lust to lead the other up to the bed he kept in a room just above.

Thoda came up behind her so quietly that she had no warning. He laid his hand on her shoulder, and she recoiled.

It was so strong an involuntary movement that there was no possibility of his overlooking or misunderstanding. She was afraid to look up at him, to see how hurt he was. And she could not explain or excuse herself. Not without wounding him even more deeply. For how could she tell her beloved that she had mistaken his touch for that of another man—a loathsome, lecherous whore-monger and slave master!

They went up to their chamber in silence and lay down, separated by silence vaster than space. Angelina knew by Thoda's breathing when he fell asleep at last, but she could not sleep. She looked back over the months of her marriage and ahead to the years. . . . Slowly and heavily it came to her that there was only one way to save herself. She could not carry her own fears and sorrows and those of her Black Sister as well. Together they crushed her hopes and her joys. Her own life was all she could live from here on. She must close and bar the door of her self. She must never again open to admit the presence that had given her voice its power.

She was punished for her cowardice the next time she tried to address an audience. It was an occasion of no particular consequence, a small group of women already in sympathy with her view. They listened politely to her feeble, stammering speech, and thanked her when she was done.

Angelina knew better than they how dismally she had failed. She preferred never to make the test again, but to find other ways to bear her share of the ongoing work, helping Thoda with other pamphlets, with petitions and letters, freeing him to return to the field as much as his health permitted, playing the woman's part, for which the world had said she was unfit.

It had been hard for her at times, easy at others. There were satisfactions—not as intense as she had been led to hope, but still very precious. There had been failures, too. . . . The only one that still mattered was her failure as a mother, especially to her firstborn, her son.

Angelina wanted children. She was a little fearful of the ordeal of bearing them at her age and in her state of health, but she conquered—or concealed—her fears, and the victory over pain was all the sweeter. Stuart was born perfect, without a blemish! And her milk came plentifully, despite her weariness and weakness. The joy of feeling her babe suck helped her begin the precarious transition from the old Angelina to the new. But before it was complete, before she could believe herself ordained as a true woman, a giver and nurturer of the divine spark of life—her body failed.

She suffered the affliction of a "gathered" breast. Her fever shot up so high that the milk stopped even in the healthy breast. She lay with one empty and the other like a stone, listening to Stuart whimper while Sarah tried to coax him to suck from a glass bottle, and she utterly despaired.

From the infection she recovered, but not from the bad start at motherhood. She performed her maternal duties, but never with confidence, never with real joy. It was to Sarah the children turned for the sustenance without which their bodies and their spirits would have starved.

Perhaps Stuart had been starved even so. Perhaps what Sarah had to give him was not enough. What he felt for his aunt was more than he felt for anyone else, either within the family or outside it, but lately it seemed to Angelina that it was only a feeble, frightened substitute for love.

Stuart was young, not yet thirty, in what should be the prime of his manhood. Yet compared to his father, he seemed spent with age. Thoda had abused his body in his own youth in ways he was still paying for, but even so, he had to struggle constantly against the impulse to commit himself to new enterprises too challenging for his strength, while Stuart seemed to have to struggle to nerve himself up to those actions that were the minimal requirements of life in the physical as well as the moral world. Ambitious for anonymity, he interested himself only in causes long dead or far removed. . . .

Angelina glanced over to see what book he had brought along to read on the journey. It was in French. Something about the conflict between the Ottoman Empire and the oppressed peoples of Moldavia.

Stuart looked up and asked, "What sort of man was my Uncle Henry?"

"What sort of man . . . ?" The question was so unrelated to what she had been thinking that Angelina did not really understand it. "He was fine looking," she said. "Rather tall. His face was long, like mine, and our coloring was much the same, except that his eyes were a grayer blue. . . ." This was not what Stuart wanted. But how could she describe Henry to him, except in meaningless comparisons? Henry was not as courageous or as brilliant as Thomas, nor as indolent or greedy as Charles, not as narrowly conventional as John. . . . "There was much good in him," she went on, uncertainly. "He truly wanted to do right, I believe. But it was so hard for a man."

"Harder than for a woman?" Stuart asked ironically.

"Yes. Women counted for so little, they could be indulged in things like pity, tenderness, Christian love. But in a man these things were dangerous. Everything was dangerous that was not useful in the government of slaves. It had to be stamped out. Otherwise the slaves would sense a weakness and be encouraged to revolt."

Stuart was shuttering himself against "preachment." But there was no way to convey the reality of terror to someone who had never been obsessed by it. She could describe the collective nightmare fear of rape, riot, arson, vengeance, but Stuart would not feel panic. He would ask her if the fears were not groundless, and she would have to say that for the most part they were but that that had not diminished their power.

"Henry was intelligent and well read. He practiced the law. He was not a leader in the profession as our father was. He had no particular ambition of his own, but he disliked being led by the ambitions of others, and he could be very stubborn in his resistance. All he really wanted was to live pleasantly, honorably, fulfilling his obligations, earning the respect of his friends and the love of those he loved."

It could have been Stuart she was speaking of!

The likeness was not a physical one, and it had never occurred to her before. But it was profound. All she had just said about Henry was true of Stuart, and something more was also true of both. Both were men placed in circumstances where their best was not good enough. More was asked of them than they had to give. Henry was destroyed by the evil around him, from which he could not escape, against which he was not strong enough to fight alone. Stuart was in danger of being destroyed by good, by the atmosphere of a household of dedicated reformers, by the demands they made on themselves and others. He had tried to live up to them, and failed, tried and failed again. He had retreated from each failure, confining himself to smaller and smaller spaces, to demands so minute that they could be met without effort, even by him.

Angelina saw now what Stuart had hoped to achieve by his stubborn refusal to fight in the War. That was *his* war. He had hoped to win a moral victory and approval, at least from Sarah, the pacifist of the family. But he had only failed again.

And she saw something else: that Stuart was still trying. That was why he had offered to come on this pilgrimage with her. He hoped to be of some help. If he succeeded—even in a limited way— he would live more easily with himself. But already, at the very start, he was being faced with challenges he had not the strength to meet. If he failed again, he would retreat still farther into himself.

"Are you all right, Mother?"

She opened her eyes and saw that he was bending toward her, frowning concern.

"Yes, my dear. Why?"

"You gave a little moan and twisted, as if you were in some sort of pain."

"Did I really? . . . I don't know. . . . I must have dozed off and began to dream."

"If you feel ill, it would be better to get off at Springfield, and go home," he said. "We could try again in a week or so. After all, we are not expected."

"The Tappans expect us in New York. Arthur is going to meet us at the depot." She patted his hand and smiled encouragement. "I shall be quite all right with you to look after me."

She was able to live out her optimistic prediction. After a restful day at the Tappans', she bore the trip to Philadelphia so well that if there had been a stage for Oxford in the afternoon she would have insisted on going on. Instead, they spent another pleasant and restful night with old friends, and started out early in the morning.

By noon, they were approaching Oxford.

"Does this road pass anywhere close to Lincoln University?" Angelina inquired of the gentleman who sat next to her and whom she judged, from his conversation, to be a native of the town.

"We still call it Ashmun hereabouts," the man said. "We passed right by it, not five minutes ago."

Angelina tried to look back, but the road was curving in the wrong direction.

"They teach blacks, you know," the man added. "Blacks and mixed bloods. I'll say this much for them, though: they stay to themselves. You could live here a whole year running and never set eyes on a one of them."

The few discreet questions they asked at the inn where Angelina and Stuart engaged rooms brought answers of the same sort. Apparently, the town held itself aloof, regarding the school as one unfortunate aspect of an otherwise desirable environment, something like the muggy cold of the south-Pennsylvania winter, upon which it was not good form for a visitor to comment.

Visually, however, Lincoln was an ornament to the landscape. Set on the highest of a group of rolling hills, it consisted of three handsome new buildings: a main one, four stories high, topped with a cupola; and flanking it, two fine residences. All three were of light-red brick; all the window trim was white; all the shutters were dark green. Young trees were planted on both sides of the drive up which Angelina and Stuart walked. A little pathetic in their winter nudity, they were—like the imposing title of "university"—a testimony to aspirations, if not to achievement. "A brave start" were the words that came into Angelina's mind.

She had insisted upon walking because she hoped the air and

the exercise would calm her and give her strength. She was not disappointed. But Stuart had derived no such benefit. He could not conceal his uneasiness as they turned up the path to the larger of the two residences.

A bright brass plate under the knocker identified it as the home of President Isaac Randall, D.D. Stuart looked to her for a final directive. She nodded. He lifted the knocker and let it fall as if it were the blade of a guillotine.

Dr. Randall, into whose office they were ushered by his wife, was a dignified middle-aged gentleman, younger than Angelina, but not by so much as his manner implied. He treated her like a relic of some distant, heroic past, piling up formal compliments and exaggerated estimates of her accomplishments without a single specific reference, till she wondered if he was not quite sure what it was she had done in the Abolition movement. He was also very careful not to ask any question that might ease the way into an explanation of her errand.

"I read in the *Anti-Slavery Standard* about one of your students," she began at last, awkwardly. "A young man who won a prize for oratory."

Dr. Randall smiled blandly. "There were a number of outside visitors on that occasion. It was, as you doubtless recall, the unveiling of a painting that had been presented to the university. Congressman Shellabarger was among our honored guests. He has taken an interest in the institution since its inception, but he had never before visited us. He was so moved by what he heard and saw, and spoke with such enthusiasm when he returned to Philadelphia, that one of the newspapers there commissioned an article by Professor Bowers. It has been rather widely reprinted."

He seemed to be talking to give her time to decide whether to go on or to draw back.

"The young man bears the name of Grimké, which is my maiden name," she said.

Dr. Randall showed no surprise. "We have two students of that name," he said. "It was Archibald who was mentioned in Professor Bowers' article, but Francis is equally promising. Indeed, he applies himself more assiduously, and I believe he may accomplish more in the end."

Why was the man treading with such elaborate caution? Could he possibly misunderstand her intention?

"They are the sons of my brother," she said.

The president made a gesture of what seemed to be polite regret.

"My sister and I knew nothing of their having come north," Angelina went on. "In fact, we knew nothing of their existence. We wonder that no one took the trouble to inform us."

"We here knew only that they had taken a name which was made illustrious by your sister and yourself."

He was not being candid, even now.

"I will not pretend that this has not been a shock," she said. "But it is too late to mend the past. We are interested only in the future and how to make it fruitful. That is why I have come."

Dr. Randall looked less, not more, at ease. "Did the boys know that you were coming?"

Angelina shook her head.

"I wonder if you will permit me to advise you in what I realize is a deeply—a painfully personal—concern," he said. "I honor your intentions, but I am very much afraid you will find obstacles you have not anticipated."

"Obstacles of what sort?"

"Your only wish is to help these young men?" He waited for her assent. "Very well. They are in need of help, and it will not be wasted on them. But they will be more grateful—or at least *it is possible* that they will be—if the help is given without acknowledging or in any way making public the relationship that impels you to offer it."

"There has been enough cowardice and dishonesty already!"

Angelina spoke heatedly, and the president halted her with a lifted hand.

"I am speaking only from the viewpoint of the boys," he reminded her. "You, as a Christian woman, can surely understand that they may prefer to draw a veil over sins not of their committing. I am not saying that this is so. But there are many—among them our most gifted and promising students—who prefer to know nothing of the circumstances of their birth."

"But these boys have taken their father's name!"

Dr. Randall gave her a look that Angelina found it impossible to interpret.

"The name signifies nothing," he said. "Most of our young men use the name of their former owners, for no better reason than that they are accustomed to being called by it. Smithers' John becomes John Smithers. Nothing is implied and no questions are asked. Not here, at any rate."

Angelina was growing confused and unsure of herself. "I shall impose nothing on them," she said quickly. "I feel they have been robbed of much—of their freedom, as long as that was possible. Of their patrimony even now. We owe them the right to their name and to whatever else we have to share."

Dr. Randall made another of his odd, regretful gestures. "I only wanted to warn you," he said. "We will put the west parlor at your disposal. The boys will be excused from their classes. You may talk, undisturbed, as long as you wish."

The photograph in Archibald's letter had prepared Angelina for the family resemblance, but it was more startling in the flesh. Both boys were very light-skinned. Many white men she knew, who lived a good deal out-of-doors, were as brown or browner, and the boys' skin color set off the blue glint in their gray eyes.

Their clothes were someone's castoffs. Francis's hung on him so that he looked like a pitifully frail young scarecrow; Archibald's had an elegance that accentuated his likeness to Henry, who had been something of a dandy in his youth. Their greeting was formal, pronounced in speech more free of Charlestonisms than her own, and utterly devoid of feeling. It was as if they were manipulating images of themselves from some remote distance.

Conversation was incredibly awkward, real communication out of the question. Angelina asked, and the boys answered all the obvious questions.

Were they enjoying their studies?

Yes, indeed, they were.

Did they do well on the midyear examination just past?

Yes, they did.

"Are you taking the same subjects this semester as last?"

Yes, they were.

"Except Greek," Archibald added. "We are just beginning the study of ancient Greek."

Stuart made an attempt to enter the conversation. He had done well at Greek, and once thought of teaching it. "You may find it quite hard at the start," he informed them in the lofty tone of a pedant. "But don't be discouraged. If you keep on till you're able to read the works of the poets and historians, like Homer and Thucydides, everything will come easy and seem very much worth while."

Archibald nodded condescendingly. "I found it to be so in Latin," he said.

Stuart stood rebuked without knowing his sin, and the conversation ran aground on a bar of silence.

"Have you heard recently from your mother?" Angelina asked. "How is she?"

"Mother is well. She is a nurse now, in the home of a family we have known for some time. A *sick* nurse."

"Does she live with the family?"

"No. She has to be home in the evenings to give John his supper."

"But John'll be coming here," Francis said.

"Yes. And then I expect Mother will go to live with our cousins so as not to be alone."

"Your brother is coming here to Lincoln?" Angelina asked in surprise. "You said nothing about it in your letter."

"We didn't know till just the other day." Archibald said, and after a short silence, asked, "Would you like to see a picture of our mother and our brother? We received one in the letter that told of his coming north."

There were two pictures, mounted on a single cardboard. One was that of a woman of middle height and slender frame, dressed in a gown that looked like silk, buttoned from chin to its tight waistline, with tight-cuffed sleeves and a long, flaring skirt. She was standing before a tasseled curtain, one hand reaching out to rest on the cover of a book laid on a small table beside her. A conventional portrait of a conventional Charleston matron, except that her skin was dark! The boy was posed beside the same table. He resembled the mother more than either Archibald or Francis did. But the characters of the two were in startling contrast: John was a dullard by his looks; Nancy was a drawn sword.

"It's a great sacrifice your mother is making." Angelina handed the picture on to Stuart. "Sending the last of her sons away."

"We going down to see her this summer," Francis said, and smiled for the first time.

"You're going to Charleston?" Angelina asked. "We thought perhaps you would be working somewhere in the North."

"No, ma'am," Francis again deferred to Archibald, but when he gave no indication that he intended to enter the conversation, Francis went on. "We got positions to teach school in North Carolina. We'll go on home at the end, leastways we will if we've saved money enough."

Archibald turned quickly and shook his head. Angelina felt— but was not sure—that he was reprimanding his brother for what might be interpreted as a subtle request for monetary assistance.

"We hoped you would find yourselves close enough to pay us a visit," she said, to keep the conversation from running aground again. Stuart was no help. His contretemps with Archibald had driven him into a silent contemplation of the double photograph. "There's so much we'd like to show you, in and around Boston."

"We been to Boston already," Francis said.

"You've been to Boston? When?"

"Before we came down here," Archibald said quickly. "We were supposed to go to school there, the way Mrs. Pillsbury had it planned. But—there was a mix-up and—well, we didn't. We came here instead."

"How long were you in Boston?"

Francis looked at Archibald, and this time their eyes met and held. Some sort of communication was taking place, but she was deaf and blind to its content.

"Quite some time," Archibald said.

No use to ask other questions. She would get no answers but those she could shake from the facts themselves. The boys had been in Boston. They had hoped to go to school there and been disappointed. Two young lads, strangers in a strange city, a thousand miles from their home, probably without funds, certainly without friends! They knew they had an aunt . . . *Miss Angelina Grimké of Anti-Slavery notoriety or celebrity!* They had chosen not to come to her. Why?

A bell rang in the cupola above the building. There was a scuffling of feet in the corridors, and the sound of voices. Both boys' eyes turned to the clock on the parlor wall. Another class period was beginning. They were hoping not to miss that too.

It was all coming to nothing. It was her own fault. She had turned, without meaning to, from the straight path.

"I want to speak to you about your father," she said. And to Archibald, "Do you remember him at all?"

For the first time the boy seemed uncomfortable. "I—think so, ma'am," he said slowly. "At least, what he looked like."

"I wish I had a picture of him when he was your age," she said impulsively. "You are so like him!"

Archibald winced as if she had slapped him, and she understood instantly how grossly she had erred.

"Will you let me tell you a little about him?" She included Francis in her question this time. "You are his sons, and you have a right to know that no matter how he sinned against your mother —and you—there was much in his character you need feel no shame to inherit."

Neither of the boys gave any sign of response, but they were no longer impatient to be gone.

"I am sure you have been taught to hate him, and it is right that you should," she continued earnestly. "But only the weakness in him. Not the whole man."

Archibald interrupted her coldly. "Our mother did not teach us to hate our father, madam. She did not hate him herself."

Angelina was too startled to hide it.

"She hates Montague Grimké," Francis said, as if this might be of some help to her. "Mauma say it's a sin to hate, but she hates him. And we do, too."

Archibald smiled tolerantly. "Frank's right. Our mother is a very religious person and she tries always to walk in the way of the meek and lowly Jesus. But she has a devil of anger to contend with, and I'm afraid Montague Grimké has the power to stir him up."

"You mean . . . ? But your mother *must* have hated Henry!"

"On the contrary," said Archibald. "She loved him very much. I have reason to feel she loves him still."

It was utterly fantastic. As if he were not the wronged son of a wronged woman, not the offspring of a man's mortal sin, but some urbane young gentleman from a country where the color of one's skin and the observance of the sacraments were matters of no consequence!

"You think she hated him because he forced her? Believe me, madam, you are wrong. If you stop to think a little, you will see it could not have been so. You've seen our mother's picture. Can you

254

imagine that such a woman would have permitted herself to be misused, not once but many times?"

It was true. The woman in the photograph was not the Black Sister of Angelina's imagination, not the passive victim who had begged her pastor to help her choose which authority to submit herself to, not a woman to be pitied or pleaded for. . . .

"But when a woman has no rights . . . none at all . . . she can be forced in so many ways," Angelina murmured.

"Mauma would have killed any man who tried!"

"What you know 'bout such things, Archy?" Frank said, so low it seemed he hoped not to be heard by the others in the room.

"I know what happened one time he did raise a hand to her," Archy answered fiercely; still looking at Angelina, as if it were she who had challenged him. "She throwed him down on the ground and held him there!"

"Him?" Frank asked in astonishment.

"That's right. Same as she done to that fat old white woman, time she come into our yard, fussin' 'bout our pigeons." Archy's old ways of speech broke through like a rush of blood from a wound. "Mauma done the same to our father! Held him down till she got good and ready to let him up."

The story that poured out of him now was incredible. Yet every detail made sense by itself. The boy had heard it from someone who had witnessed the whole scene, a slave woman on the Bellemont plantation, when Selina was still living.

"It was Miss Selina said he was to whip Mauma in the first place."

"Selina?" Angelina could not suppress her disbelief.

"That's who," Archibald insisted. "Miss Selina wanted Mauma to take a husband, and Mauma wouldn't. So Miss Selina told our father to give Mauma a whipping that would change her mind."

That was what Angelina could not accept. The rest was all credible. Even Nancy's fanatical pride and physical strength. But not the roles assigned to Selina and Henry. They might have done—*had* done—many wrongs, but not of this sort. Someone else—not Selina—wanted to see Nancy mated like a brood mare. Someone else—not poor, gentle Selina—wanted her whipped when she refused. Someone else—not Henry—pronounced the ludicrous threat that was supposed to cover his humiliation.

". . . he stood up and pulled his clothes straight and said to Mauma, 'Go 'long 'bout your business, and don't sass you' missis again, or I'll have to give you another whippin'.'"

Archibald spat out the final line as if it had a foul taste. He looked defiantly at Angelina, his eyes hot and dry of tears.

"When was this supposed to have happened?" she asked.

"Long before! It was even before Miss Selina took sick. She grew much attached to our mother during her illness." Archibald had gone back to his cold, didactic tone. "She would have set Mauma free if that had been possible.

"It was not till four years after Miss Selina died that our father bought the place in St. Paul's Parish. He left Miss Eliza to look after the house in Charleston and took Mauma to Caneacres. I was born at the end of the first summer. Frank was born the next."

Angelina could not grasp the import of this arithmetic. Both boys were watching her as if they expected her to say something; to explain the paradox—the two Nancys, one larger than life, a heroic figure that was both mother and father to her sons, overcoming unbelievable obstacles to keep their bodies alive and teach them the Christian values and the Puritan ethic, defending them and herself with reckless ferocity; the other, a concubine who invited—or, at the very least, made no resistance against—a fate that thousands of her sisters, weaker in every way than she, fought at the cost of their lives.

The bell in the cupola rang again.

Frank got to his feet.

"We ought not to be absent from our next class," Archibald said stiffly. "We are sensible of the honor you have done us by coming."

"We want to help." Angelina felt tears swelling in her throat.

She wanted to offer them money, enough to make sure they could go home after their summer's work, but she was afraid to say so. "If you will tell us what you need—"

"Thank you, madam, there is nothing."

"I think we had better go now, Mother," Stuart said. "You must not overdo. You'll make yourself ill."

He was right. She was already feeling dizzy. The doctor said she must lie down and stay quiet if that happened. Stuart was making her excuses and saying their good-byes.

They drove back to Oxford in Dr. Randall's carriage, Stuart talking with animation that was as real as it was rare. He had been very much impressed by both of the boys. They had fine stuff in them, he thought. Much promise.

More promise than Stuart himself, Angelina thought sadly. If not finer stuff, surely more fire . . . What had their slave mother given them that she had not been able to give her son?

"The young one is very sensitive. Very proud, of course, and not at all anxious to take any sort of favor. But you can feel a warmth under his reserve. Didn't you think so, Mother?"

Angelina nodded, and found that even so slight a movement made her head throb.

"I was curious about one thing," Stuart continued. "Why was it, do you suppose, that Archibald had never told his brother that story?"

"Because it is very painful," Angelina said slowly. "It was much easier to believe the other . . . what I believed. . . ."

"Then why did he tell it today?"

"He was angry. He wanted to inflict pain."

"On whom?"

"On us . . . on all white people."

"But he is half white himself," Stuart objected. "That's the great difference between him and the young man Father was telling us

257

about in Cincinnati. *He* at least could hate white people with a whole heart. . . ."

Angelina could no longer pay attention to what Stuart was saying. She was having to breathe rhythmically to keep the blackness from engulfing her. She could hear his voice, but only disconnected snatches of his thought came through.

Then the carriage stopped at the inn, and Stuart was helping her down, all solicitude, now that he saw how pale she was. He would have carried her up the steps if she had let him. His arm supported her all the way down the hall to the door of her room.

"Let me have a light supper brought to you, Mother."

"No, thank you, my dear. All I need is to lie still and quiet. It's nothing to be alarmed about. I'll sleep if I can."

"You don't want me to sit with you?"

She thanked him again and pressed his hand. He saw her inside the room, drew the blinds, kissed her, and left her. Angelina lay on the bed and waited for the blackness to well up again, or the terrible hammered dome of pain to close down.

It was perfectly quiet—inside her body as well as outside it—the sort of quiet that seemed to presage storm. But no storm broke.

The suspense extended itself until it was transmuted into something else, a state that was neither waking nor sleeping, both more and less than full consciousness. She seemed to be adrift on a stream like one of the tidal rivers of her childhood, so calm and slow that one could hardly say whether one moved up with the tide or down with the current.

There on the bank were the two boys—Archibald and Francis—staring at her with blue Grimké eyes in brown faces. How coldly they looked at her from the first! How finally they rejected her at the last! Did they blame her for crimes committed against them by others?

The current gentled her away and around a bend, into a country as desolate as an old battleground. The dead that lay on it, unburied, were hopes—hers, Sarah's, Thoda's, the hopes of the heroes and prophets of Abolition, and of a million slaves. . . . The war that had been fought here was fought for the wrong reasons, and it was bearing the wrong fruit.

Lincoln had commanded its armies. Lincoln, who found an excuse for every evil but disunion, had written the Proclamation that called forth the jubilee. Lincoln was the one chosen for martyrdom. It was for him the liberated thousands wept and prayed, for him the freedmen named their sons and the schools in which their sons prepared for freedom. What irony!

And yet it was not all irony.

The current carried her on, and the shape of the man changed as a mountain changes when it is approached on a long curve from the plain. He took on a stature greater than the sum of all his parts. The very quality she and the other radicals had denounced as weakness loomed as awesome strength. The strength to love. . . . It had served to bind the disparate parts of the North together for the agony of war. It was needed now in the aching void of peace. Without it there would be no peace. There would be a division more fearful than the one Lincoln had fought to prevent. Far worse than two nations growing beside each other in hatred was the prospect of two nations growing one inside the other, unless they were bound together by love.

Now Lincoln was gone, leaving no one to take his place. Who was to splint and bind the broken limbs of the nation, North and South, black and white? What hands could reach across the ravines and gullies, and grasp hands on the other side? Not the old Abolitionists! That was the true irony.

Few as they were now, weary and frail, they were still fighting. Fighting each other if there was no enemy within their sights. They had learned to hate righteously and well. They could not unlearn the lesson, now that the time for hate had passed.

It was part of the terrible cost of reform that those who gave their lives to it should be so often twisted and warped. Denied the normal joys and satisfactions of life, doomed to a dreary repetition of failure, they had to confront an enemy within as dangerous and far more subtle than the one without. In the face of universal scorn, they had constantly to declare to themselves that they were better, righter! than those who scorned them. They became rigid, jealous of each other, envious of the pitifully small rewards the movement had to bestow. Faith they preserved through the long ordeal, and hope, but not charity!

And the greatest of these is charity. . . .

So it was that now, at the end of their lives, and the beginning of that for which they had sacrificed their lives, now when they were most needed, they were least used. Now, when the chains just broken were being secretly reforged, when the victors were confused and distracted, and the enemy was stealthily rising from his knees to his feet, the old warriors should have been recruiting their replacements, black and white, teaching what they knew before it died with them, sifting what was good and true from the chaff in the legacy of their lives.

But no one was listening to them. They had lost their voices, as she had lost hers.

The current swung her in a wide, slow circle back to the two Grimké boys. There was fear in their eyes, along with the coldness. They looked to her to save them from the story Archibald had told. It had done terrible violence, and it threatened more.

And it was not true!

It might not be false, but it was not true, either. Not enough of the truth to be true.

. . . and don't sass your mistress again, or I'll have to give you another whippin'.

If Henry said anything like that, it was not to cover his shame. He was not fool enough to think that could be done by an empty threat. For whose ears did he speak, then? To deceive or to appease whom? Someone who was listening, but not watching . . . not Selina, who would never have stayed to witness the punishment . . .

Eliza!

You know what they are! As immoral as animals, even the ones who make a big fuss about being Christians! It was one of Eliza's dearest dogmas. *There isn't a Negro woman born who won't feed a man's lust if she thinks there's anything to be gained!*

Eliza might very well have demanded that Nancy be mated— for Henry's protection! Eliza would have nagged and wheedled and hinted till she got Selina to issue the order, bullied and prodded till she got her to demand punishment for Nancy's refusal to obey. Henry knew how Eliza felt. He knew whom to blame and whom to appease, and that it could be done cheaply, with words alone! For Eliza did listen at keyholes. She was ashamed of it, but she did it; and shame made her stupid, easily gulled.

Poor Eliza! Twisted into an evil thing by the life force in her that was denied. How many Elizas were there in the slave South? Disappointed in their own hopes, condemned to live always in the shadow of that disappointment, circling the sun of some other woman's fulfillment! Sarah had escaped such a fate by coming away, but the Elizas stayed on and grew bitter. And they were denied a channel even for their bitterness. Whom were they to blame? The masters who had not chosen to make them mistresses? That was dangerous, for they must live on the sufferance of those same masters, live on a dole not much more generous than that meted out to a favorite mauma or a concubine. No wonder they so often chose to hate the slave sister who shared their fate!

You have to watch them all the time, and even so they get round you. Men are so weak. . . .

Angelina came back to Archibald's story, circling it warily, poking a question here, another there. Why did Henry let himself be overpowered in the first place? He was a strong man. He might have been caught off his guard by the suddenness of Nancy's attack, but once the shock passed, he would have been angry. Anger was the trigger to violence in his nature. If he did not give way to it, it was because he was possessed by something stronger than anger.

Love?

Was it possible in such circumstances? Could a man—a master—love his "property"? And Nancy? What did she feel? Could a woman, not mistress of her own person, feel love for the man who held title to it?

There was only one way to know. She must invoke the presence she had been resisting. She must open herself to the anguish and live it! The anguish and the ecstasy and the consequences of both! She must be Henry and Nancy too, stretched on a rack of which one end was passion, the other, guilt.

* * *

It was not hard to imagine the start: Nancy, the mauma, the second mother, the subdeity of the home, moving always in the charged atmosphere of its innermost sanctuary; Henry at his most loving there, and his most lovable.

As Selina sank into the first stages of illness, Nancy must have taken on the small, intimate services that were a wife's office, as well as the management of the house and the other servants in it. She watched Henry reach out in tenderness to the dying woman who could bear and return nothing more than tenderness. She could read the hunger in his eyes because it matched her own.

They could have fed each other's hunger, filled each other's need, but for the commandment Thou Shalt Not Love—a person whose skin is of a different color. But for that, Selina's death would have ended the dilemma her illness had helped to create. They could have married with the approval of a community that held it a man's duty to give a second mother to his children if the first died. The same community that would go mad with outrage if he chose the woman he loved!

She saw what it cost him to put the thought away, over and over again. She saw it drive him to vices for which he had little taste: to drinking and keeping late hours with low company; to cards and cockfights; anything that would deaden his desire and stupefy his senses.

262

And so they lived.

For how long?

It was not till four years after Miss Selina died that our father bought the place in St. Paul's Parish.

And five years before Nancy bore him a son.

She must have believed it would go on forever, this living two separate lives that could not overlap, except in death. In one of them she paid and repaid her debt of guilt to Selina and Selina's children for the sin committed against them in the other life, the dream. She must have fought and won the same battle every day of those years, only to lose it at night. But inevitably there came a time when the two lives did overlap.

It could have happened in any of a hundred ways, but it must have been at night, when that which stood between them was blotted out. If Henry was late coming home and had forgotten his key . . . Stephen should have been sleeping in the downstairs hall till the master was home, but he might have sneaked off to the greater comfort of the quarters. . . . There was a racket at the street door that would soon have the whole household roused. She snatched a shawl to throw around her nightdress and ran barefoot down the staircase. Not truly awake. Still that other Nancy, mistress of the house whose peace she was guarding as she threw open the door. Henry had been leaning against it, and lurched forward when it gave. Her arms went out to steady him, and his were around her. Their bodies touched and fused. . . .

Angelina came to herself for an instant and knew who she was and what was happening. She tried to wrench herself free from the woman into whom she had entered, but she was too weak. She was Nancy, too weak to wrench herself free from Henry's embrace.

"This can't go on," he said. There was the smell of brandy on him, but he was not drunk. He was as much himself as she, as much as either could be in the precarious privacy of this moment when all other reality was suspended. "You know it can't go on any more."

She knew it couldn't if he said so. She could resist for herself, but not for both of them. She said nothing, for to speak or to move would be to commit herself, to deny everything she had been taught to believe, to affirm an imperative that she could not accept . . . or reject, either.

Then someone called—or moved—somewhere in the house. Stephen had waked and was shuffling in to beg pardon for his fault. Or there was a creaking on the floor of Eliza's bedroom just above.

She tried to pull away.

"I can't stand it any longer," he said. "I can't live in the same house with you."

"Then sell me!"

The words hissed out like snakes.

He let her go, and she ran from him, ran all the way upstairs, stopping only when she came to the door of Henrietta's bedroom, making sure she was breathing quietly when she opened it and slipped into her cot at the foot of the white girl's bed.

She had told him to sell her, but he would not. Eliza must have tried long ago to persuade him to that step. But even Eliza knew that the children would raise an outcry to prevent it. Grown as they were—Henrietta already a young lady and thinking about getting married—they still looked to her as their mauma, still preferred her to their aunt. Besides, selling her would have been a confession of guilt to the onlooking circle of his peers, the judges who prevented the honorable solution to the dilemma.

Since that was prevented, it was only a matter of time before the dishonorable solution would force itself. With or without their intending or planning, there would come a night when they were alone in the house. . . .

At Christmas, when the family was bidden to the Draytons' place on the Ashley. Nancy might be left behind to manage the other servants and see to some heavy cleaning or minor repairs. . . . Or it might not be till July, when they all went up to the mountains to escape the heat. She would have to stay at least a week, to pack away clothes and put dust covers on the furniture. There would be a great bustle of activity during the days, but in the evenings she would be alone. She would let the others go, to visit with their friends and kinfolk or to hear the new preacher at the Second Presbyterian Church, who was leading special services for his black communicants. . . .

Alone in the quiet, empty house, she could let the dream take over. She could wander through the chambers, dusting her hand along the rail of the beds and the backs of the chairs, setting this vase in place, arranging that curtain's folds. Anyone watching would see only the mauma, putting the last touch of order on the master's room. No one could tell that it was the mistress who moved through her own realm. . . .

She might go out on the upper veranda to smell the sea breeze that scraped the palms against each other and sent the perfume of Cape jessamine in clouds through the darkness. Standing there, bemused, she might not hear him come. Not if he left his horse in the stables and came in the back way, mounting the stairs quietly, because he knew what he had come home for, giving her no warning till he stood behind her, his fingers catching her by the shoulders, pressing so hard into her flesh that she could feel her own pulse under them. As it quickened and she ceased to pull against his hands, they moved down, down, over her breasts, cupping them so that the nipples tightened and ached. Down, down, till they grasped the bones of her hips and forced them back against him.

Everything was changing. Shape flowed into shape. Struggle to resist him dissolved into a struggle to reach him through a maze. Monsters and hags—furies!—were all around them, reviling them, threatening, striving to part them. But she beat them back. Together they beat them back. For the agony of that giving and taking was his as much as hers. It was an act of destruction as well as of creation. Each had to strike off a part of the selves they aspired to be, and throw it to the furies! It was an act of violence as well as of love.

Afterward they must have tried to go back to the old forms, the rituals of mastery and servitude, following them more rigidly than ever because they were no longer anything but forms. But it was not possible to undo what had been done, and living under Eliza's eternal, suspicious surveillance must have become unbearable.

So Henry bought a plantation a day's drive from the city. He bought Eliza's consent—or at least her silence—at the price of the title she had longed for. He made her mistress of the Charleston house. She carried the keys at her waist and her head high, and Charleston took its cue from her.

Some may have wondered that a man who had refused for so many years to follow the proper calling of a Carolina gentleman should suddenly succumb. If Henry had chosen to become anything but a planter, there would have been murmurings. But this was the tradition, and if he followed it for the wrong reason that was his own affair. The gentry of the split-souled South had learned to be grateful for the option of ignoring whatever spoiled its self-portrait. If the surface was preserved, that was enough.

Life could not have been easy for such lovers as they now became. From what Archibald had told her—face-to-face this morning, and before that in the letter he wrote—and from her own experience, Angelina could guess what it had been like at the start. She knew the small, self-contained world of an upriver plantation, diked against the incursion of the world outside. . . . Sun and moon, cool and warm, storm and calm—these were all that marked the passing of time. . . . Life and death! Plants, men, and animals came into being and left it, each at a different pace, in unending sequence, like the days and hours. . . .

For Nancy it must have been a dream, a hard dream, terrible with joy. Not an hour went by without some threat to remind her that it was only a dream, that she must live each hour of it fiercely, for the time was short. But that gave substance to the joy, as the dikes along the rice fields gave substance to the land they stole from the

266

river. For if the time had not been stolen, if they had not been so cut off from the real world, she would not have had the whole of Henry's life to share. He would not have needed her in so many ways. There would have been white men, planters, from whom he could have learned the lessons that were Nancy's to teach him now. For it must have been Nancy who went through the settlement, quarrying the knowledge of the oldest and wisest hands. It would have been beneath the dignity of the master to admit ignorance. She must have brought her gleanings to Henry to be sorted, sifted, framed into plans and orders to carry out those plans. They must have learned the lore of rice and cotton together, exulting together in each success, consoling each other for each failure.

This was not living like a white woman. Nancy had seen enough to know how small was the portion allotted them. It was not marriage. She had seen Henry's marriage at close range; she knew the difference, and that all the difference was gain. She was living as a whole woman, mate of the man she loved, mistress of his home, partner in all his enterprises.

And then her baby was born . . . the son who looked so like his father . . . the brown-skinned baby with gray-blue eyes . . . Archibald Henry! . . . Henry, because it was his son; Archibald, because he could not claim him. The boy must have a public name, one by which he could be called before the people of the settlement as well as the white visitors who came out now and then from Charleston and who would surely see the little lad running about the yard.

The name was a subterfuge like the little house in which Nancy and her babies must have lived. There had to be a little house. No matter what a white man did, obeisance must be made to the blind god of public opinion, black as well as white. A gentleman could live with his black mistress, could sell her husband into death or exile like a latter-day David, to possess his Bathsheba. It could be known to all his fellow Brahmins, and he could keep his place of honor in his caste so long as he kept his outcaste wife and children under a different roof. If he moved them into the house in which he lived, he was forever beyond the pale. It mattered not how remote the plantation might be. News would be carried to Charleston. He would be tried *in absentia,* the verdict of excommunication rendered. . . .

While Nancy was mauma to his white children, she lived in his house because she was needed to protect the white parents' rest. That was the one post in which black women were permitted to cross the line that was supposed to divide the races in sleep. She slept first in Henrietta's nursery, then in Montague and Tom's, then in Selina's sickroom, and finally in Henrietta's again, as a duenna. But at Caneacres, where she was in fact mistress, she could not live under the master's roof. Even the hands would have resented it, would have felt it a reflection on the "name" of the small community that was their country, would have talked spitefully.

But the little house across the yard from the big one put everyone at ease. And probably Nancy did not mind. She could accept it as she accepted the other inevitables, like pain in childbirth, like bondage itself, because her pride was not touched. Not by that or anything else. Not even the moments when the outside world invaded the dream. When there were visitors from Charleston, and Nancy had to leave her babies in the care of one of the old aunties in the settlement and resume her public role as mauma, supervising the serving of the dinner, or even serving it herself. . . .

Her pride could not be touched because it was not founded on the good opinion of others, neither her own peers nor Henry's. But his was. That was what made the dream so fragile.

Each time there was an invasion from the outside, he must have been twice shamed: once, before his friends, who might or might not be deceived by the flimsy camouflage, and again and more deeply before Nancy. What had it done to his love? To his soul?

Did shame drive him away from her sometimes? Back to the city in attempted repentance for the sin that, strangely, did not feel like sin at all? What did Nancy feel when he went? She must have known that he might not come back, that he might try to forge a chain to keep himself from coming, might marry a white woman whom he did not love. What did she feel each time that he did come back, condemning himself for weakness? Did she condemn him too? Or did she give herself to him with passion that left both of them quiet, but only one at peace?

What killed the dream in the end, and Henry with it? . . . Eliza had written at the time . . . something about the country fever. . . . Was it true? Or was that only a euphemism to cover a harder truth? Was Henry driven to another sin by his despair? Did he put a bullet into his head to quiet the pain in his heart?

Angelina's questions had been feeling along the wall of the unknown like the river's fingers seeking a weak place in the dike. Now she made a supreme effort, and the wall seemed to crumble. She flowed through the darkness and came out into light. She could see very clearly, as if she were living—not remembering the past or imagining the future—living her own life. . . .

Some of Henry's friends had come out for a holiday on the plantation. They had begun drinking there, very heavily, and the carouse had gone on when they returned to Charleston, Henry with them. . . .

When he came back to Caneacres, he looked as she had not seen him since the old bad days after Selina's death. It showed in his face and eyes, and in the way he made love to her. Not tenderly, as it had been since they came to the plantation, but like that first time, when love was an act of violence committed against himself as well as her.

He came down with the country fever a day or so later. Most white men who stayed on rice plantations in hot weather got it sooner or later. It could be serious or not. With Henry it was fatal, because he was already sick to death in his heart.

He tried to talk to her, wildly when the fever was up, quietly when it dropped, always about the same thing.

"I've put it in my will that you and the boys are to go to Montague."

He watched her face for the answer to questions he could not bring himself to ask. Was it right? Was it the best thing to do? Was she content?

Nancy gave him no answer.

"Henrietta will marry," he explained, "and who knows whether her husband would regard such a trust? Tom's a good lad, but he's not yet of age. Montague is my heir. I can trust him to carry out my wishes."

Again he watched her face.

What could she say? That she wanted to be free? That was impossible unless she left the South. She had two small sons, and her body was growing big with another. How could she venture into the unknown world of the free North? How could she earn her way? Who would protect her? If she stayed in the South, someone must stand as her master before the law. Montague was as good as any. . . .

Later, when Henry's fever went up again and his dreams were nightmares, he insisted that a messenger be sent into town. "I want to see my son. Bring Montague to me. I must tell him what he's to do."

When the messenger had left, he said to her: "I've done wrong, Nancy. . . . I know it. . . . But I mean to make it up to you now. . . . Montague is to treat you and the boys like his own family . . . see you never want . . . no harm comes to any of you. . . ."

He fell back to sleep, and she left him, left someone in her place beside the bed, and went out of the house.

Eyes followed her across the yard. Eyes peered into the doors and windows of the little house, and read the signs on her face. Terror spread to the settlement. People stole up to the big house and hung around the foot of the steps. Some came into the little house with their questions. Was it all up with the maussa? What would happen if he died?

She knew little more than they did, and nothing that would give them comfort. They brought bulletins from the sickroom: that he was resting easier, that his fever had gone down some. But she knew he would die, because he did not want to live. The love that had straightened and strengthened her had broken him. He had lost his way between his world and hers, lost the poles of right and wrong, the direction of his life.

He was out of pain when she returned. His face seemed suffused with light, but she could guess from what direction it fell. He was at peace because the war was over. He was tender and trustful with her, because he was past shame and fear.

He died in her arms.

Let himself die. Without waiting for the son he had summoned. Without delivering the final injunction and extracting the final promise. Had he already said all that was needful on that last visit to town? Or did Montague know nothing more than the words he would read in the will? She would not ask. That was her last gift to him: the illusion that he had made all things right, that she was secure and content.

His gift to her was a jewel he had never possessed for himself— pride. He had loved her as his wife. He had made her his peer. She had reached her full stature, and she knew now what that was. No mysterious gulf separated her from the master caste. She had functioned as one of them, functioned better than most of them. No one could awe or cow her again. Least of all, poor unfulfilled Eliza, who was the enemy she must now ready herself to meet.

She laid her love's hand at his sides, and drew the sheet to cover him; went out of the chamber in which so much had been born, so little had died. Down the stairway to the yard, nodding to the silent men and women who waited for the word she did not have to speak aloud. A low moaning sound went up, but she did not join in it.

All through the night of mourning, the little house was crowded with dark forms, with people who came, whispered a while, and went away.

"We goin' to run off," some of them said. "Better than stay an' be sol'." . . . "There's places on the islan's where no buckra ever come." . . . "We got a good chance to make it if we start now."

There were always runaways at times like this. Nancy was tempted to be one of them, for to the woman she was now it was better to live free in the swamps and palmetto jungles than to eat the bread of charity, half slave and half free, better for her and for the sons she had to raise. But how could she run with the two of them and the new one on his way?

So she waited for the Grimkés: for Dr. John and young Montague, and Miss Mary and Miss Eliza. Eliza triumphant and vindictive, but powerful to do only what Nancy wanted done: to make the funeral arrangements, to say all the words, to make all the small, meaningless decisions, to burn the incense, and bury the truth under a cloud of sacrificial smoke.

It was Eliza who decided that Nancy and the boys were to return to Charleston and live in the family house, at least for a time. It was not generosity. It was safer that way, easier to lock out the specter of scandal, if everything was kept within the closed circle. That was why the funeral had to be in town, at a safe distance from the people of the plantation, who knew and might speak what must not be spoken.

Nancy sat in the black pew at St. Paul's Episcopal, and listened to the rector pronounce a eulogy that Eliza might have composed. She stood beside the grave with his white children, holding on to Henrietta, who was weeping, while the coffin was lowered so that Henry could lie beside "the wife of his bosom." She visited the graveyard later and read the words on the white stone slab that covered the double grave, his and Selina's:

MADE PERFECT THROUGH SUFFERING

She did not weep.

She knew when the will was read, but she did not hear it. No one told her what it said. But Montague treated her from that moment on as if she were free. Free to fend for herself, with her three nameless, fatherless sons.

When Caneacres was sold—the people, the land, the animals, all put up for bid at public auction—the livestock that had been Nancy's was treated as her legal property, and a slave could not own property. The money it brought was given to her.

"It's enough to buy you a house," Eliza told her. "You can stay with us till you've found one or had one built."

It was not enough to buy a house. Not enough to buy the boards to build one. But Nancy did not dispute. She neither thanked them nor protested. Nor did she beg. Not from them!

Her own people helped her. One gave her a corner of his lot to build on. Others gave her their labor to raise the tiny shack. And while they worked, she earned her keep at the Grimkés by washing and ironing for them.

"You can make a good living as a laundress," Eliza told her. "We'll let you have our work, and recommend you to other families."

And so it began, the long, long travail. Chained on a long tether, but chained all the same. Free, but forced to slave for the master of hunger, her own hunger and her sons', all the years of her young womanhood, till at last, when the boys had grown strong enough to share her burden, suddenly the chain was pulled tight. Her sons taken as slaves!

How had she borne it? How had she kept from going mad with grief and anger?

"If we had known . . . if we had only known . . ."

Angelina spoke the words in her own person, and they brought her to herself, but not the self she had been before. She was changed. Whether it was by revelation or by the intensity of her effort of imagination she did not know, but she had the sense of having passed through the most profound and secret depths of the other woman's life. Perhaps she had imagined some of it wrongly; perhaps there was much that she had not been able to imagine at all, but it was all she could bear, and it was enough. She knew Nancy Weston as she had never known the Black Sister, as a real woman—flesh and bone as well as heart and mind. She knew herself the better for it . . . and Henry, too. . . .

Except that she was so tired. She had not really slept, and she must sleep now. It was very late. There was one dose of laudanum in her satchel, brought along to dull the pain of headache if one should strike. She swallowed it in some water, and sank almost at once into the healing deeps.

Some time before morning she rose into a dream.

She was at home in Charleston. It was early spring. Morning. Sunday. The willows were in canary feather, and grape hyacinths and crocuses were gay among the graves.

The church doors stood open. The organ was being played inside, very slowly, like a dirge.

Henry was standing with his back to her, his hands gripping the bars of the churchyard fence. He was staring at the headstones. He was angry.

"If we had known . . ." she kept repeating. "If we had known, we could have helped. Why didn't you tell us, Henry?"

"You were gone."

He would not relent. Not even enough to turn and look at her. People were beginning to drive up in their carriages. There was not much more time.

The low tones of the organ shook the air like sobbing.

Henry was not dressed for the services. He wore riding breeches and a linen shirt that made him look very young, very slim and elegant. Angelina felt uneasy about her own choice of dress. She had put on the severest of her Quaker grays. It was hot and tight. But it was not so much the physical discomfort she minded as the sense of giving offense. She ought not to be lingering here in front of St. Paul's in a costume that would be construed as a rebuke or an insult by her mother's friends.

And Henry was not ready to forgive her.

"It was you wanted me gone," she reminded him. "You said I made life miserable for everyone."

"So you did. You harrowed our feelings till we didn't know what we did, and then reproached us."

"Henry, why must we quarrel when—?"

"Don't go feeling sorry for yourself," he interrupted irritably. "You can call a person the blackest of villains, in that smug, soft way you have, as if you were doing him a favor and expected to be thanked for it. But let anyone breathe a word against you, and you're in tears with one of your headaches coming on."

"Henry, Henry . . ."

"Very well, then. Cry, if you must. It won't mend matters."

It was all trivial and terrible. Everything was veering off in some new direction in which her purpose would be lost. And the music blew like a cold wind out of a sepulcher into the warm, weak morning sunlight.

"You're going away," she said. "And we may never see each other again."

She had got it wrong. It was she who was going away, wasn't it? But Henry didn't contradict her.

"That's your fault," he said. "You're driving me away."

"I only did what I thought was right, Henry. I love you too much to let—"

"What do you know about love? You were as unloving as a stone! Unloving and unforgiving!"

"I had to be!"

"You gloated over our sins! You confessed them for us! Out loud, so everyone could hear! And damned us when we didn't kneel down and say you were right!"

"I didn't! I didn't! I had to be harsh with you as I was with myself. You remember how I cut away all the trimmings from my bonnets and dresses? Gave up my flower garden, and all the things I loved to eat and drink and touch and smell? All for the same reason.

Because it was so hard to keep my feet on the path, with wickedness all around like a swamp. . . ."

"You pushed us deeper into it to raise yourself."

She was sobbing now. "Why do you only blame me? You don't blame Sarah. She did the same."

"Sarah would have helped me if she had been here," he said sadly. "But she was gone, too. You were both gone when I needed you."

A spasm of grief shook him, and his hands pulled at the bars as if he were trying to wrench them loose. The music was throbbing so that it shook the walls of the church, threatening to tumble stone from stone.

"You made me sin!" Henry cried. "It's your sin, too. Yours and Mother's and Father's and Sarah's. You can't buy yourselves free of it. None of you can.

"It was committed by no one and by everyone, the sin against my sons."

He was lost in the wildness of the sobbing. People pushed in between them . . . voices . . . carriages . . . thunder. . . .

She was on her way into the church. She stopped once to look back, but Henry was gone. It was up to her.

She woke, refreshed, knowing what it was she had to do. Her purpose was fixed, and strong enough to support her.

"We must go back to the college," she told Stuart, when he came for her. "I have to speak to them again before I can leave."

As the boys entered the visitors' parlor, Angelina rose. "I want you to come with me," she said, and held out a hand to each of them.

Reluctantly they came, submitting only because it involved less commitment than a refusal. Angelina took their hands and, holding them tightly, led the boys out of the room, out of the hall, all the way to the door of the president's house. The gentleman himself opened to them.

"I have come to commend my nephews to your kindness," Angelina said. "Yes, these two fine young men are my nephews, Dr. Randall. The sons of my brother, Henry Grimké, and his wife, Nancy Weston Grimké."

Francis turned to look at her, and then quickly away. Archibald did not move his eyes. No one said anything for a moment. Then Stuart spoke.

"I hope you'll write to me," he said to Francis. "I'll write you. Just as soon as I get home. But you don't have to wait for my letter. Just put down anything that comes to your mind."

Francis smiled at him, diffidently, but still said nothing.

"I'll read any of your compositions that you want to send me," Stuart went on, "and tell you just what I think. I'm very fixed in my opinions, I'm afraid. But you tell me straight out where you think I'm wrong, and we'll have a debate."

It was the longest reach in the direction of another human being that Angelina could remember his ever having made. But it was not enough.

"We still hope you will come to visit us," she said. "Our home is yours, whenever you wish to make it so."

Both boys said, "Thank you."

Archibald was looking at her now, but she could not read his thoughts.

"I want to say this one thing to you before we take our leave. . . ." (She wanted to reach out to him with her arms. Sarah would have done so, if she had been here.) "You have taken the name of Grimké. It was once honored in this land. Some day I shall tell you of those who gave it luster. But that was long ago, and the luster is dimmed now.

"I charge you most solemnly, by your upright conduct, by your devotion to justice and humanity, to lift it out of the dust where it lies and set it high.

"There is no one who can do it but you."

"Thank you," Archibald said very softly. He wanted to say more but he seemed unable to. He took a step toward her, but seemed unable to take another.

A great wave gathered in her heart, caught her on its crest, and carried her the intervening inches. She took the boy's grave face in her two hands, and kissed him.

They were both weeping now.

"Thank you . . . Aunt Angelina," he said. "We will try to do as you ask."